FALLEN HEARTS

CISSY MECCA

B
Boldwood

First published in Great Britain in 2025 by Boldwood Books Ltd.

Copyright © Cissy Mecca, 2025

Cover Design by Jane Dixon-Smith

Cover Images: Shutterstock

The moral right of Cissy Mecca to be identified as the author of this work has been asserted in accordance with the Copyright, Designs and Patents Act 1988.

All rights reserved. No part of this book may be reproduced in any form or by any electronic or mechanical means, including information storage and retrieval systems, without written permission from the author, except for the use of brief quotations in a book review. This book is a work of fiction and, except in the case of historical fact, any resemblance to actual persons, living or dead, is purely coincidental.

Every effort has been made to obtain the necessary permissions with reference to copyright material, both illustrative and quoted. We apologise for any omissions in this respect and will be pleased to make the appropriate acknowledgements in any future edition.

A CIP catalogue record for this book is available from the British Library.

Paperback ISBN 978-1-83656-247-4

Large Print ISBN 978-1-83656-246-7

Hardback ISBN 978-1-83656-245-0

Ebook ISBN 978-1-83656-248-1

Kindle ISBN 978-1-83656-249-8

Audio CD ISBN 978-1-83656-240-5

MP3 CD ISBN 978-1-83656-241-2

Digital audio download ISBN 978-1-83656-244-3

This book is printed on certified sustainable paper. Boldwood Books is dedicated to putting sustainability at the heart of our business. For more information please visit https://www.boldwoodbooks.com/about-us/sustainability/

Boldwood Books Ltd, 23 Bowerdean Street, London, SW6 3TN

www.boldwoodbooks.com

To the readers who have followed me from Bridgewater to the Finger Lakes. Hope you enjoy Cedar Falls!

The Bachelor Pact Rules:
    Never stay the night
    Never date the neighbor
    Never fall in love
    Never say "I Do"

1
PIA

Cedar Falls, Finger Lakes Region, NY

"Want your regular?"

The cashier didn't even look up as a woman about my age approached the counter.

"Mmhmm," the customer murmured, looking as if she was about to cry. As someone who cried at sappy commercials, among many other things, I could empathize.

Making a quick decision, I jumped up from my seat.

"I've got this," I said to the woman. "You head to the ladies room."

Although it was an odd offer from a stranger, she didn't seem to mind. Swallowing hard and giving me a quick nod, she bolted in the direction of, I assumed, the ladies room. It was my first time in the place, new to town and all, so I knew very little about the Coffee Cabin or even Cedar Falls itself. Except that, as of last night, it was my new home.

When the cashier looked up—a college kid, from the looks of him—he appeared confused.

"I've got her coffee. And..." I didn't need to look at the pastries again to know what I wanted. "A blueberry crumble muffin."

Paying for both, I brought them to my corner seat and went back to people-watching. So far, nothing out of the ordinary. Just a cozy coffeehouse in a town even smaller than the one where I grew up. One I'd be seeing a lot of since my new apartment was just upstairs.

"Thank you so much," the woman said when she returned, clearly unsure what to do.

"Join me," I offered. "Got a muffin top."

She looked a bit like that actress from the funny movie with Ryan Reynolds. What the heck was the name of it? Ugh, how could someone be so bad at remembering names?

"You look like someone," I started, about to explain the movie.

"Emma Stone."

"That's it. I guess you get that all the time?"

"I do. But I take it as a compliment, so thank you."

I would too. Emma Stone, and my companion, were both extremely pretty. Red hair in a long bob and a smattering of freckles across her cheek, just like me. It was rare to meet someone with freckles. We also shared unusually bright eyes, hers green and mine blue. I wondered if it meant anything? Like maybe we were destined to be friends?

"You're welcome," I said.

"And thank you for the coffee."

"My pleasure. Please help yourself to the muffin. It looks too good not to eat."

"Oh, they're good, alright. Deadly so. Try some."

I helped myself and silently agreed. This would be dangerous. I'd have to limit myself to one a week or special occasions or something. Sweet treats were my downfall.

"I appreciate the rescue. Delaney," she said, offering her hand.

"Pia." I shook it, smiling.

"Passing through?" she asked.

"Actually, no. I just moved here. I'm renting the apartment upstairs." I motioned above us. "Got here last night from Oregon."

"Oh wow. You must be exhausted. Welcome to Cedar Falls."

"Thanks. So you live here?"

"I do. Born and raised. Although I just came back to town myself after a few-year hiatus." Delaney took a sip of coffee, looking over the rim sheepishly. "Sorry about the waterworks."

Clearly she'd been crying, but I hadn't planned to mention it.

"No apologies necessary," I said. "No one is a bigger crier than me. Though I definitely don't look that good after a cry. More power to you."

Delaney laughed. "I don't believe you. The guys in town are going to lose their minds. We haven't had anyone new to Cedar Falls as pretty as you... ever."

"Stop," I said, never able to take a compliment well. I'd gotten comments on my dark hair and clear blue eyes my whole life. But it wasn't like I'd done anything to earn it, so I was never sure what to say. I supposed "thank you" would suffice, but somehow I never managed to say the words.

"Although, fair warning. There are more than a few heartbreakers out there."

Ahh, so that was the source of the waterworks. "Breakup?"

"Yup. Five months hot and heavy, and boom. Just like that, he goes back to the ex. I feel silly. Five months isn't very long, I know. But I liked him. A lot. He was a commitment phobe, and in the worst twist of fate, mutual friends of ours say he's planning to propose."

Breaking off a piece of muffin, I prepared to do one of the things I did best.

Overshare.

"I get it, trust me. Last year I dated a guy for the summer. Knew it wouldn't last since he was only there for a seasonal job. But the fact that we were never on a collision course for a long-term relationship didn't seem to matter to my traitorous heart. There was something about him that I connected with, almost from the start. An attraction, of course, but something else I could never quite put my finger on. Getting to know him was one of the easiest and most fun few months of my life."

"Why do you think that was?"

I'd asked myself that so many times. "I'm not sure, to be honest. We just clicked. Our chemistry was off the charts. I told him things I'd never shared with another living soul, trusting him completely even knowing it was a dangerous thing to do."

"So what happened?"

The pang in my chest at the thought of having lost a man I'd been convinced would play a role in my life, even though I knew from the beginning such a thing was impossible, never dulled when I thought of him.

"He left. We tried for a long time just to be friends, which worked for him, but never for me. I know he really liked me, and enjoyed getting to know me too, but only one of us caught feelings. Turns out, it's really fucking hard to be friends with someone you could envision waking up to every day. Who you'd have given everything to be with."

"You were willing to move for him?"

"I was. But he wasn't ready for that kind of commitment. So I know a thing or two about commitment phobes and do my best to avoid them." I remembered why I was telling this gut-wrenching story, one that I'd worked for so long to forget. "There were days I questioned everything. How I felt about him, how disappointed I was in myself for taking too long to let go. Aside from losing my grandparents, it was honestly the most difficult period of my life. One I never saw coming." And finally, my point. "But I eventually got over it. And you will too. I promise."

Delaney reached across the table, tears in her eyes once again, and smiled in a way that erased any doubt. We weren't going to be friends.

We already were.

"Thank you for sharing that with me."

It should have felt odd to squeeze a stranger's hand, but it didn't. I truly believed there were no such things as coincidences, and the two of us were meant to be in this coffeehouse together today.

"My pleasure."

Letting go of my hand, she took a deep steadying breath. "So tell me how you ended up here in this little corner of the world."

"Well," I said, taking a sip of coffee. "I was hired as the new manager of a struggling inn. The owner seems like a great guy who I can't wait to meet in person on Monday when I start."

"What's the name of the inn? Who's the guy?" Delaney smiled wryly. "Trust me, if it's in or around Cedar Falls, I'll know him."

"Heritage Hill," I said as a vision of the beautiful, if older-looking inn popped into my head. "The owner's name is—"

"Thomas Bennett."

The way she said his name sent a shiver down my back. "What is it?" I asked, knowing without a doubt something was wrong.

"Oh, Pia," she said, as if feeling really sorry for me. "Thomas Bennett is dead."

2
MASON

What does a person do the day after they bury their father?

I wandered from my old bedroom at the inn where I grew up down to the kitchen. Esther, the elderly woman Dad had hired a few years ago to cook breakfast when he decided to start marketing Heritage Hill as a B&B, used the second kitchen Dad had added to the expanded part of the inn. This one, in the original house, was used only by my father and me. It was strange to walk into the kitchen without a pot of coffee brewing, courtesy of Dad.

It was even stranger to imagine not seeing my father walk through the door saying, "Mason, get up to the Heather room and see about unsticking the window."

Just as the coffee began to brew, a different voice filled the room.

"How you doing?"

Beck had stayed the night, along with a few other of my close friends.

"Alright," I said, reaching into the cabinet for two mugs. "Black, right?"

"Yep."

Only the sound of coffee brewing broke the silence. With someone you'd met in kindergarten, there wasn't always a need to talk. A few minutes later, I slid my friend a mug and sat across from him at the kitchen island.

"How many years has death been a part of my life?" I asked, not really expecting an answer. "But it still doesn't prepare you."

"Yeah, but we're not talking about terrorists or criminals. This is family. Hits different."

The only close family I had left. "True."

More silence. Some of those deaths Beck mentioned flashed through my mind. Eight years as an Army Ranger and four with the NYPD still hadn't prepared me for when I walked into the morgue and saw Dad lying on that cold metal table.

A fucking heart attack. Sure, he'd eaten his share of unhealthy food, but my father had always been an active guy, like me. He even went to the doctor every year and had gotten a clean bill of health just a few months ago. I only knew that because he'd texted me to get my own ass to the doctor, something I hadn't done since the medics forced me into their tent on my last tour.

One thing I did know about death, though, was that it came for all of us at some point. Lamenting the fact that he was gone wouldn't bring him back. And it certainly wouldn't solve the problem of Heritage Hill.

"What the fuck am I going to do?" I asked, as if Beck would have the answer.

"I don't know, man. That's your call. How many days did you clear the calendar?"

It might be more rundown than when I was a kid, and my father's lakeside inn certainly made less money than it had in its heyday, but it was late fall in the Finger Lakes. Which meant the inn was at least half full for the rest of the month.

"For the week," I said. "I should probably clear another."

"Ya think?"

We were opposites in just about every way—

Beck's dirty-blond hair to my black, his openness and easygoing personality to my sarcasm and private nature—and the only thing we had in common was a sense of humor. And our friendship.

"I think I'm fucked. That's what I think."

"How many bereavement days do you get?"

"Five."

"Hmm. It does seem like you're a bit fucked."

I rolled my eyes. "Thanks, bud."

"No problem."

Neither of us said anything for a few minutes, and though I wasn't usually the kind of person to work out a problem out loud, this one wasn't going to solve itself anytime soon.

"Even if I sell, that'll take time. Either way, I need someone to run the place in the meantime."

"If you go back, you mean."

Our eyes met. He'd said aloud what I'd been thinking. We both knew I was less than thrilled in Manhattan. Though I'd wanted to be a cop since my mom died, city life wasn't as glamorous as a young kid from Cedar Falls once thought it would be. Sure, there was more to do. Better restaurants. More women. But there was also more crime, fewer cops being hired every year, mandatory overtime and more bullshit than the army, which is a fucking feat. I'd even explored a position up here, in the Finger Lakes, in another town that had an opening in their department just to get out of the city.

"Even if there was an opening in CFPD, I could never do both. Law enforcement officers in New York can't work anywhere where alcohol is served," I said, voicing what Beck already knew.

"Right. Which means you'd be playing Papa Bennett in the meantime."

"So I put in a request for unpaid leave to keep the place up and running until I can sell it?"

"Or don't go back. Don't sell."

The thought had crossed my mind. But I was no innkeeper. That was all Dad. He'd loved this place. Poured his heart and soul into it.

Now, it was his legacy.

"I don't know. Leaving the NYPD is one thing. But running the inn? It's never been my thing."

"When you were a teenager? No, it wasn't." He shrugged. "Who knows? Now that you've seen the worst of humanity, maybe it's time for a change."

"Quite a fucking change."

Beck sipped his coffee and said nothing. He'd only laid out what I already knew was a shitty set of options. Problem was, I wasn't sure what I wanted, and unexpectedly having Heritage Hill fall into my lap complicated matters.

"Either way, I'm gonna need more than five days."

"For what?"

Parker breezed into the kitchen with his signature mismatched socks the same way he'd breezed into our friend group in college. With a perpetual smile on his face, he was the guy everyone adored. Women. Men. Mothers. (Especially mothers.) Little old ladies.

Everyone.

"To figure out what the hell to do with the inn."

Parker slapped Beck on the back, looked into his coffee mug and, apparently deciding there was enough left to make it worth his while, snagged it from him, saying, "Thanks."

Beck was too good-natured to do anything other than make himself another coffee. If that had been me, I'd have taken it back and told Parker to fuck off.

Although he probably never would have taken it from me in the first place.

"You're such an asshole," Beck said to Parker, who ignored him.

"I'll put in for a leave today and figure out the rest later."

Parker sat on the other side of the island from Beck, who shook his head at our friend.

"I could stick around," Parker said. "While you're off. Help out when I can."

Parker worked in construction, which meant crazy hours. But I still appreciated the offer. "Thanks, but I know how little time you have."

"I'm staying," he said, as if he hadn't heard me. "Moving to number two though."

Although the guest rooms were named, rooms one through four were in the main house and had always been kept open, reserved for family and friends. Since number two was a lakeview room, I didn't blame Parker for moving if he was going to stay.

"Are you serious?" I asked.

"Abso-fucking-lutely. Your dad died; you have zero direction in your life." He shrugged. "You need me."

"Jesus, Parker." Beck laughed. "Make the guy feel like shit, will you?" Beck focused back on me. "I'm staying too."

As a bartender, Beck's life in Cedar Falls was as carefree now as when we were in college. In fact, he basically acted just about the same, despite being an actual adult. This place was about to get spicy with the two of them staying on.

"You guys are nuts."

"Tell me something I don't know."

All three of us looked toward the kitchen door. Cole, the fourth member of our lifelong bachelor group, sauntered inside. Unlike the rest of us slobs, he was already dressed, signature dark-rimmed glasses firmly in place. Looking every bit like the history professor he was, Cole also headed toward the coffee pot.

"So what are we up to?" he asked no one in particular, pouring himself a coffee and sitting.

"Mason is having an identity crisis," Parker said. "So we're going to stay here until he figures out what to do with his life."

"Papa Bennett just died, asshole," Beck said. "Cut the guy some slack."

"We're staying, aren't we?" Parker shot back. "I'm not completely heartless."

"Staying, as in, living here?" Cole asked, turning to me. "What about your job?"

"He's taking a leave," Parker said. Apparently he was my new spokesperson. I'd always talked a lot less than him and Beck, so the two of them had a habit of jumping in to speak for me. The pair loved to hear themselves talk, so it worked out.

"Until he figures out what to do with the inn," Beck added.

"Are you thinking of keeping it?" Cole asked me.

"I have no idea what I'm going to do," I admitted.

"Which is why we're staying," Parker said. "You are too."

"Oh really?" he asked. "And what exactly do you propose I do with my job?"

"Pfft." Parker made a face. "You like the city about as much as Mason. If he's leaving, you have no other option."

"Right," Cole said, taking off his glasses and polishing them, as if they needed it, with his shirt. "I'll just quit my job at Columbia despite the fact that I worked like hell to get a tenure-track position. And come back here, to the metropolis of Cedar Falls, and what? Maybe get a teaching position at the high school? So I can live with you degenerates?"

Parker nodded as if it sounded like a perfectly reasonable plan. "Works for me."

"You're ridiculous," Cole said to him. But then, sobering, he asked me, "How you doing this morning?"

"I'm okay. Just a lot to figure out."

"I bet. And though I'd love to live at Heritage Hill and recreate our college years, I'm headed back Saturday. But I took the week off."

That surprised all of us.

"You did?" Parker asked.

"I did." He looked directly at me instead of Parker. "I knew you'd be staying for a bit. It was as long as I could get off in the middle of the semester but—"

"You didn't have to do that."

His answer was automatic. "Of course I did."

And that was that. No other words were said. None were needed. When we made a pact to stay bachelors together for the rest of our lives, it was only half-jokingly. No four guys had each others' backs more than us, and this morning proved it.

These fucking guys were everything. And now that I'd lost my only immediate family member, that wasn't just an expression. They were, literally, all I had.

3

PIA

There was no help for it. I had to go to the inn and talk to the son. Showing up at a job I may or may not have any longer, less than a week after the guy's dad died, wasn't high on my to-do list, but what option did I have?

After Delaney told me that Mr. Bennett had a heart attack and died suddenly last week, I'd honestly had no idea what to do next. She said the entire community had come out for the funeral, that he had been both respected and well-liked, having lived in Cedar Falls his whole life. Delaney also said he'd run the inn himself, but that his son was in town and was probably the person I needed to talk to about next steps.

Had I packed up my life on the west coast and come here for nothing?

I felt like a selfish asshole worrying about it when the poor man was dead. He seemed like such a nice guy, genuinely concerned about the fate of Heritage Hill and wanting to turn it around. I'd worked for bad bosses before, and it sucked. One of them passed me over for a promotion that had gone to a man much less qualified, and it still burned my butt. That Mr. Bennett and I jived so well had been one of the deciding factors in taking this job. And now he was gone.

Life truly was unpredictable and cruel, sometimes.

Turning the corner, I followed my navigation and estimated it was not too far ahead on my left. Mr. Bennett had assured me I didn't really need a car right off the bat since the apartment in town was a short walk to the inn. He'd even offered me a room so I didn't need to leave the inn at all, but sometimes it was good to have a little separation from work.

Pictures didn't do it justice.

Just ahead, right on the lake, was the old mansion that was Heritage Hill. I knew from my research that it had originally been built as a private residence in the late 1800s, and then added onto and restored nearly twenty years ago, expanding to the inn that loomed in front of me. With a large circular porch off to the right that looked almost like an attached gazebo, the massive structure framed with trees in every shade of now-fading autumn colors, Heritage Hill was everything I'd envisioned.

Though it was showing signs of aging, with some updates, a little focus and the right marketing, there was no reason it couldn't be the crown jewel of Cedar Falls. With enough land to accommodate wedding parties—something Mr. Bennett said wasn't currently on their list of services—the historic inn had every chance to turn around its finances and be as successful as Mr. Bennett said it had been when he'd inherited the property from his own father.

Heritage Hill just needed a little TLC.

Having talked myself into coming, now that I stood on the wraparound porch of the inn I was supposed to manage, I froze up. How could I possibly knock on the door and wait for the son to answer? What the hell would I say to him? Sorry about your dad, do I still have a job?

Maybe I'd come back tomorrow.

Good plan.

Turning around, I was two steps away when the door behind me opened.

Crap. I'd been totally snagged.

"Can I help you?"

I turned back. Standing in the doorway was a good-looking guy, probably my age-ish, around thirty, with short brown hair. He certainly didn't look like his dad had just passed away. The guy was grinning at me in a way that made it impossible not to smile back.

"My name is Pia Russo. I'm so sorry about your father. I just—"

"Not my dad," he said. "But thanks."

Not my dad? What did that mean?

"Excuse me?" I walked back toward the door. "He wasn't your father?"

Delaney had said the son was in town and Heritage Hill had been closed for the week. He was the right age, so obviously this was the guy.

"Nope. My father is a complete asshole. Papa Bennett, the total opposite. Great guy."

"I see." Except I didn't, at all. Was Mr. Bennett his stepfather?

"Parker," a voice said from inside the house. "Who are you talking to?"

The door opened all the way. Another guy, about

the same age, looked me up and down. Also good-looking, this one had dirty blond, almost surfer-looking hair. With scruff on his face and a smile that was only a breath away from leering, he positively screamed ladies' man. I was pretty sure if I stood on the porch long enough, he'd be asking for me to come inside to use one of the bedrooms for a little fun. Though he was extremely attractive, I wouldn't fall for a guy like that if someone paid me a million dollars. How many hearts had this guy broken? And why was he, too, smiling like he hadn't just lost his father?

So this was Mason Bennett. Great.

"Hi, you must be Mason. I'm really sorry about your father."

"Not Mason. But I can be, depending on what you want Mason for."

Yep, I'd completely pegged him. No thank you.

"Are you Mason?" I asked the first guy, already suspecting the answer.

"I'm not," he said, confirming my suspicions and explaining why he'd claimed Mr. Bennett was not his father. "You're looking for Mason?"

"No, she's here to see me, obviously," surfer-dude said.

"Actually..." I didn't want to insult him since

these were most likely Mason's friends. "I would like to speak with Mason, if that's possible."

"I'll get him," the first guy said. "Actually, I better not leave you alone with this one. Beck, go grab Mason."

"Yeah, okay." Beck didn't move. Obviously these guys were good friends, or maybe even family members, though they didn't look alike.

"Mason," the first guy boomed into the house. "Someone here to see you."

Beck backed away from the door but didn't go far.

"Who is it?"

Finally, Mason.

He was exactly like what I might imagine Mr. Bennett's son to look like. Also extremely handsome. Refined. Like he belonged on a Yale campus.

"Hi, I'm Pia Russo." I stuck out my hand, more at ease. He took it, appearing confused. "I am so sorry about your father," I began.

"She thinks you're Mason," Beck said.

I dropped his hand. "You're not Mason either?"

"Nope. Sorry to disappoint you."

"Where's Mason?" the first guy asked Yale.

"In the bathroom," Yale answered. "Pia, would

you like to come in? I apologize for my friends, who obviously have zero manners."

"Sure," I said. Yale wasn't the only confused one. Was this an inn or a fraternity? And how was it possible Mason had this many hot friends, if they were indeed his friends?

I followed them through the entranceway, already familiar as I'd studied pictures of Heritage Hill for weeks, and we made our way to the kitchen. No sign of Mason.

"I'll get him," Yale said. "Can you guys behave yourselves in the meantime?"

"No promises," Beck responded. That one was a firecracker.

"I'll keep him on a leash," my original Mason, the one who didn't care much for his father, said, smiling at me. He was cute. Really cute, actually.

I smiled back.

"I'm Parker. This is Beck and the stiff is Cole."

"Nice to meet you," I said, meaning it. I was about to ask him how they all knew Mason when a gravelly voice from the doorway asked, "Who are you?"

I looked up.

Jesus, sweet Mary and Joseph. He was like a cross between Henry Cavill and Ian Somerhalder. The cheekbones. Dark hair. Big, like Henry. Smoldery like Ian, though less playful. And of course, when I said Ian, I meant Damon Salvatore. As if the two didn't go hand in hand.

He watched me as if expecting me to say something.

Any one of his friends could stop a girl in her tracks. But there was something about him that was almost biblical. Suddenly Delaney's small smile when she'd talked about Mason made sense. And here I thought the two of us would be friends. She was a devil to not have warned me about him first.

He waited. His friends waited. What was the question?

"Pia," one of them said. I didn't see which since my focus was 100 percent on the man filling the entire doorframe. "Pia Russo."

He'd asked who I was. Shit. "Pia Russo," I repeated, as if his friend hadn't already said my name. Double shit. His dad. "I am very sorry about your father's passing."

"Thanks," he said, frowning.

So he was a man of many words. I rushed to explain why I'd barged in here and tried to forget my audience of frat boys.

"Your father hired me a few weeks ago to manage

Heritage Hill. I just got to town yesterday and learned of his passing."

His eyes narrowed. One of the guys whistled, a kind of "oh boy" sound.

"My father would never hire an outsider to manage the inn."

That took me aback, but I remembered the guy had just lost his father. Summoning more patience than was typical of me, I ignored the curt tone. "I can assure you, he did. I have the email chain to prove it. Restoring hotel properties is a specialty of mine."

"Heritage Hill isn't a hotel."

He might be good-looking, but the guy was also kind of a dick. "Inns too."

"Sorry you came all the way here, but no thanks."

No thanks? Was he serious?

I looked around at his friends. Clearly they didn't want to get involved. A second ago, all three of them had stood in a semicircle around me, but now suddenly each of them had somewhere to be. Muttering everything from "Nice to meet you," to "Have to move my stuff," the three scattered. Even Beck.

What the hell was I supposed to do now? Clearly he didn't want me here. And he'd just lost his father.

But I'd quit my job and moved across the country to be here.

Deep breaths.

I'd start there.

"I quit my job to take this one. Gave up my apartment, sold my car and moved from Oregon to be here."

He blinked but didn't say anything. The guy was a freak of nature, he was so good-looking. Too bad the personality didn't measure up. How could he be Mr. Bennett's son? They were like night and day.

"That's across the country," I added.

His biceps were much bigger than the average man's. And he had those bodybuilder veins on his forearms. I couldn't look away.

"I'm aware," he said dryly.

He just lost his father. He just lost his father. Patience, Pia.

"I am sorry about your dad," I said again. "I only spoke to him twice on the phone after a string of emails, but he seemed like a really nice guy."

"He was. But he also loved this place and ran it himself his entire life. I can't imagine he would hire someone and, no offense, but he didn't mention you at all."

He didn't mention you at all either.

"Maybe he wanted to surprise you?" I ventured sweetly.

"He hates surprises as much as I do."

Charming.

"I can show you the emails, if you like?"

"No thanks. And I really am sympathetic to your predicament, but circumstances have changed."

"Please—"

"I'm taking over for the time being, and Heritage Hill is bleeding money. It can't afford someone like you."

"As I told your father, with a few small tweaks I really think this place would be easy to turn around."

"Thanks for coming." He walked toward me, giving me no choice but to back up and walk with him. "But I've got a lot to take care of. Leave your card, and I'll gladly compensate you for your traveling expenses. Are you renting in town?"

I nodded, mortified that he was actually going to send me packing. "Above the coffee shop."

"I'll take care of your deposit and talk to the landlord to get you out of the lease."

I didn't want to get out of the lease. I wanted this job. But Mason was walking me toward the door. I couldn't very well refuse to leave.

"I..." What else was there to say? He didn't care that his father hired me. Or that I'd quit my job and moved across the country to be here. Part of me wanted to curse him out, but I had to remind myself —again—the guy had just lost a parent.

"Thanks for coming by. I'll be in touch."

He looked right through me, as if not even noticing I stood in front of him. The guy would be impervious to arguments of any kind. I could see that clearly. He was almost militant.

"I guess... that's it then?" It couldn't be. Had I really moved to New York for absolutely no reason?

"Have a good day, Miss Russo."

Yep. That was it. I wouldn't grovel. "Same to you, Mr. Bennett."

With that, I was hardly out of the door before he closed it. Not quite on my face, but close.

What. The hell. Had just happened?

4

MASON

"Show-off."

Beck shot me a "no shit" look from behind the bar. He knew full well his bottle-flip antics were impressing the girl sitting in front of him. I'd never seen her before, which meant she and her friends were probably tourists.

"Anyway," I continued to Parker, "they said I'll know about my leave request in a day or two."

O'Malley's Pub sat on the east corner of Cedar Falls town square. Although Heritage Hill had been built well before the town of Cedar Falls was established, the location couldn't be any better, within walking distance. Since O'Malley's was one of only two bars in town, even during the off season it was pretty much packed most days of the week.

"That seems quick," Parker said, taking a swing of beer.

"Captain called my situation an extenuating circumstance."

"By 'situation' you mean Papa Bennett?"

"Apparently."

My father loved coming to O'Malley's and meeting new people. He really was tailor-made for the service industry, unlike me. He had also enjoyed busting Beck's ass. More often than not, my friend would text me things like, *Papa Bennett is at the bar tonight. He just told a woman who I had a 100 percent chance of taking home to stay clear of me. You've got to do something about him, dude.*

So of course I'd text my father, who'd gotten a good laugh over his cock-blocking success. That time, he'd said the woman was too young for Beck anyway.

"What is it?" Parker was watching me.

"Just remembering the time Dad warned away that blonde tourist Beck tried to take home."

"The twenty-one-year-old?"

"Yeah, that one."

"Your dad was something else."

That was an understatement. "I can't believe he's fucking gone."

"Wild Turkey, neat," Beck said, sliding a glass toward me. I hadn't even noticed my first drink was gone. "On the house."

I lifted the glass in thanks to him and took a sip, the rich whiskey sliding down my throat.

"Isn't that the woman from earlier today?" Parker nudged me in the arm. "Pia?"

Sure enough, the stunning brunette was pulling out a seat at the opposite end of the bar from us. She hadn't seen us yet, but it was impossible not to notice her. I'd never met anyone in my life before with such clear blue eyes. Coupled with dark hair and the fullest fucking lips on the planet, Pia Russo had made one hell of an entrance earlier that day. Having just buried my father, I had no business imagining tearing the woman's clothes off, clearing the kitchen island with my hand and laying her down atop it. But that was exactly what I'd been thinking the entire time we talked. She was sexy as fucking hell. No wonder Beck had been panting after her all day and was in full-blown stalking mode now as he served her.

The guy was an absolute manwhore. We all

loved women, but Beck simply couldn't stay away from them.

"Beck isn't wasting any time," I said.

"She doesn't seem to be into him." Parker's surprise mirrored my own. Most women loved Beck. Like Parker, he could charm the habit off a nun with his sense of humor and good looks, but that didn't seem to be working. Part of my Ranger training showed me how to read body language, which in the field could be the difference between life or death. In this particular instance, it signaled the difference between interest and non-interest.

And she was about as interested in him as I was in hiring a manager for the inn. No one had run Heritage Hill but my dad, with the exception of my mother, when she was alive.

Pia finally looked our way, our eyes locking.

As expected, she didn't seem pleased. Just the opposite, in fact. I could tell she wanted to be nice, probably because of my dad, but her anger was as palpable now as it had been this afternoon. The woman should really stay away from poker.

"She's not starting a Mason fan club anytime soon."

"Agreed," I said without looking at Parker. Damned if I would break eye contact first.

"Man, did you see those eyes of hers?"

I was looking into them right now. "I did."

"I still can't believe you tossed her onto the street."

Finally, Pia looked away. She'd lasted longer than expected.

"She's not a street urchin. The woman is clearly capable and will be fine. I already talked to Paul and got her deposit returned and rent cleared for the month."

"Yeah, but still. She quit her damn job and moved from Oregon."

I couldn't help but smile. "Which is clear across the country."

"And what's so funny about that?"

"Never mind."

"I still think you should reconsider. Seems to me the perfect solution. You're about as personable as this coaster." He lifted up the coaster from under his glass as evidence.

Unlike a lot of people, Parker wasn't intimidated by my frown.

"What? It's true and you know it."

"Fuck off," I said, as lovingly as possible.

"Suit yourself. But I think you're nuts. Clearly Papa Bennett thought it was a good idea, and if you decide to go back to work but keep the inn open, boom. Problem solved."

"If I go back to work, I'm selling it."

"Okay, genius, let's think this through. You sell it. And the new owner runs it. Either way, someone other than you will be the new innkeeper."

I fucking hated that. "You mean someone other than my dad."

"That too."

"Stop making fucking sense, will you?"

Parker smiled. "Someone has to have two brain cells to rub together in this group. And it's obviously not that one." He nodded to Beck, who'd moved on from wooing Pia and was back to his original target.

Poor woman. She didn't stand a chance.

"At least we know he'll never break the pact."

My gaze shifted back to Pia. "I never worried about him breaking it."

"I never worried about any of us breaking it. You're a mean bastard. Cole wouldn't get married if you paid him ten million dollars to do it. And Beck and I like variety too much."

All true.

I watched as Pia sipped her red wine. She didn't glance my way, but instead sat alone and looked really fucking miserable. My doing, unfortunately.

"I never thought we'd actually do it," I said, going back to the pact we'd made in college never to marry. It had been Cole's idea—not surprising, since his parents had a pretty shitty marriage. Everyone, including Cole and his sister, agreed they should have gotten divorced years ago, but they stayed unhappily married for convenience's sake. And for appearances too.

"I did."

I looked at Parker. His characteristic smile was gone.

"If my dad could cheat, anyone is capable of it. Marriage just doesn't work."

"Or it works too well," I said quietly.

That was the one thing about Dad's death I wasn't sad about. Finally, after all these years, he was back with the woman he loved. The one whose death he never recovered from.

"Or that."

We fell into a companionable silence until Parker blurted out, "You should keep her."

Pia.

Truth was, it did make sense. But I wasn't sure about working so closely with a woman as beautiful as that. I'd been able to keep up my end of the pact by dating women who I couldn't see myself with for more than a night. Pia did not fall into that category. My attraction to her was so fucking strong, the second she started talking I knew I was in trouble.

"I should. But I won't," I said with a finality that Parker accepted.

She finally met my gaze.

And stood up.

5

PIA

Screw it.

No one ever got ahead in life by sitting on the sidelines and letting other people carry the ball. If I wanted this job to be my fuck you to the jerk who passed me over for a promotion I deserved, one I'd more than earned, then I actually needed the job.

Also, I didn't want to move back home, tail between my legs, and basically tell everyone I was let go before I even started the position.

"Mind if I join you?"

He was even hotter up close, but I knew that already. Too bad the guy apparently hated smiling, at least at me. Catching a glimpse of him laughing with his buddies, the bartender unfortunately one of them, I'd been taken aback. A smiling Mason was a devastating sight indeed.

"Actually," he began, but his friend cut in.

"Not at all."

I took the seat next to Mason. "Parker, right?"

"You got it. And you remember Beck, I'm sure," he said as the bartender sauntered over to us. I knew more than my share of women who'd fawn all over the guy. Good looks plus that kind of confidence? Luckily, I'd had my heart broken enough times to know how to avoid it.

"Hello, Beck," I said as if bored. In truth, I didn't even dare reach for my drink in front of me for fear my hands might shake. I could feel Mason looking at me.

"Hello, Pia," he drawled back. "Fancy meeting you on this side of the bar."

"Does that usually work?"

"To pick up women?"

"Yeah."

"Always. Except tonight. I have a feeling you're not into me."

Laughing at his appalled expression, I took the bait. "Do you really? That's so strange since it's very untrue."

"Now you're just toying with me," he accused.

"As much as I'd love to continue this extremely enlightening conversation," I said, "it seems there's a woman who you might actually have a chance with boring a hole into your back."

Chuckling, Beck turned toward the woman he'd been flirting with all night. She lifted her empty drink. "Seems like you're right," he said, winking at me before walking away.

Sitting back on the stool and grabbing my wine, I finally turned to Mason. Though he wasn't smiling, exactly, his frown didn't seem to be as big as when I first sat.

"So," I began.

"The answer is no."

What a bastard. A gorgeous, gruff bastard.

"I'd say something about your lack of manners but will cut you some slack. Given your circumstances."

"His attitude," Parker said from the other side of Mason, "has nothing to do with his dad. Mason's always like this."

"Good to know," I said, rethinking my plan. Maybe not a boss I'd care to have.

"Were you going to ask me something else? Like if you can have the job?" Mason asked.

Like I said. Bastard.

"I was going to ask how you managed to snag these two as friends," I said sarcastically, "since they apparently like to smile and you do not."

I was wasting my time. Clearly he wasn't going to reconsider, so the gloves were off. This wasn't my potential boss but a guy being a complete dickhead to me.

"We met in kindergarten," he said of Beck. "And this one"—Mason nodded toward Parker—"in college."

Surprised he answered without a hint of sarcasm, I had no comeback.

"I see." Finding my words, I asked, "Where did you go?"

"University of Rochester. You?"

"Oregon State University for hospitality management." And though I probably shouldn't, I added, "You know, to manage hotels *and* inns... things like that."

Parker snickered. Leaning forward, he smiled in a way that was almost encouraging. As if he was rooting for me.

"You don't say?" Mason asked, the sarcasm back in full force.

Mom always told me you catch more flies with honey, but I was over here full of piss and vinegar.

"My parents own a restaurant in Oregon, which got me interested in the hospitality business. Since graduating, I've worked in various places, mostly lodges, up and down the coast."

"Never been to Oregon." So much for his acknowledging my credentials.

"It's beautiful. I'm an ocean girl at heart and got used to being by the water."

"Yet you came here?"

I met his gorgeous eyes that all at once seemed to both beckon me and push me away. "I was ready for a challenge."

"You think Heritage Hill is a challenge?"

"Have you seen your father's books?" Oops. Too much vinegar.

"I meant it when I said it was a surprise that he hired you. My father did not like change, with a few exceptions when he updated the place. He wanted to keep Heritage Hill running much the same as when he was a child. I have seen the books and tried to talk to him about making some updates, but the man is... was... as stubborn as they come," Mason said, wincing at that last part.

"Something made him change his mind. I spoke to him twice, after a string of emails, and he was ready to do, in his words, 'whatever it takes' to get Heritage Hill back in the black."

"Interesting." Mason turned to Parker. "Does that sound like Dad?"

"No," Parker said. "It doesn't."

"Sure it does." Beck braced his hands on the bar in front of us. Where had he even come from? "He told me about a month ago that there would be some changes coming. Admitted he'd been too slow to keep up with the times."

"That's about when he first contacted me," I said.

Mason studied Beck closely. "You didn't think to mention that today?"

"You mean after Pia had left? When you locked yourself in the office for the afternoon?"

Mason's jaw flexed. Beck might be a player, to the extreme, but he wasn't intimidated by the very intimidating Mason Bennett. If they'd been friends since college, that was a long time. My guess was that Mason was in his early thirties.

I'd just hit the big three-oh this past summer. Hooray for me. They said age was just a number, but it still stung. I never imagined myself starting a brand-new life at thirty. Or flying cross-country to attempt as much, only to be turned away by the hottest, most emotionally unavailable man on the planet.

"Were you in the military?" I blurted.

Both Mason and Parker looked at me. It was just an instinct, but it seemed like a good one. Parker's knowing smile gave Mason away.

"I was. Why do you ask?"

"Mr. Modest won't tell you, but he was more than just military. Army Ranger. My boy is as badass as they come."

A former Army Ranger. That explained a lot. Though I didn't know as much about them as the Navy SEALs, I did know the average person wouldn't have the grit or discipline to accomplish such a thing.

You are not impressed. The guy's still a dick. Not. Impressed.

"No reason," I said, turning away.

Watching Beck very capably run the entire bar himself, I decided to finish my drink and leave. I was done begging for this job. A guy like Mason, a Ranger, wouldn't change his mind. He would be impervious to any form of manipulation or persuasion, not that I was trying to manipulate him.

It was done.

Pushing my glass away, I stood up and grabbed my purse.

"Where are you going?" Mason asked, almost like he didn't want me to leave.

"Back to Oregon," I said. "There's nothing for me here."

I couldn't stay another second. Mason smiling was a sight to behold, and one that would be burned onto my brain for life. I all but ran from the bar, realizing I'd never said goodbye to Parker. Or Beck for that matter. They seemed like decent guys, but I just had to get out of there.

Pushing open the door of the bar, I stumbled out into the chilly fall night but didn't move. I leaned against the brick building, closed my eyes and imagined getting off the plane in Oregon. Failing. Again.

"Pia?"

My eyes flew open.

Apparently Mason had used his stealth training to follow me. I hadn't even heard the door open. "Do you still want the job?"

6

MASON

Sometimes you made a decision that was guaranteed to bite you in the ass. This was going to be one of those times. It didn't matter how much training I'd gone through for the department and as a Ranger, learning to avoid making split-second calls that I might later regret. Every once in a while, we all just ended up doing stupid shit.

Hiring Pia fell firmly into that category.

First of all, if I sold the inn, she'd likely be out of a job anyway. The most likely candidate for a buyer would be Paul Baker. He collected real estate in Cedar Falls like other people collected baseball cards or pennies. For years he'd told my father that Heritage Hill was the top on his list of properties he'd love to own. And for years my father had told Paul that it was not for sale. Knowing he'd pay top dollar, I'd almost contacted him earlier today but held off. If he did purchase it, Paul had more kids and grandkids to run the place than anyone I knew. Better to let Pia head back to Oregon before establishing a life here and having the rug pulled out from under her, as it certainly would be if Paul bought the place.

Second, I was attracted as hell to the woman. Having her work for me was not ideal. Mixing business and pleasure was never a great idea, especially when I had no intention of ever sealing the deal with a woman, long-term commitment and all. My friends and I may have been college kids, but I'd agreed to the bachelor pact for a reason.

"I do," she said now to my stupid fucking question. What the hell had I been thinking?

"You sure? I'm not my father."

Her eyes narrowed. "What does that mean, exactly?"

"I'm pretty sure you know what that means."

"That he was nice and you…"

I raised my brows. "Go ahead."

"Fine," she said, lifting her chin. "You are less nice."

Refusing to smile, I inwardly gave the woman credit. She was quick. And honest. I liked both of those things about her.

"I might not have put it exactly like that."

"No?" she asked, back to herself. The fire in Pia's eyes had gone out just before she ran out of the bar. Even if Parker hadn't pushed me off the bar stool, I'd planned on coming after her anyway. Seeing her defeated, eyes closed, when I opened the door hadn't felt... right.

"No. As long as you realize we're two different people, and that there's every likelihood you'll be out of a job sooner rather than later anyway—"

"Jesus," she said. "You're planning on firing me again, even before I start?"

"No, but I haven't made any long-term decisions about keeping the inn. If I do sell, the most likely buyer will just as likely hire a family member to manage the place. That's one of the reasons I didn't want you to stay."

"Oh."

"Did I take the wind out of your sails, Pia?"

As if she'd admit it. "You could have told me that earlier rather than, 'No thanks. Go home,'" she said, her hands flailing up in frustration.

How I'd love to take those pretty hands, hold

them above her head and pin them to the wall, our bodies pressed together. I would devour those full lips of hers and absolutely not think of them wrapped around my dick.

Fuck. This was such a bad idea. "I don't remember it quite like that."

"Close enough."

Stalemate.

Damned if I didn't want to go back inside. With her.

"Come back in," I said. "We can talk specifics." Remembering Parker and Beck, and not wanting to endure the two clowns' commentary, I had a better idea. "Did you eat dinner yet?"

"No. I was actually planning to grab something in there."

"O'Malley's is fine if you like chicken fingers and fries." I pointed to a restaurant on the other side of the town square. "The Big Easy has much better food."

She hesitated. Not that I blamed her.

"Let me tell the guys, and I'll grab you dinner. It's the least I can do after this morning."

"That is true."

I smiled. Pia didn't pull any punches. Before she could change her mind, I headed back inside.

"Hey, taking Pia to the Big Easy," I said to Parker as I walked up to him. "You're on your own for the night."

"The whole night, huh?"

"Don't be an ass. I'm rehiring her. We have some things to discuss."

"Did he just say he's rehiring Pia?" Beck asked.

The innuendo in Beck's tone was one of the reasons I hadn't taken her back inside. "Tell Cole I'll catch him at the house later."

"Will do," Parker said.

Back outside, glad to see Pia was still there, I resolved to try to make up for earlier. While it was true I still didn't think working with Pia was the best idea in the world, what was done was done. I'd make the best of it, stop picturing her naked and keep our relationship professional.

"This is the best of the three restaurants in the town square, but there are a few others within walking distance that aren't bad. And you probably already know the Coffee Cabin has decent coffee but even better coffee cake."

"You don't look like a guy who eats a lot of coffee cake."

"Eh, not usually a fan of empty calories, but I indulge every once in a while."

"That's what I thought."

I opened the door to the Big Easy, a New Orleans-themed restaurant with colorful shutters and wrought-iron accents that more than hinted at its roots.

As usual, the owner was standing behind a hostess stand.

"Pia," I said as we walked up to the stand. "Meet Maggie LeBlanc. She's graced Cedar Falls with her Cajun and Creole cuisine for more than twenty years."

Pia stuck out her hand, which Maggie took. "Pleased to meet you."

"Same here." Maggie frowned at me. "I'm so sorry again about your father, Mason."

Dad. For the briefest of moments, I'd almost forgotten, pretending my life was the same as it had been last time I visited home. But nothing would ever be the same again. Fuck, but it hurt. "Thanks, Maggie."

"This place is incredible." Pia was looking up at the ceiling, where beads hung from every corner. Light jazz played in the main dining room.

"On weekends there's live jazz," I said. "That's usually when I like to come."

"And during crawfish boils," Maggie added.

I couldn't argue that. "True. Maggie, this is Pia Russo, the new manager of Heritage Hill."

Maggie's eyes widened. "And who's the innkeeper?"

"Me for now," I said. "So do you have a table for two?"

"Sure do, come with me."

We sat, ordered food and drinks and dove right in. Nothing personal. All business.

"So tell me everything you and Dad discussed. What you planned to do for him and the inn. What his thoughts were. Bring me up to speed."

Pia talked about some of the same things I'd considered. Renovation to improve aesthetic appeal and functionality. A fresh color palette to appeal to modern travelers. Identifying target markets. Utilizing local partnerships to hit that market.

But her ideas went a hell of a lot further along. "I also think elevating the inn's dining experience by hiring a chef would open up a whole new world of possibilities."

"You're talking about adding a dining room. That's next-level renovation."

"Not a dining room, necessarily. Somewhere for special events that can be incorporated into the inn's existing structure. Wine pairings, themed tasting nights, and of course the biggie, weddings. But that could be phase two. Partnering with local restaurants, like this one, would be a good start."

"My father hated the idea of weddings. Said it would ruin the experience for other guests."

"He mentioned that, and to be honest..." Pia became more and more animated as she talked. "I know he wasn't sold on the idea. But I'm positive there's a way to include them as a part of our offerings while maintaining the serene environment your father insisted on for other guests. It would bring the income we need to make the other necessary changes and could be done tastefully."

"We'll have to talk more. What else do you have?" I could tell Pia was still bursting at the seams.

"Well, I'd love to lean into the idea of community involvement and partnerships. Offering joint packages for guests to explore the region. Maggie mentioned a crawfish boil. That's the exact kind of thing I'm thinking—hosting community festivals and events to increase visibility and build relationships. Think seasonal celebrations and holiday packages. And obviously beefing up a customer loyalty program."

"Obviously," I said as our meals were brought out.

Pia's enthusiasm was difficult to ignore. I could easily see why Dad hired her, even if I was still surprised he'd reached out in the first place.

"I'll be honest, this sounds like a lot."

"That's why you have me."

Of course she meant professionally, but for the briefest of seconds I imagined Pia was talking personally. I should have let her go. Leave the bar, leave Cedar Falls, and not look back.

What I should do, and would do?

Two very different things.

7
PIA

"Morning, Pia."

"Good morning, Beck," I said as he opened the door.

"Dude, Mason is a lucky guy. You look amazing."

"Beck," I said, stepping inside, "you are aware I'm Mason's employee, right?"

"Right. But not mine, thankfully."

Mason was nowhere to be seen. He had said nine o'clock, and Mason didn't strike me as the kind of guy to be late. I pulled out my phone. Eight fifty. Oops. I'd overestimated how long it would take to walk here. Just the fact that I could walk to work was a huge change from any other job, and one I was going to enjoy.

"Are you insinuating that because I'm not your employee it's okay to hit on me?"

Beck plopped down onto a couch. "Yep. Exactly. Glad we're on the same page."

This guy was something else. "We're actually not on the same page at all. The only thing I'm interested in here is making Heritage Hill the premiere Cedar Falls destination."

"And that's it?"

"That's it."

"If I were to ask you out—"

"I'd politely decline."

"Beck. May I speak with you?" a voice called from the hallway.

If I remembered correctly, this one's name was Cole.

"Sure, go for it."

Since Beck clearly wasn't moving, he stepped into the room. "Beck?"

Sighing like a wayward child, Beck didn't move. "Is this about the dishes in the sink?"

Cole cleared his throat. "Yes, it is."

"Then you're gonna want to talk to Parker. Those are his."

"Please ignore both of them," a deep voice said from the entranceway.

Mason. My heart had no business thumping as if my current crush had just entered the room. Yet that's exactly what it did. Though Mason was not—I repeat, not—my current crush. In addition to being borderline brash and smiling too rarely, with a few exceptions at dinner last night, he was also my new boss.

"Do they live here?"

"Nah, they're just staying temporarily."

"We do live here," Beck said.

"Speaking of." Cole crossed his arms, still glaring at Beck. "I have to head back in a few days. No time like the present to clean out the basement."

"We did say we'd tackle that today." Beck didn't seem pleased by the prospect, though I didn't blame him. It sounded like a daunting task.

"You guys don't have to—" Mason started, but Beck cut him off, standing.

"Not listening." He breezed by Mason and Cole, presumably to tackle the basement. Cole looked like he was heading to a polo match and not at all ready for the task at hand. As they left, Mason shook his head.

"Are they really cleaning the basement?" I asked.

"Apparently. Though I have no idea how they

plan to accomplish that. Not even I would be able to make heads or tails of what's good down there."

"That's actually really sweet of them."

Mason pushed away from the doorframe where he'd been standing. With a fitted pair of navy sweats and white tee, he was more casually dressed than I'd seen him yet. Unsurprisingly, it was a good look on him.

Not that I noticed.

"Sweet isn't the first thing that comes to mind when I think of those two."

"I'd say what they're doing is pretty nice. But don't they have jobs? Or at least, Cole. I guess Beck works at night."

"Come take a tour of the property," he said. "Like you said, Beck bartends. And Cole is a professor at Columbia. Tenure track."

Mason sounded proud of his friend.

"Isn't he a little young to be a tenured professor at Columbia?"

"Cole's not tenured yet, but he's on his way. His father is a Yale professor, so it runs in the family. He was pretty much groomed for this. In case you hadn't figured that out already."

"He does look the part." I followed Mason through the kitchen to a back door. We stepped outside onto a wraparound deck that ran the length of the place. The lake view took my breath away. "Pictures don't do it justice."

With the leaves changing color, the property couldn't possibly look any more picturesque.

"It's so beautiful."

"Agreed," he said.

I could tell from the corner of my eye that Mason had been looking at me, not the property. But obviously he was talking about the landscape. There was not a hint of interest there, which was more than fine, of course. Since that would be inappropriate.

So why are you wishing he fawned all over you like Beck?

"This was my father's favorite spot," he said, hands gripping the railing in front of us as we looked out. "You can see most of the property from here."

"He clearly loved this place. That was obvious when we spoke."

"It was his life." Mason paused. "My mother died when I was eleven from breast cancer. After that, he poured his heart and soul into Heritage Hill. The people who stayed here were his family."

Though I didn't want to ask, I got the sense Mason's father never remarried. "Do you have any siblings?"

"No." Mason shook his head. "Mom got sick less than a year after I was born. The cancer came back twice and... no, I don't have any siblings." He looked at me. "Do you?"

"Three sisters, all younger."

"Four girls. Sounds like fun for your dad."

I laughed. "Five with Mom. And yeah, tons of fun. He's married to his work, but I think the restaurant is more of an escape than anything else."

"I don't blame him."

Was Mason teasing me? I didn't think he was capable of it.

"We're all close," I added, almost uncomfortable with nice Mason. "But I fight more with the middle two. They drive me crazy sometimes, but I'll keep them."

"Are they still in Oregon?"

"Yep. One lives on her own, the others are still at home."

"You don't mind being out here with your family all out west?"

Good question. At first, I had been resistant to the idea of moving so far away. But the job had been a perfect fit for my skill set, and I needed to get away, so I took it. "It'll take some getting used to but..." I waved a hand in front of me. "Working with this was too hard to pass up. There's so much potential here."

Catching myself staring at the veins in Mason's forearms, I quickly looked away.

He pushed himself up and started down the back porch, all business now. "So as you know..." He began retelling the history of Heritage Hill. I'd studied before interviewing with his father so already knew all of this, but I listened carefully to him. We toured the grounds first and then the inn, beginning with the family and friend rooms and ending with the guest ones. "So, eight rooms, each named after a female in my family, starting way back with Elizabeth, my great-grandmother. The first Heritage Hill matriarch."

"Three lakeview guest rooms, one village view with the fireplace, and the others are all village views with no extra amenities?"

"Yep."

We stood in the Eliza room, considered the best of all eight. It boasted both a view and a fireplace but was definitely outdated.

"What are your thoughts on updating the rooms?"

"That we need more money to renovate than Heritage Hill's coffers will allow."

"So you're on board with some updates?"

"I am, but we need to work within a budget. I've thought about asking Parker to handle some of the bigger renovations—he's in construction—but he's still in building season."

"So maybe over the winter, weather allowing?"

"Maybe. If we sectioned off some of the rooms while renting others, it could work since the winter is less busy anyway. But the main rooms downstairs? I don't see how to get that done without closing. The outside is tricky too. No one wants to pull up to scaffolds on their romantic getaway."

When he said the word "romantic," our eyes met. And for the first time, something in his look set off alarm bells. And fluttering in my stomach. I wanted to look away but found it impossible. He was so damn sexy.

When his jaw flexed, I could tell Mason was annoyed, probably with himself for showing any kind of interest in me.

"Hey, oops, sorry." Beck leaned against the doorframe. "Didn't mean to interrupt anything."

"You're not interrupting anything," Mason said, his tone annoyed. "We're touring the property."

"Uh huh, okay." He put up his hands as if giving himself up.

Beck was one of the only people who had more animated hand gestures than me.

"I think it's really incredible, what you're doing," I said, my meaning clear. He was dusty as hell and actually had a cobweb in his hair.

"You realize I heard that as, 'You are incredible,' right?"

"Ugh," I asked Mason, "is he always this impossible?"

His answer was automatic. "Always."

"Now that we've established I'm pretty incredible and impossibly magnetic—"

"That's not what I said."

"There's a lot of shit down there. Cole and I are putting it in good, trash, and 'ask Mason' piles. Does that work?"

"Sure," he said. "I'll come down after I get Pia settled."

Beck's grin meant he was about to say something spicy. "Want me to get her settled for you?"

Mason looked pissed. "She is my employee, asshole. Keep it professional."

The irony of that statement wasn't lost on either Beck or me; we both laughed. But I stopped immediately as I turned back to Mason. He was not laughing. In fact, he looked even more off-put than the first time we met.

"Good luck with that one," Beck said, walking away.

"It's okay," I assured Mason. "I don't offend easily and can handle him. Honestly, it's no big deal."

"You shouldn't have to handle Beck. I'll talk to him later. I don't know how long he's staying but he won't make you uncomfortable in the meantime."

"I'm not uncomfortable at all," I reassured him. "Seriously."

Mason looked like he was going to argue. Instead, he nodded toward the door. "Come on, I'll take you to your office."

Without looking back to see if I was coming, he took off down the hall. I'd have to convince him it really wasn't a big deal, but if there was anything I'd learned spending the morning with Mason, it was that he didn't convince easily of anything. Once his mind was made up, it was an uphill battle to unmake it.

Especially concerning me.

8

MASON

"Pia thinks we renovate in phases but prioritize the ground floor and kitchen so that, by spring, we can begin hosting bigger events, including weddings."

The guys and I sat around the kitchen island, takeout containers and empty beer bottles littered everywhere. Thursday nights didn't get any better than this. The only exception would have been if my dad were to walk through the door and say something like, "Looks like a beer bath in here. Get it? Beer bath, not blood bath?"

"Look at him smiling when he talks about Pia," Parker said.

"Yeah, like you're talking about a fish you caught." Beck reached for a cold French fry in a Styrofoam container. He kissed the fry. "You gorgeous thing."

"I haven't once kissed a fish. Or called it 'gorgeous.' You're ridiculous."

"That's more like you," Cole added, drinking beer instead of Scotch for a change, "with any marginally pretty customer."

"Marginally pretty?" Beck popped the fry into his mouth. "My standards are much higher than that."

"Too high with Pia. Not sure if you noticed." Parker took a swig of beer. "But she's not into you. Despite your best efforts. She is, on the other hand, very into the boss man."

It took all of my discipline not to ask, "You think so?" like some eager fifteen-year-old. And that was the exact reason I shouldn't have hired her. Instead, I said, "First of all, that's not true. Second of all, it doesn't matter. She's my employee."

"Third," Cole said, "she isn't going to be for long if you sell, so what does that matter?"

I hated when Cole got logical on me.

"I got the leave," I reminded them. "And intend to follow through as if that leave might be extended. Or maybe Pia will be so good I can keep the place and my job."

"Is that what you want?" Parker asked.

"Who the fuck knows?" I reached for my beer. "In the meantime, what does your calendar for the next few months look like?"

Parker screwed up his face the same way he always did when he was thinking. I could practically see steam coming from his ears. "Busy. But I have a thought."

"Look out," Beck teased.

"What if I stay here? Work on the place in my spare time. With the rent money I save, I can work for materials only."

"No way," I said, automatically rejecting the idea. "You can stay, of course. But you're not doing a job without getting paid."

"I will be getting paid cause you'll be feeding my ass too. Honestly though," he added quickly, knowing I was going to refuse again, "I've been talking about starting my own construction company for too long. Renovating Heritage Hill would be my job alone, something to put on the resume if I do venture out."

"Oh shit." Beck looked impressed. "I honestly never thought you'd pull the trigger. No offense, but I thought Jack had you by the balls."

"Jack does have me by the balls," Parker said. "As bosses go, he's not great. But he's also the biggest player in town and pays the bills." He shrugged.

Parker was being nice. His boss, the owner of the construction company he worked for, was a total dickhead.

"Anyway." Parker actually looked serious. "Let's do it."

I could tell he was for real. Being friends for an entire lifetime with someone meant you could read them pretty easily. Though I didn't love the idea of him working for free, I needed the job and was short on cash. But I did have a place for him to stay and guests' mouths to feed for breakfast anyway, and if it was a stepping stone for Parker...

"I'm in."

"Hold on a second." Beck leaned forward. "In case you forgot, we're roommates. You honestly think the two of you are going to recreate college days here in this massive inn without me?"

Funnily enough, the second Parker tossed out his idea, I knew Beck was going to want in. Thankfully there were four rooms in the main house, and none were occupied. "You can take number three."

He pretended to be offended. "The smallest, nice."

"Also far enough away," Cole added in his typically dry manner, "no one has to hear the"—he cleared his throat—"guests you take home."

"Exactly," I said. "And maybe you can make yourself useful with the renovations too."

"Of course." He did not sound at all convincing. "I did spend two days cleaning a damn basement."

"True." And I appreciated it, even if I didn't say the words. The guys knew saying such things out loud made me uncomfortable.

Cole took off his glasses to polish them. "If only I could partake in this interesting adult male bonding experiment."

"Whatcha mean?" Beck asked.

"I mean," he said, as if giving one of his famous lectures, "it's one thing to declare we will remain bachelors for life. But quite another to actually live together at our age."

"You say that like we're seventy." Parker shifted on his stool. I looked down, unable to unsee the brightest pair of pink and blue socks imaginable. Even though it was sort of his thing, those had to go.

"It would be more acceptable if you were seventy," Cole said, popping his glasses back onto his face. "It would be like a retirement home."

"And this will be like a very fancy frat house," Beck said.

"Exactly my fear." I took a long swig of beer.

"Frat brothers are not thirty-one and thirty-two," Cole pointed out.

"You should totally join us." Beck was unrepentant.

"Sure. Great idea. Maybe O'Malley's is hiring."

Beck could have taken offense to that, but he didn't. With a college degree and parents who had more money than God, Beck chose to sling drinks because he liked it. Not because he had no other option, which would also be fine in my opinion. My father taught me never to look down on a person because of how they looked or what they chose to do for a living, and it was sage advice. I'd met cops who didn't deserve the respect they got and custodians who deserved a hell of a lot more.

"You hate the city almost as much as Mason," Beck accused instead.

"Clarification," I added. "He hates it more."

Cole was more like Parker. Loved the outdoors, played ice hockey growing up and in college. His family moved from Cedar Falls when his dad got the position at Yale, but of all of us, Cole enjoyed small-town living most. But when Columbia came calling, he answered.

"That's neither here nor there."

"Sure it is," Beck pushed back. "Being a tenured college professor is your father's dream, not yours. You can leave anytime."

Now we were treading in dangerous territory. "We're getting off track," I said, refereeing. "Are the two of you actually moving in? What if I decide to sell?"

"Apartments in Cedar Falls aren't that hard to come by," Parker said.

"So we're really doing this?" Beck asked.

"We're doing this," Parker said, looking back and forth between Beck and me.

"Can we please remember the end game?" Cole broke in. "No wives."

The bachelor pact had been his idea, and anytime one of us had come close to breaking it, Cole stepped in with one of the myriad of reasons marriage was a bad idea. As if we had to be convinced.

I was allergic to the kind of lifelong heartbreak my father suffered. Parker's dad cheated and his parents divorced, making him as bitter about the institution of marriage as any of us. Beck's had divorced too. Ironically, Cole's were the only set of parents intact, but it was almost worse because everyone knew it was for appearances and convenience only. Cole basically resented his parents almost as much as he resented people who didn't read for pleasure, which included me, but... whatever.

"Who the hell wants a wife?" Beck asked, bottom on the list to ever actually settle down.

"Not me." Parker stood up and went to the fridge for another beer. "Someone to complain I'm fishing all day? No thanks."

"Mason?" Cole peered at me through his dark-rimmed glasses.

"Cole?"

"You're still on board?"

"Obviously." Was that really a question?

"Even if a certain dark-haired inn manager makes the move on you?" he countered.

"Seriously? Not you too."

"Sorry, buddy, I'm with them on this one. I've seen the way you two look at each other."

I sighed. "How many times do I have to remind you she is my employee?"

"So you don't mind if I take a shot with her?" Beck asked.

He had no chance. She wasn't interested. "Not at all. But please just don't do it here. This may be your new home, but it's work for her, and I won't have her be uncomfortable at work."

I caught Parker looking at me strangely. "What?" I asked him.

"What about me? There's a lack of hot women in Cedar Falls, if you haven't noticed. And Pia fits that bill very well."

My chest tightened. Parker was every woman's type, unless she hated the outdoors. As good-looking as Beck without the cockiness. Pia could easily go for a guy like him. Not that it mattered. Except, the thought of Parker and Pia naked in bed together made me want to vomit.

But with all of the guys, Cole especially, looking at me so intently, waiting for my answer, there was only one to give. "Same as I said to Beck. Keep work and play separate, please."

"You sure?"

I couldn't tell if he was serious or testing me. Either way, the answer was the same. Even if I didn't like it much. "I'm sure."

With that matter dropped, Beck and Cole went back to fighting about whether or not Cole liked his job. For my part, I tried like hell to get Pia with any of these guys out of my mind.

Unfortunately, it didn't work.

9
PIA

"Yes, Mom, things are fine."

I popped her on speaker and glanced around the office, which had clearly been Mason's father's. He'd emptied the desk but his bookshelf was still intact, something I was inclined to leave even though Mason told me I could box anything else I'd like.

It was a cozy, well-appointed space with a view of the lake that Mason assured me he didn't need, saying there was a desk in his bedroom, though he hardly seemed to use it. Anytime I had seen Mason doing paperwork this past week, it was at the kitchen island.

"Your apartment looks small in the picture you sent yesterday."

I logged into my computer. "It's fine, trust me. I'll send one of my office. It's got a gorgeous lake view."

My mother was a sucker for the water, just like me.

"Oohhh, nice. Have you met anyone there yet?"

"That woman I told you about, Delaney. We have dinner plans Saturday night."

"That's great."

Mason appeared in the doorframe, filling it, as he always did. In jeans and a navy distressed T-shirt, his arms were on full display. I waved him inside.

"What about any boys? Oh, and I forgot to tell you, I saw Richard Sterling yesterday."

Oh my God. Quickly pressing the speaker button, I picked up my phone. "Seriously, Mom. I've been here less than two weeks. Have to run though, the boss is here."

A smiling Mason slayed me. It was so much easier when he was being a jerk, something he did from time to time, though never quite as much as that first day. But sometimes his short, curt responses jarred me. We were opposites in so many ways.

Getting my mother off the phone, I was prepared to pretend he hadn't heard part of our conversation and thought quickly what I could ask him instead.

"Boys, huh?"

So much for that.

"My mother is very... curious."

He sat down in the plush evergreen cushioned chair opposite my desk. "Curious?"

"Yes. My sister calls her intrusive, but I don't see it that way. She just cares and wants us to be happy."

"Hmm."

He was so difficult to read. Did the Rangers teach him to do that? Make his expressions completely neutral?

"So I guess that means no boyfriend?"

It was the last question in the world I'd have expected from him.

"No boyfriend."

Did he have a girlfriend?

"You?"

Oops. It slipped.

"Do I have a boyfriend?"

"Sure. Or girlfriend. Whatever."

At least he was still smiling. "No girlfriend at present."

Alrighty then.

"I actually came in to see what you thought of this." He leaned forward, putting a color palette on my desk. "Parker is going to start working on the reception and foyer area next week, so we need a wall color. It's similar to the one you sent, maybe a shade darker."

"Next week already? Wow, that's quick. How are you thinking to reroute guests?"

"What do you think of some sort of wall divider as soon as they enter, taking them into the parlor? I could have the reception desk moved in there."

"I think it's a great idea, and I love the color too." I handed the swatch back to him. As I did, our fingers touched. Brief enough to hardly notice. But I noticed. And the way Mason looked at me, it seemed he did too.

At first I thought it was my imagination, but every day the charge between us grew stronger. There was no doubt at this point he was attracted to me, and I was to him. Big time.

Boss.

Jerk.

I tried to remember those two things, but when he wasn't all sulky and reticent, thinking of him like the big jerk he was that first day became more and more difficult. Added to the fact the poor guy's father just passed away... it was a dangerous train of thought.

Mason cleared his throat.

"I also wanted to mention," he said, as if that exchange hadn't happened, "Cole's heading back tomorrow. You're welcome to come to O'Malley's tonight with us to celebrate."

That seemed like an odd word to use. "Celebrate? That he's leaving?"

"He's a pain in the ass sometimes."

"But you said he's one of your best friends?"

"Also true."

"So why are you best friends with a guy who's a pain in the ass?"

Mason shrugged. "Because he's also loyal to a fault and a lot of fun when he loosens up. Not to mention, he's the smartest guy I know."

"I see."

"Come out with us tonight. You'll see what I mean."

I had no plans and would love to, but... "Are you sure that's a good idea?"

Mason appeared genuinely confused. "Whaddya mean?"

Shit. "You know, boss. Employee. All of that."

"That's not a concern for me at all. We're a team of two, three if you count Esther. I think it's perfectly reasonable for us to be more like friends, but if that's not what you want—"

"Oh no," I reassured him. "That would be great. I just never want to overstep."

Mason sighed, not like he was annoyed but more as if trying to sort through his response. "I invited you, so no worries about overstepping. Plus, you're going to be seeing a lot of Parker and Beck, so might as well get used to them."

Mason had told me about their arrangement, how they were moving in with him. I hadn't seen much of Parker these past few days, but Beck popped his head into the office periodically. Asking me out, and me saying no, had become a running joke between us. At this point, I didn't even think he really wanted to go out with me but did it more for laughs. It felt as if we were becoming friends. And I actually liked friend Beck a lot better than potential date Beck. That guy was as cocky as they came.

Actually, they were both pretty cocky.

"What's so funny?" Mason asked when I didn't respond but laughed instead.

"I was just thinking about Beck's latest attempt at getting me to go out with him," I said, pointing to the vase of white roses on my desk.

"Are you fucking kidding me? I told him not to make you uncomfortable."

"Oh no, no, it's not like that. Honestly, I don't

think he even wants to go out with me at this point. It's sort of just a running joke."

Mason raised his brows. "I might not get too comfortable with that idea. Trust me, if you said yes, Beck would go out with you in a heartbeat."

"You think?" I teased, not caring really about the answer since it was never happening. He simply wasn't my type.

Mason was about to say something more but stopped. Looked pointedly at me.

"What is it?" I prompted, curious.

"Nothing," he said, standing.

It wasn't nothing. I was sure of it. And just as sure that Mason wasn't going to spill the beans.

"What time tonight?" I asked.

"Seven."

"See you there. If it's okay, I'm taking off early today for a dentist appointment."

"Like I said on your first day, there's no set time or days. As long as we're on the same page with what we're both responsible for, think of your schedule as flexible as mine."

In other words, just get the job done. Not a problem at all.

"Thanks. I'll email you my final proposal for

some of the things we discussed yesterday before I leave."

"Sounds good."

He walked out, Mason's incredibly well-shaped ass impossible to ignore. At my door, he stopped, though, and turned back to me.

"I don't think so. I know."

With that, he was gone.

Know what?

I replayed our conversation.

Ahh. Beck. Mason knew for certain he'd go out with me. But was I crazy to think there was another layer to that? Like maybe because Mason would too? It was a train of thought I should definitely not spend any time exploring, just like I should not be excited to hang out with Mason tonight at O'-Malley's.

If only the mind worked like that and you could turn off your thoughts. Fat chance of that happening anytime soon.

Especially when it came to Mason.

10

MASON

"Here comes your girl," Parker quipped.

Unfortunately, inviting Pia tonight had given the guys some ideas about us. Namely, that I liked her. Which wasn't altogether untrue. Maybe it was the grief, having a distraction for my mind as I lay awake at night thinking of all the things I'd never say to my father. The questions I never asked him or the life events of mine he'd miss. In the midst of those thoughts, Pia's face often appeared. Usually smiling, sometimes laughing, always using her hands to convey a story.

I'd think of a hell of a lot more too, but since I didn't exactly need her to walk in just as I acquired a hard-on, I pushed those thoughts aside.

"She's not my girl," I said.

"Right. Because she's mine." Beck gave Cole another Scotch. Apparently he was going to tie one on tonight despite the fact that he'd be driving back tomorrow. Should make for a fun night.

"Not from what I've seen." Cole took the glass and pushed his empty hand across the bar.

"Zip it," I said, not wanting Pia to hear them talking about her that way. She might have said she was totally fine with Beck's advances, but they were annoying. And I was not fine with them. Trouble was, Beck didn't listen very well. Or at all. He'd make a shit Ranger.

"Damn, she's looking hot tonight." Parker gave Pia a look that I liked even less than Beck's advances. At least I knew she wasn't interested in Beck, but Parker was a big unknown.

He was also right. She did look hot.

It wasn't her understated outfit—jeans, a white button-down shirt and black boots—or the red lipstick, something I'd not seen her wear yet, which was sexy as hell. It was the way Pia walked into the bar, as if the world were her oyster.

"Hey, guys," she said, heading toward the empty seat next to me. "Guess this one's for me?"

She peered at the alcohol behind the bar as Beck

came up to her. "Do you have limoncello, by chance?"

"No, ma'am. But I'll get it for you. Will you go out with me then?"

She laughed. "Nope. Will you still get it?"

Beck rolled his eyes. "Obviously. What are you planning to do with it?"

"Um, drink it," she quipped back.

"Straight-up shot? Or do I also need to get you some Prosecco?"

Pia seemed impressed. "How very astute of you. Yeah, I was thinking more of a limoncello spritz. I guess an Irish pub doesn't stock Prosecco either."

"Not yet, but it will."

As she and Beck went back and forth, coming up with a new drink for her, I unsuccessfully attempted to tamp down an annoyance that had no business rearing its ugly head. There was a friendly banter between them that seemed easier and more natural than ours. So what?

"Perfect," she said as they settled on a vodka soda drink for her.

"No red wine tonight?"

"I'm a mood drinker," she said.

"That tracks."

"How?" Pia asked, waving hello to the other guys.

"I dunno. It just seems like... you."

"Because I have big moods?"

As if I would answer that one.

"It's not an insult to me. I do have big moods. If I'm happy, I'm really happy. If I'm upset, there's no hiding it."

"In that case, yes."

True to her word, Pia didn't take offense. "Which I've noticed is the complete opposite of you." She cocked her head to the side. "Is that your Army Ranger training, to be all stoic and mysterious? I looked it up online. Seems pretty intense. And competitive."

Understatement.

"I guess that has something to do with it. But it's my personality too. Dad was a much better candidate for innkeeper than me."

Beck re-joined us. "Here you go, *señorita bonita*."

"Beck, get the hell out of here," I said in response to his dramatics.

He bowed, making Pia laugh. I refused to care that he seemed to do that so easily. All three of my best friends were good-looking guys, and there'd been plenty of times we eyed up the same girl. But not once had any of us stepped on each other's toes, and I certainly wouldn't get worked up about a woman I couldn't date anyway.

"So, Pia." Cole leaned forward. He had enough Scotch in him to make this interesting. "What do you think of Cedar Falls so far?"

She'd just taken a sip of her drink, her tongue sticking out to retrieve the straw, making me wish I was a straw.

"It's not all that different from where I grew up, just smaller than my hometown and no ocean nearby. But I like it."

"You're from Oregon, correct?"

"Yep. Newport."

"My parents took me to Newport, Rhode Island a few times as a kid, but never Newport, Oregon."

"I haven't been to Rhode Island. Or a lot of places out east, really."

"You should definitely check it out. It's a great place, known for its Gilded Age mansions and yacht-filled harbor. They hosted the America's Cup for years."

"Sounds idyllic."

As she and Cole talked, I imagined myself strolling the docks of Newport with her. This time of year would be chilly, so we'd duck inside for clam chowder and a drink.

Where the fuck had that come from?

Also, I was tired of my friends monopolizing her.

"Do you like to dance?"

The live bands on weekends were a definite benefit of coming to O'Malley's. This one was pretty good too.

"I do."

"Good. Come on."

Without giving her a chance to say no, I headed to the dance floor. To say Pia looked surprised when she joined me was an understatement.

"You... dance?"

"I do."

There wasn't much of a dance floor but tables had been cleared out to make one. Though it was too loud to talk, we danced two songs before Pia made a drinking motion. I wasn't ready to get back to the boys, so when we stepped off the dance floor, I said, "I'll grab our drinks," as Pia leaned against a narrow counter against the wall to listen to the band.

"Oh, look who's back."

Ignoring Parker, I grabbed our drinks and headed back to Pia. There was a 100 percent chance I'd catch major hell for this later. But that was one of the benefits to seeing some of the things I had, both on the streets of New York City and during my deployments... very little truly fazed me.

"Here you go," I said, handing Pia her vodka soda. "You seemed to be enjoying the band."

Not that she couldn't enjoy it from the bar. O'Malley's wasn't that big of a place. But still.

"Thanks. They're really good. Do they play here a lot?"

"Pretty regularly," I said, taking a long swig of beer just as the band took a break. O'Malley's had crap whiskey, so beer it was.

"So," I said. "Who's Richard Sterling?"

Pia startled. "Oh, my mother's call," she said, recalling how I knew the name. "He's my old boss."

I wouldn't mention that I thought he might be an old boyfriend. There seemed to be a lot of me caring about things I shouldn't going around tonight.

"I assume your new one is better?" I asked.

"Mmm, he started out a bit rough," she said, turning fully toward me.

"I won't argue with you on that one."

"As if you could. But yes, much better. Richard was the owner of a luxury resort where I'd worked my way up to Assistant Director of Guest Experience. Despite glowing reviews from my team, and even one from Richard that said, and I quote, 'Pia has developed a reputation for attention to detail and creativity with the ability to create memorable experiences for guests,' I was passed up for the director position."

"You memorized his review?"

"Word for word."

"Why do you think you got passed up?"

"Easy. There was another guy below me who smoked the same kind of cigars and played golf with Richard. Didn't seem to matter that he had multiple complaints filed against him by guests or that he was wholly unqualified for the position."

"Well, at least you're not bitter about it," I teased.

"Not even a little. And I certainly didn't take this job just to turn Heritage Hill around as a challenge to myself. I have nothing to prove."

"Obviously."

"Right. Glad we're on the same page."

Pia was more upset than she let on. I could read facial expressions and body language well, and had been trained to do both. I had a mind to invite Richard Sterling to the inn just to punch the fucker in the face. He was the kind of dickhead that gave men a bad name.

"I'm sorry that happened to you," I said, noticing she was empty. "Another drink?"

"Sure. Should we go back to the bar?"

"No." I said it much too quickly. "We should stay here," I amended, "so I can get you back on the dance floor. You're pretty good."

"You are too. I have to say I'm surprised."

"We'll talk about your low expectations of me when I get back."

For the second time, I headed to the bar without Pia. Ignoring both Cole and Parker's ribbing, I asked Beck for two more drinks.

"We don't bite, you know," he said, handing me a beer and making Pia's vodka soda.

"That's not actually true," I said.

"The last time I saw you dance like that," Parker began.

I shut him down with a look.

He smartly didn't continue.

"You know where to find us," Cole said dryly as I walked back toward Pia.

"Thanks," she said, putting her old drink on the counter and taking a sip of the new one. "So, you asked a question. Is it my turn?"

If I didn't know better, I'd think that sounded almost flirty. "Shoot."

"In my office today, we were talking about Beck asking me out."

"Aw shit, what did he do now?"

Pia's laugh crept into my very soul. "Nothing, I swear. But I could totally tell you were going to say something more about it."

Yep, she was flirting. There was no way Pia would bring up this particular topic unless she already suspected the answer. And this was where I should shut it down. Stop this very dangerous dance.

"You said, 'You think?'" I quoted her.

"Of course, I was teasing. I know he would." She laughed. It was a nervous laughter, and Pia seemed to regret having brought up this discussion. She wouldn't look me in the eyes.

I waited until she finally did. And responded. "I *was* going to say something more."

Pia waited.

I hesitated.

It would be the shot across the proverbial bow. Saying this might have repercussions. But she blinked at me in a way that tempted me to continue.

So I did.

"I was going to say, I know so because any guy in his right mind would want to go out with you."

Yet Pia already knew that. Or at least suspected.

"Ah, well... that's nice of you to say."

I let her play it off as a casual compliment to cap

a casual conversation. But it was anything but, and I was pretty sure she knew it.

What did it really matter? There was very little chance Pia couldn't feel my attraction to her anyway. But that didn't change the fact that she was my employee.

"See?" I teased instead. "Your new boss is much nicer than the old one."

Pia smiled, and before I got lost in that smile, I reluctantly added, "Band's starting up. Another dance or should we head back to the boys?"

I could sense she wanted to stay. Maybe dance. But thankfully Pia's foray into the forbidden forest of topics seemed to be at an end. "Let's head back to the boys. Cole is leaving tomorrow."

Cole could eat a sack of rocks for all I cared at that moment. But it was as good an idea as any given the current state of affairs. Every muscle in my body was tense and fine-tuned as if ready for action.

Of which there would be none, tonight or any night. At least not with Pia.

"Sounds good," I said as we headed back. And it would have been all well and good until Pia glanced back at me on our way to the table, and those blue eyes of hers beckoned.

11
PIA

"Hey, girl," Delaney said, coming up to our table.

I'd arrived earlier, so I stood up and gave her a hug. She seemed to be in much better spirits than the last time we spoke.

"Is this place amazing or what?"

Delaney sat across from me just as the soft jazz started. This time, it was live, the sax player pretty surprising for a small town like this. "It is. And actually my second time here already," I said. The Big Easy was becoming my favorite dinner spot. Although, aside from takeout, I hadn't actually gone anywhere else in Cedar Falls. Unless O'Malley's counted, but that was just bar food.

"Get out. When were you here?"

"Last week."

With my boss. Who I was pretty sure I had a very inappropriate crush on. Not only had I gone and blurted that stupid question last night, but at one point we'd exchanged a look that nearly had me ripping my clothes off in the middle of the bar.

"We're gonna need drinks for this, aren't we?"

"Um, definitely."

Thankfully the waitress came by just then and we both ordered French 75s. Though gin wasn't usually my go-to, it was apparently a popular New Orleans drink, and who didn't love champagne?

"Sooo?" I prompted.

"I kinda, sorta got back with my ex."

Based on what she'd told me of him so far, that didn't seem like the greatest plan in the world. But in matters of the heart, we all did pretty stupid things. Myself included. So I would be the last one to judge.

"You say that like it's a bad thing?"

Again, Delaney scrunched her nose, my bubbly new friend making me laugh. "Because it probably is."

At least she recognized the fact.

"First of all, he broke my heart, and usually I

don't think the person who broke your heart is a great candidate to fix it. Second of all, now that I've moved back, we're long distance. And third, my gut is saying it's a really bad idea."

Which meant it probably *was* a really bad idea. "One you're doing anyway?"

She sighed. "Yeah. I'm also madly in love with him. I swear every text he sends is like a little cocaine rush. Not that I've ever had cocaine," she added. "But I just can't explain it. He lights me up in a way no one ever has before. When we broke up, I was devastated. And now I'm on cloud nine despite the fact that it could easily all come crashing down again."

"What about the whole engagement to the ex thing?"

"Just rumors."

Our drinks arrived.

Lifting mine, I tried to make the best of her situation. "Well, you know what they say. Better to have loved and lost than never to have loved at all. Hopefully, it will work out this time. But if it does come crashing down, at least you can say you tried."

We clinked glasses. "Tell me what you've been up to," she said. "I'm sorry we couldn't get together before now. I've been swamped at my new job."

"I don't think you told me what you do?"

"I'm a pharmacist," she said. "And I honestly had no intentions of coming back to the area. But a position opened up, and I did miss my family, so..." She shrugged. "Here I am."

"Funny, I don't see you as a pharmacist."

Delaney laughed. "Everyone says that." She cocked her head to the side. "Do I give off more artist vibes?"

Actually... "Yes. You do."

"That's my first love. It started with painting pottery when I was little, and then I started sculpting my own pieces. One thing led to another"—she stuck out her wrist—"and I started painting and designing jewelry. This is mine."

It was one of the most unique bracelets I'd ever seen, and I immediately wanted one. "Please tell me you sell those."

"Someday, maybe. Happy to make you one though."

"Why don't you sell it?"

"I dunno, it just feels weird to charge people I know. I'm not good at that sort of thing. I guess I could do something like a craft circuit or something, but there's not a lot of time for that with work. I've thought a lot about selling online or something, but there's a million places to buy jewelry there, and it just seems like a dime a dozen. And pieces like this take so much time, I'm just not sure it's worth it. Maybe it's better to keep artistry as a hobby."

"I get that."

"But seriously, enough about me. How's it been going so far? I couldn't believe it when you told me you were going home. What happened?"

I told Delaney all about my arrival and Mason's change of heart. And about the job, my old boss and why I wanted to succeed at this one so badly. She listened intently but nearly spat out her drink at one thing I'd said.

"Beck Claymont?"

I'd told her about Mason's friends and how well I surprisingly got along with the one that I thought I'd dislike most.

"Actually, I didn't even know his last name."

"Dirty blond hair, sort of surfer-ish style? Tattooed arm? Super hot and extremely flirty?"

"Good description. That's the one. You know him?"

"Know him. Dated him. Well, sort of. It was middle school, so I can't say we went on any actual dates. In my defense, Cedar Falls isn't that big. The pool of men is pretty pathetic."

"I could totally see my younger self having done the same, before recognizing his type."

"Heartbreaker, you mean?"

"Exactly."

"I don't know Parker though very well."

"He and Mason met in college, so he's not from here."

"Ahh, makes sense."

When the waitress came, we both ordered red beans and rice. "Speaking of men, and the small pool of them in Cedar Falls, has anyone else caught your eye yet? One of Mason's other buddies that *isn't* Beck, maybe?"

I swallowed, knowing I should not answer that question, as if saying it out loud made it less true.

"Pia?" she prompted.

I looked at her guiltily through my eyelashes, choosing to take a sip of my drink instead of answering.

"It's one of them, isn't it? The cute professor?"

I shook my head.

"The sexy construction worker, Parker."

"No, not him."

"Oh no." Her eyes widened. "Pia."

"I'm not doing anything about it," I rushed to explain. "And I certainly didn't ask to be attracted to the same guy who pretty much tossed me out on the street. But..." I thought about him leaning against the wall last night after we danced. If I could have stopped staring at his strong jaw or forearms, I would have. Never mind his ass in jeans. "There's just something about him. I can't explain it."

She put her drink down and leaned forward, as if getting ready for a speech. "I totally understand and probably should have warned you about him. Mason Bennett is a certified hottie. And no, I didn't date him. But I have a friend who did in high school, and that guy is as emotionally unavailable as they come."

"I can tell. But also just plain old unavailable too, being that he's my boss and all."

"That too."

"You asked," I defended myself. "Was just being honest."

"And I'm glad you told me so I can talk you out of it."

I shook my head. "No need. I will not be acting on that particular impulse. I've had enough heartbreak to last a lifetime, and I'm pretty sure he's not a commitment kind of guy."

"He's not."

"And let's reiterate, my boss."

"That too."

"So completely off-limits."

"Completely." Delaney looked over my shoulder. "Just making sure we're on the same page."

"Absolutely we are."

"Good. Then you won't care that he just walked in."

12

MASON

"Thanks, Maggie," I said as she sat us close enough to the small stage to hear the sax player but far enough away to still be able to talk.

"We should get down there again," Parker said as we sat.

"New Orleans?"

"Yeah. Maybe when Cole gets his tenure."

We ordered drinks, and I looked around the room. Seeing Paul Baker with his family, I waved. Paul returned it.

"Did he talk to you yet?" Parker asked.

"Since Dad passed? Nah, though I don't doubt he will."

"What'll you tell him?" he asked as our drinks came.

"The truth. That I haven't made any permanent decisions, but for now we'll be moving forward with some renovations. After my leave is up, it's anyone's guess."

"If you do end up selling, I wonder if you can negotiate Pia to stay. She seems like a great fit so far."

I hated to admit it, after the first impression I made, but my father had really done Heritage Hill one last favor when he hired her. She was smart, a hard worker and efficient. With damn good ideas.

"I've thought of that already. He'd be crazy to lose her." There was no other way to interpret the look Parker gave me. "Don't start."

"I'm just saying," he started anyway, as if I hadn't had plenty from all three of them, even drunk-off-his-ass Cole, last night when we left O'Malley's. "I've seen the way the two of you look at each other."

"What are you getting for dinner?" I asked, changing the subject.

"'What we've got here is a failure to communicate.'"

"*Cool Hand Luke*," I said. Parker's proclivity for movie quotes was a thing with him, though I only caught about 50 percent of his references.

"Yup."

"There's no need to communicate anything," I insisted. "Pia and I are nothing more than employer and employee. Period. End of story."

Parker's smile was concerning.

"What?"

"It's just... you should probably stop talking about her." If possible, his smile grew. Parker looked as if he were about to burst out laughing.

"And why's that?"

Parker cleared his throat and nodded. I turned in that direction.

Fuck. Me.

Her hair was back in a ponytail for the first time, making Pia look slightly different. An immediate vision of me grabbing ahold of that ponytail and using the leverage to kiss every bit of skin on her neck, and lower, proved Parker's point.

"Hi, Mason."

She stood next to me, having come from nowhere.

"Hey, Pia. You just get here?"

"No," she said. "I'm here with a friend who noticed you come in. Hi, Parker."

"Sup?" Parker stood. "Take my seat. I have to make a quick call."

Before Pia could argue, Parker, like the good wingman he was, headed toward the front of the restaurant. Only problem was... I didn't need a wingman. Pia was not a potential date.

"Mind if I do?" she asked, eyeing the empty seat.

"Not at all."

If by "mind" she meant "are you going to find it hard to concentrate on dinner now?" the answer was yes.

"I guess you liked the place?" I asked, trying not to stare at her lips. They were glossier than usual, a perfect pale pink I'd dearly love to kiss off.

"I did, but Delaney actually suggested it."

Her secret smile was easily interpretable. "She told you about Beck?"

"Yep. I guess it's inevitable, running into exes in a town this small."

"I wouldn't exactly call them exes. They were honestly just kids. Where is she?"

Pia pointed to a table on the other side of the restaurant behind me. I turned and waved at Delaney, who was, indeed, watching us. She was all grown up, but as bubbly as I remembered. I turned back to Pia.

"So she's back in town for good?"

"Pretty much. She got a job at a local pharmacy."

"You mean, *the* pharmacy. We only have one."

"The pharmacy," she amended. "So whatcha getting?"

"Not sure yet. You?"

"Red beans and rice."

"A sure bet."

"Yeah, I tend to do that. Get the same thing at restaurants, if I know I like it."

"So not a risk taker?"

Pia didn't immediately answer. Was she suddenly thinking the same thing as me? By her expression, it seemed likely.

This wasn't about red beans and rice.

"Not usually."

There was an expression Rangers used when playing with fire: *dancing with the dragon*. That's exactly what I was doing by pursuing this conversation.

"Never?"

"I wouldn't say that. Maybe some things are worth taking a risk for."

"Such as?"

Pia swallowed. "Nothing specific comes to mind."

Liar. But I didn't call her out since I wasn't willing to dance with this dragon any longer.

"Jambalaya," I said.

It took her a second to recalibrate.

"Sounds good. Well, I better get back to Delaney."

"I'll have to say hello to her before we leave."

"If we go first, we'll do the same," she said. "But I can't say I'm rushing out of here anytime soon." Pia stood. "The sax player is amazing. So much good live music in a town of this size. O'Malley's. Here. It's awesome."

"Cedar Falls is known for it. At one point, there was a push to make music a selling point of the town. Though it's not quite Nashville, the sentiment sort of stuck."

"I've heard that's a great city."

"Nashville?"

"Yeah. I've never been."

"Do you like country music?" I asked as Parker rejoined us.

"I do."

"Then you'd love it. Actually, they have music of all kinds, but for a country fan, there's nowhere like it."

"Mason loves country music," Parker said, sitting.

"So we have at least one thing in common," she teased me.

I didn't correct her, but it was at least two.

"Maybe you should do a company retreat in Nashville," Parker suggested.

I was going to fucking kill him.

"Company retreat," she said, giggling. "With two people." Pia never giggled. She was nervous. The tension between us that had been ignited last night had only been more inflamed by this conversation. Starting tomorrow, I was going to avoid any innuendos or flirting, no matter how innocuous it seemed.

"Good idea, Parker." Then, to Pia, "Talk to you soon."

"See ya," she said, leaving.

I glared at my friend just as the music began.

"What?"

"I'll give you 'what.' Are you trying to get me to break the pact?"

Parker eyed me carefully. "You only truly break it if you get engaged or married."

Although there were "rules" to the pact, we'd agreed that if anyone got engaged, they would have to add $250 to the kitty. Marriage was $500. Not to mention the shame of backing out on a promise we'd made for one damn good reason.

Marriage didn't work.

"Maybe you haven't noticed, but Pia isn't exactly a one-night stand kind of girl."

"Ahhh, so he finally admits it."

I was done with this conversion. "I admit nothing. Now pick something out before the waiter comes back. I'm hungry."

Parker had a bad habit of being indecisive with his meals.

"And grumpy."

I ignored that.

And also tried to ignore the fact that Pia was sitting in the same restaurant as us. The first was easy. The second, absolute fucking torture.

13

PIA

Since I didn't technically have days on or off, even though I'd worked every day this week, I walked from my small apartment toward the inn anyway. It had nothing to do with seeing Mason and everything to do with the fact that guests would be coming back tomorrow.

As I approached, I was still far enough away that when I heard banging, I decided now was a good time to panic. Parker was making mostly cosmetic changes to the foyer and reception, so what was with this noise?

Unfortunately, I didn't have to open the front door of the inn side of the building to see the cause.

"No," I said, walking up the stairs. "No, no, no."

I knew the renovation log by heart at this point. We hadn't discussed new flooring, since the downstairs flooring was actually one of the newest additions. The bedrooms were another story altogether, but... what the hell?

"Parker," I called over the noise. "What is going on?"

He looked up, protective eyewear intact, and turned off the very loud saw. "What's that?"

"What is going on? What is that?"

He looked from me to the tile and back again.

"A grout saw?"

A grout saw. Fabulous. "Why are you using that on the flooring?"

He looked at me like I'd lost a marble. "Because this is how you replace tiles."

Deep breaths. It looked like he'd just gotten started. There was no way this was a one-day job, and even if we rerouted guests into the parlor, they'd have to walk past this. Never mind the noise.

"Why," I asked, trying to stay patient, "are you replacing the tile?"

"Because I can't install the hardwood flooring without taking this out."

I peered inside. No sign of him. Deep breaths. "Where is Mason?"

"Hardware store."

Remembering this was a problem for Mason, and not the guy doing pro bono work on the inn, I remained calm. "And where is the hardware store?"

"Block off the square behind the Sugar Shack."

Right, the candy store on the same block as my apartment. "Thanks."

I got back up the hill and was two blocks away from the town square when I saw him. Mason was just heading into Casa Di Vino, across the street from O'Malley's.

By the time I got there, he was already at the register. With a bag in the crook of his arm, Mason was just checking out.

"Pia?" he asked as I approached.

"We need to talk," I said, glancing at the older gentleman checking him out. His friendly smile and bright eyes made it hard to look away.

"Hi," I said.

"*Buongiorno, signorina.*"

I knew it. He was Italian.

"*Buongiorno, signore?*"

"Emilio," he said, completely ignoring Mason.

"Pia," I said. "*Al tuo servizio.*"

"*No, sono da te, Signorina Pia.*"

Mason cleared his throat.

"He's Italian," I said, by way of an explanation.

"I'm aware." Mason's dry tone was very much in line with his current mood, which seemed to be on the surly side. His eyes suddenly widened. "I just realized, you guys have the same last name."

Emilio and I locked gazes. "Russo?" I asked.

"No," Mason answered, even though I wasn't looking at him. "Your other last name."

I gave him a look.

"You are a Russo," Emilio asked. "From where?"

As he talked, I could detect a slight accent. Unless I was mistaken, he was first generation but had been in the States for many years.

"My great-great-grandparents on my father's side were from Matera. You?"

"I was born in Bari. My wife and I came here nearly twenty-five years ago."

"Isn't Bari the one with the white houses?"

"It is," he replied. "Have you been there?"

"I wish. I've never even been to Italy before."

"*Un peccato,*" he said. Though I didn't know the phrase, he was clearly disappointed. "You must go someday. *Belissima.*" He kissed his fingers.

Emilio's boisterous and gregarious greeting made

me feel instantly at home. "I would love to, especially Matera. I've heard Sicily is beautiful."

"Not nearly as beautiful as you."

"*Grazie*." I accepted the compliment.

"Who is this beauty, Pia Russo?" Emilio asked Mason.

"Heritage Hill's new manager. She's from Oregon, moved to Cedar Falls last week."

"Very good," he said. "Do you drink wine?"

"Do I drink wine? Is that even a question?"

Emilio laughed. "You'll come back and sample a new vintage Barolo wine a childhood friend of mine produces in the Piedmont region. Northern Italy," he said, as if the two words were ash in his mouth. "But he is a good guy. The wine is made in a small batch from an obscure grape clone with exceptional terroir. I'll have it by the weekend. You'll come to try?"

"Of course," I said. "So this place is yours?"

Though I spoke with Emilio, every nerve ending in my body hummed with awareness of Mason. I couldn't smell his signature cologne today. Instead he smelled like soap. The visual on that one almost had me shaking my head to clear it.

"*Sì, signorina*. My wife's family owns a small vineyard back home. We spent many years there, winemaking, and now have it shipped here."

"That's incredible. So some of this wine is yours?"

"Indeed. And others, by some friends back home. I even have local wines," he whispered, leaning forward as if telling me a secret. "For the folks who like the 's' stuff."

I made a face. "Sweet wine. No thank you."

"I don't use the word here since every other lake in the region produces the stuff. But you'll find Keuka has more dry than most. Have you done a tour of the region's wineries yet?"

"Nope." I shook my head.

Emilio put his hands on his hips. "Mason. Your manager is a dry wine drinker and you haven't taken her to Ravines? Or Keuka Springs?"

"I have not."

Emilio didn't seem to take exception to Mason's dry tone. "Fix that, son."

He handed Mason back his credit card just as a person got in line behind us.

"Yes, sir," he said, his deference and politeness to the older man oddly appealing.

"It was a pleasure to meet you, Pia Russo."

"And same to you, Emilio Russo."

"She's a keeper, Mason."

"See ya, Emilio."

As we walked out, I couldn't help but point out, "You didn't agree with him."

"That you're a keeper?"

"Exactly."

"It's too soon to tell." He held the door open as I walked through it.

"Funny," I said, remembering why I'd come to find him in the first place. As soon as we hit the street, I stopped walking. "Not funny, the fact that we have guests coming tomorrow and Parker is ripping up the foyer floor."

Mason stopped with me. "You were at the inn already?"

"I was." Why was he looking at me funny?

"On a Sunday?"

"I just wanted to make sure everything was set for tomorrow. Which, I might add, it is not. We can't have that torn up, never mind the noise, with guests coming."

Realizing both of Mason's arms were full between his hardware store and wine purchases, I reached for the wine bag.

"I got it."

"I'm not carrying anything," I argued.

"I got it," Mason repeated, as if he hadn't heard me.

"You are so frustrating."

We began walking toward the inn.

"So I've been told."

"Soooo?"

"We decided to do it last night. Parker thinks he can hammer the whole thing out today with mine and Beck's help."

"The whole thing, as in ripping up the tile and replacing it with hardwood floors? In a day?"

"That's what he said."

"But that wasn't even on the list of renovations."

"I know. But I finally finished going through my dad's things and found some notes. Including…" His sidelong gaze wasn't lost on me. "Ones about you."

Oh boy.

"He had a list of renovations too, including the foyer and reception area's flooring, with a star next to it. Apparently having a more updated and appealing entrance was top on his list."

Now I felt like a shit for making such a big deal. "So you wanted to honor his wishes?"

He shrugged off my tone, acting like it wasn't a thing. But I'd begun to know Mason a bit, and it was. His tone had gotten gruffer, if such a thing were possible, when he talked about his dad.

"I mentioned it to Parker, and he was like, 'Let's

do it.' Since we didn't have guests today, and it's Parker's day off, he thought it would be a good time to get it done. I was going to mention it to you last night before we left but didn't want to mix business and pleasure."

I nearly tripped on the sidewalk at that one. Moving on...

"I don't mind," I said.

"No?"

He said it with just enough innuendo in his tone that it was difficult to ignore. But I did, of course. Though my imagination would probably not stop racing when I was home tonight in bed.

Like last night, touching myself, thinking of him.

Focus, Pia.

"No. This isn't a typical job, and I know that." We stepped onto the inn's property. "I'm invested in making Heritage Hill a success, whatever it takes. That's why I'm here today. On a Sunday."

We could still hear Parker's grout saw from the walkway since the inn's front door was open. As we made our way into the kitchen, Mason put his bags on the island, just as Beck stumbled in looking like death warmed over.

We both stopped to stare. He wore only a pair of

boxers, and there was a lot to look at. Beck clearly worked out regularly. But mostly I wondered what Mason would look like in a pair of boxers too.

Pouring himself a coffee, Beck leaned against the kitchen counter. "When does Esther start back? I could really use some scrambled eggs with cheese."

I stifled a laugh.

"Tomorrow," Mason said dryly. "You could actually make them yourself, you know?"

Beck didn't answer.

"Rough night?" I asked.

"Late night." His smile told me I didn't want to know any more. Bottom on my list of morning topics were Beck's hookup stories, and I could guarantee that was what he meant.

"Are you still up for the floor project? We got most of the materials last night and Parker's already ripping up the tile."

"I hear that." Beck walked to the fridge, opened it, looked inside and closed it.

He was a real piece of work. "Get upstairs," I ordered him. "Get some clothes on, and I'll make you eggs with freaking cheese."

"Seriously?"

"Yes, seriously. Now go. I need this project

wrapped up today. We're not getting bad reviews the first day on my watch." I shooed him out of the kitchen. "Go."

Surprisingly, he listened, but not before refilling his coffee mug.

"You don't need to do that," Mason said. "It's not part of the job description."

"Making eggs and cheese for your hungover friend? Are you sure? I swear I saw that somewhere in the original posting."

"Funny," he shot back in the same exact tone I'd used back at the wine store. "So how do you know so much Italian if you've never been there?"

"My grandparents and some of my aunts and uncles speak it. They and their friends are in the restaurant enough that I've picked up a few things over the years."

"More than a few things, I'd say." Mason crossed his arms and leaned back against the same counter Beck was at a few minutes ago. Two good-looking men. Similar stances. Only one I wanted to touch.

So badly.

"Mostly food and wine stuff. I can order red wine with the best of them."

Mason didn't say anything for a second. "I like it."

His tone was at odds with his words, like he was angry or something.

"When I talk in Italian?"

"Yeah."

I'd like you to toss me over your shoulder and carry me upstairs.

"Thanks," I said instead.

"Ahem." Parker cleared his throat at the door.

I quickly looked away from Mason and headed toward the fridge to grab the eggs.

"Anytime you want to join me. Did you get the leveling compound?"

"I did. Coming in now."

I closed the fridge.

Parker was gone already.

"See me before you go," Mason said.

"I'm gonna do some work after the eggs. Want some?"

"Sure, thanks."

Mason just nodded and left the kitchen, but for my part, I couldn't breathe. That entire exchange was next level. Not the words, exactly, but the way he'd looked at me. It was as if Mason was fighting the same battle as I was, and this morning, we both emerged losers.

Mason wanted me to see him before I left. What

did he want that we couldn't have talked about just then? Part of me dreaded the answer and another part of me wanted to leave sooner rather than later just so I could find out.

Be careful what you wish for, Pia.

Sage advice. Now I just had to follow it.

14

MASON

"Mace." Beck nodded to the door.

Pia stood there, watching me. For a second, I couldn't decipher her expression... until I realized. I'd taken off my shirt, and Pia had definitely noticed. Trying not to smile—what guy wouldn't be thrilled to have a beautiful woman looking at them like that?—I stood up and made my way toward her.

Grabbing a hand towel, I stepped over hardwood planks. "Let's head outside."

We walked around to the back deck, the cool air like heaven after working up a sweat. "What time is it?" I asked.

"Almost four."

"Shit. It feels like we were working for a half hour."

Pia rested her hand on the railing, looking out over Heritage Hill's property. Even more leaves had fallen in the last few days as autumn quickly inched toward an end.

"I can't believe how much you guys got done. The new floor will look incredible."

"Parker's a beast. He's crazy talented."

"And went to college with you?"

"Yeah, for business. He wants to start his own company."

"Seems like a good idea." She paused. "So, you wanted to talk to me before I left?" Her eyes dipped to my chest and quickly flew up to my face. She didn't want to look, that much was clear. Which was exactly what I'd planned to talk to her about. We had to address the obvious, that the two of us were insanely attracted to each other, but that attraction couldn't go anywhere. We both knew it.

The words wouldn't come. Instead, I pretended to look confused.

"Oh yeah. Can't remember why now."

She waited until I said again, "Nope. Nothing."

"Hmm. Alright then. Well, I'm taking off. Big day tomorrow."

Say goodbye. See you tomorrow. Sounds good. Something. Anything.

Except, I didn't want her to go. Pia was like the rainbow after a storm. Since I'd come home, the quiet moments were filled with memories of my father, but when she was around...

I took a step toward her. "We only have a couple of guests. Shouldn't be too big of a deal."

"I know, but still. They're your first guests as innkeeper." Pia smiled knowingly. "Are you ready for that?"

"Am I ready to be nice to them? Is that what you mean?" I teased, something I seemed to be doing more with Pia than was typical for me. I wasn't normally the teasing type.

"I wasn't gonna say it, but..."

Another step, as if I were willing her to stay by my presence. Pia didn't move. Again, her eyes dropped to my chest, and then lower. A final step, this time coming close enough to her that if Pia reached out her hand, she would be able to touch me.

When she looked up, our eyes met. The air sizzled between us.

Do it, Pia.
Touch me.

"You have a lot of…" She cleared her throat. "Muscles."

"Have to stay ahead of the curve."

"A cop thing?"

"Sort of."

So much for my vow of keeping more distance between us. I'd done the exact opposite. My eyes fell to her lips. Most women with lips that full used fillers, but Pia's were 100 percent real. What I wouldn't give to slip my tongue between those lips, devour them so completely that Pia was unable to stand.

"Mason," she said, her voice thick.

"Yes, Pia?"

How I wanted to grab her hand, put it on my chest and tell her to have a field day. Touch. Explore. Anything she wanted.

"I liked it better when I thought you were an asshole."

Better she understood her instincts had been correct. "I am an asshole."

"Maybe," she agreed, making me smile and cutting into some of the sexual tension between us. "But not as big of one as I thought."

"There you are."

Fucking Beck.

Pia stepped backward.

"We need more vapor barrier."

Our proximity hadn't been lost on Beck. He'd basically written the playbook on seducing women. Not that I had been trying to seduce Pia.

Well, maybe I had, a little.

"I'll go grab it. Maybe some takeout for dinner too."

"Sounds good. You taking off, Pia?" he asked.

Her demeanor completely changed with him. "Why do you ask? Need something?"

"Just you to agree to a date. Just one date."

"Not gonna happen."

Pia's shoulders shook as she walked away, toward my fucking asshole of a friend. He would stop asking her out... today.

Patting him on the back like an errant toddler, Pia called, "See you in the morning," to me. And just like that, she was gone.

I glared at Beck, who, unapologetically, leaned against the banister and crossed his arms.

"So what the hell was that?"

"What?"

"Really? Come on, man. I've known you since kindergarten."

"As if I could forget, especially the day you pulled

your pants down in the hall waiting for the bathroom."

We'd been in a line, the teacher taking us all to the bathroom at once, when Beck's pants were suddenly around his ankles. The teacher screamed as if he'd just stabbed someone. Beck had been making women scream with his dick ever since. According to him, anyway.

"First of all, I was goaded into it. Second, you don't actually remember that, just the story. No one can remember being five."

"I can."

"Whatever you say."

Beck claimed a girl dared him to pull down his pants. If nothing else, it made for a memorable story. His mother had not been pleased by that phone call.

"I say, you are attracted to Pia."

It wasn't the first time he or the others had accused me of much, but denying it now was pointless.

"Doesn't matter."

"So you admit it?"

I sighed. "I need to go get a vapor barrier."

Attempting to walk by Beck, I was stopped by a hand on my chest. Beck could be so fucking annoying sometimes.

His hand dropped.

"You're finally admitting it?"

"Beck," I said with an attempt at patience. "Like I've been saying since Pia started working here, she's my employee. I'm her boss. It doesn't matter if I'm attracted to her."

"Sure it does. I'll back off if you just admit it."

Power move. Beck knew I wanted him to back off. He'd likely seen it with the daggers I'd shot him a few minutes ago.

"Fine. I admit it. But she's free to date whoever she wants, just not me. So if you have a shot with her—" I was going to say "go for it," but the words stuck in my mouth.

Beck's silly grin was so typical of him.

"First of all, she doesn't want to date me, obviously. It's a joke between us at this point. Second of all, consider it done."

Good.

I just wouldn't say that out loud.

"It's a bad idea," I admitted for the first time to anyone but myself.

"Agreed."

"Because she works for me."

"Nah, not that."

My eyes narrowed. "What the hell does that mean?"

"It's not ideal," he said, Beck's more serious side making a rare appearance. "If you get together and end up staying here, and it doesn't work out." He shrugged. "But aside from that, who cares? You're consenting adults. And it's not like you have some board of directors or someone to answer to. You're a literal staff of three."

I didn't get it. "So why isn't it ideal? In your mind." Because in mine, screwing around with one of my only employees, and a good one at that, wasn't a good idea at all.

"Because there's more between you than a simple attraction. I've known you long enough to tell. And that, Mason, should scare the hell out of you. Or anyone who knows the success rate of long-term relationships."

Leave it to Beck to force the truth down my throat.

"I like you better when you're not so serious," I said, echoing Pia's comment about liking me more when she thought I was an asshole.

"Everyone does," he said, slapping me on my shoulder and walking away.

Great. Now what?

Damned if I had any answers. Just more questions.

15
PIA

"Someone's here to see you."

Beck stood at my office door, which was always open. After a successful first week, I'd just been wrapping up, planning to head back to my apartment for a long, hot bath. Avoiding Mason during our opening week had been impossible. After that near... whatever it was... I'd just wanted to crawl in a hole. Instead, we had to navigate our roles, he as innkeeper and me as manager, and ensure all went smoothly when Heritage Hill opened for the first time in decades without his father greeting guests.

"To see me? Is it Delaney?"

She was the only person I knew in town besides the boys.

"Who?"

"Never mind."

"Oh, Delaney Thorton. That's right, I forgot you guys were friends. No, it's not her. But speaking of her, did she tell you—"

"That you guys dated in middle school? Yeah, she did. Said you were a terrible kisser."

As expected, that gutted poor Beck. Hand to his heart as if I'd wounded him, he groaned. "That's a low blow, Pia."

I was so bad at keeping up a joke. "Fine. She didn't say anything about kissing you."

He smiled. "Knew it, because we never kissed."

"You didn't?"

"Nope. I was too scared to try. Was a late bloomer, if you can believe that."

"I don't believe it at all, actually." I closed my laptop. "Did you say someone wanted to see me?"

"Oh yeah. Your mom and sister are here."

My head snapped back up as I shoved my laptop in its case. "Excuse me?"

"You mom and sister are here."

So much for pulling more info out of Beck. I stared at him, trying to make sense of his words, but he didn't say anything more. How was that possible?

I'd just talked to Mom, and she didn't say anything about this at all.

"What the hell?" I grabbed my stuff and rushed from the office.

"How old is your sister?" Beck asked as we headed down the stairs. I stopped and glared at him. "What? She looks just like you."

"So discriminatory. Twenty-four. Too young, so stay away."

"I will," he acknowledged as we made our way to the reception room. "But not because she's too young."

I can't even with him right now.

"Mom?" I turned the corner and, sure enough, my mother and sister Sophia were standing there talking to Mason. "Soph? What the heck are you guys doing here?"

My mother opened her arms. "Surprise!"

Hugging them one at a time, I looked them up and down. Sure enough, they were real.

"You've met Mason?"

"Sure have. You never mentioned how handsome your boss is, Pia."

This was just what I needed. "Really, Mom? Maybe because he's my *boss*?"

"You can be seriously embarrassing," Soph said, backing me up.

"Well, I certainly don't mean to be. Did I embarrass you, Mason?"

He looked ready to crack up laughing. At least he didn't take offense. Thankfully, Mason wasn't offended easily. And also, he looked really good in navy. I wished I could tell him to stop wearing it.

"Not at all, ma'am."

"Why didn't you tell me you were coming?" I asked them.

"Duh," Sophia said in her "my big sister is so clueless" tone. "Because it's a surprise. Mom wanted to make sure you're all settled in."

"I'm perfectly settled," I said, trying to ignore how good Mason smelled. "But my apartment is tiny. How long are you staying?"

"Just the weekend. And if you have plans, don't worry about us. Sophia and I will get to know the town. Don't change them for us."

"Pia, can I talk to you a sec?" Mason asked.

I stepped off to the side with him just as Beck walked from the foyer upstairs. I saw my sister looking. "No. Absolutely"—in case she didn't get it the first time—"no way."

Sophia rolled her eyes.

"He already asked about her," I said, defending my tone to Mason. "And that's not happening."

"Don't blame you. If I had a sister, I wouldn't let Beck date her either."

"He is a real piece of work," I admitted when Mason and I were fully out of range from my mother and sister. "So what's up?"

"Let them stay here. We have open rooms."

"You sure?"

"Positive. Why wouldn't they? Unless you're dying to sleep on your couch for the weekend."

"I'm actually not," I admitted. "But I do love staying up late with Soph after Mom goes to bed and having a wine, or two, with her. Of all my sisters, she and I are the closest. I still can't believe she's here."

"You stay too. Take number one."

No. Absolutely a terrible idea. Especially in the main house. Why hadn't he suggested one of the inn's rooms that were empty for me? Didn't matter. The answer was no.

The word stuck on my tongue.

Our eyes met.

I thought of saying no. I thought of saying, "That's a bad idea." And yet, of all the responses that ran through my head, my mouth was about to blurt out the most dangerous one.

"Sounds good. As long as you're positive."

"I've been meaning to tell you that, anytime you're here late and want to stay, number one is open for that reason. Friends and family only."

"Beck keeps calling it Cole's room, as if he'll be joining you three soon."

"Beck just wants to recreate college, in every way. Cole's not coming back to Cedar Falls."

"It seems like you're right." My heart raced. "Looks like you'll be having some unexpected guests this weekend."

"Works for me."

Neither of us moved. I could tell he wanted to say more, but words were not always Mason's strong suit.

"What is it?" I prompted.

"It was a good week," he said. "Thank you."

It was a good week, and despite Mason's concerns that his dad was the affable one, he'd "turned it on" every time he was with a guest.

"You're welcome," I said simply, having learned to accept a compliment. It wasn't always the case. So often when I was young, I'd say things like, "no big deal," or minimize my accomplishments. But after what happened with Richard, I'd promised myself to knock that shit off.

"Beck and I are painting tonight though. I hope that won't bother you."

"Not at all. I'll take them to dinner, and Soph and I can hang out late at night in my room."

"Let me know if you need anything."

Besides you?

"Will do."

I reluctantly pulled myself away from Mason and back to my mom and sister. "Okay, so here's the scoop. We're all going to stay here for the weekend since my apartment is tiny. You two will take rooms over there." I pointed toward the inn section of Heritage Hill. "And I'm going to stay here in the main house. That way," I said to Soph, "we can have a late-night wine with the kitchen close by."

"Or two or three wines?" she asked.

"Your mother would like to be invited to the late-night wine session too," Mom said.

"Sure. We'll just drag you from the bed where you'll be snoring after three seconds of watching the Hallmark channel over to my room. And also, you don't like wine," I pointed out.

"True," she admitted.

"Ladies," Mason called from where I'd left him. "Welcome to Heritage Hill, and Cedar Falls. I'm sure I'll see you around this weekend."

"Thank you, Mason," my mother said sweetly as he left.

The second he did, both Soph and my mother started in.

"Holy shit, Pia. He's gorgeous."

"Watch your mouth, Soph," my mother said. "But she's right. He really is. Does he have a girlfriend?"

"Have you two hooked up? I'm picking up some vibes." Sophia picked up her overnight bag.

"No. No. And knock it off," I answered. "Come on. I'll show you two ying-yangs to your rooms and will try to make a reservation at a restaurant you'll love for tonight. Or tomorrow, if I can't get it tonight."

"Italian?" my mother asked, as if there wasn't any other kind of food.

"No, Creole."

Her face was priceless.

"Trust me, you'll love this place."

As we walked toward the hallway that connected the main house and the inn, neither of them let up about Mason, asking question after question. Thankfully, neither one of them asked pointedly if I liked him *in that way*, because I didn't make it a habit to lie to my family. And the answer was yes.

I did.

16

MASON

"Beck still sleeping?" Parker asked, handing me a coffee. He was an early riser, like me. Some habits were hard to break, and waking up before the crack of dawn in the army was one of them.

"What do you think?"

He sat at the kitchen island, pushing his stool in close. "I think he's not the only one sleeping upstairs this morning, a fact that hasn't eluded you, I'm sure."

"I never should have admitted anything to that asshole."

"Oh, okay." Parker laughed. "Because otherwise I had no fucking clue. Come on, man."

Glaring at him did absolutely no good. Unlike the perps I dealt with, ones who weren't accustomed to bracelets and could be intimidated into behaving, my old friend couldn't give a shit.

"Like I told Beck, it doesn't matter. I'm her boss, and it wouldn't be right."

"Is that the real problem, though? I mean, it's just the two of you here, really. This isn't a corporate America job where you guys have to look over your shoulder because the big boss might be offended. Consenting adults and all of that."

He sounded just like Beck.

"Yeah," I insisted, leaning against the kitchen counter, "that's the problem."

"Not the pact?"

"I don't give a fuck about losing a few hundred dollars."

"But you do believe in the reason we made the pact in the first place."

I couldn't argue with that. No way I would go through what my dad endured. "True." I added, "Who knows if I'm even staying."

"You're staying. No way I'm moving back into that apartment with Beck. I like not being able to hear his nighttime antics."

I rolled my eyes. "You could get your own place, you know."

"I could try. But Beck is like the little brother I

never asked for. He'd be pissed. I've never met anyone who hates to be alone so much."

I thought of Beck's family situation. "There's a reason for it, as you know."

"True. But back to Pia..."

"I thought my ears were ringing."

Lord have mercy. She wore sweats and a tee, her hair up in a messy bun. No makeup. Not a stitch. Pia looked like she'd just rolled out of bed. Sexy as fuck. Unfortunately, it hadn't been my bed.

"Morning," I grumbled, aware of a tone I hadn't intended.

"Is he always so happy in the morning?" Pia asked Parker.

"Time of day doesn't matter much, or haven't you noticed?"

"Oh I've noticed."

"I'm standing right here," I said, not taking my eyes off Pia.

"Oh look, you are," she teased. "Two things," she said, all work efficiency now. "I found the bathroom but it doesn't seem to have any towels. And I popped my head into the second kitchen and Esther's preparing breakfast already. Does she always start so early?"

Second kitchen was what we called the inn's kitchen that my dad had added on years ago, though it had never been utilized for anything more than breakfast.

"Yeah, why?"

"I think she may be underpaid. The woman works seven days a week and for more hours than I realized if she's already in there prepping."

"Let's talk about it," I said, more than open to the idea of increasing Esther's pay, since it was something I'd already considered. "And I'll grab some towels for you."

"Coffee?" Parker asked Pia.

She smiled and nodded. "Yes please."

"Cream and sugar are there." He pointed to the counter after hopping off his stool to grab her a mug. "Did you guys have a good time last night?"

After painting into the night and grabbing some takeout with Parker, I'd passed by Pia's room. The sound of muffled voices told me she and her sister were inside, which made for a mostly restless night, Pia so close to my bedroom. At least three times my eyes popped open as I wondered if Sophia was still in there. Or if Pia was already asleep.

Or was she lying awake, thinking of me?

Unlikely.

"We did. Mom loved the Big Easy, even though it's not Italian. But I have a horrible wine headache from staying up way too late with Soph."

Pia was avoiding eye contact this morning.

"If your mom likes Italian," Parker said, "take her to Bella Luna. It's in a restored historic building on Lake Street. Very rustic with the best wood-fired pizza around. Oh, and make sure you get the tiramisu. It's incredible."

"You wanna come?"

Parker looked at me. Finally, Pia did too.

"You're more than welcome," she said.

I began to shake my head—being around Pia more was the last thing I needed—when Parker answered and opened his mouth first.

"Sure, we'd love to. Mason and I will be painting all day, so later is better."

"I'll call and see if I can get a rezzie for five of us after seven. I assume Beck is working?"

"Always," Parker said. "But maybe your mom and sister would like to visit the fine Cedar Falls establishment of O'Malley's Pub after dinner?"

Listening to Pia's tinkering laugh was one way to start the day. I was getting fucking hard watching her. Listening to her. Imagining her under me.

"Maybe just Soph. My mom will more than likely want to be dropped off. But who knows."

Fucking great. Dinner. Pub. And she was literally sleeping down the hall from me.

"You okay?" Parker asked. The fucker actually smirked. He knew I wasn't okay, and only the fact that he would be painting with me on his day off would save him. And he knew it.

"Come on," I said. "I'll get you those towels."

Without a backward glance, I headed up the stairs.

"Someone is extra cranky this morning."

"I'm not cranky," I said, in a tone that defied my statement.

"Whatever you say."

I headed to the towel closet in the hall next to my room. Pia paused at the open door and didn't hide the fact that she was peeking inside.

"So this is where the cranky Mason Bennett lays his head, huh?"

I froze, closed my eyes and prayed for strength, and then turned. There was only so much a man could take. Especially one that tuned up for the very woman standing... at the entrance... of his bedroom.

Fuck me. "Nothing special about it."

"Is that Luke Skywalker?"

I moved closer to her. "Dad remodeled a few years back," I said. "But I kept that poster from when I was a kid."

"*Star Wars* fan, huh?"

I stepped inside the room, fully aware she would follow.

"For life," I said, thankful I'd made my bed. Aside from that poster, most of the room was nondescript.

"No kidding. Can't say I'm a huge sci-fi fan. But he is cute." Pia looked around. "Very neat."

"Army habit."

"You seem to have a lot of those. What are some others?"

"Punctuality. Resilience. Respect for authority. There are lots of them."

We stood much too close for comfort.

In my fucking bedroom.

Every muscle in my body screamed for me to reach out. To pull her into me. To throw Pia onto my bed and make her scream my name.

"We should go," I said, not waiting for her to respond. Once out in the hall, I closed the door.

"I'm sorry," she said as I reached for the door to the towel closet.

"Why?" I asked, pulling out two towels and a hand towel. "You have nothing to be sorry for."

"Wandering into your bedroom like that."

I handed Pia the towels. "Pia, there's a lot of ways I could respond to that, but being respectful," I said truthfully, "of our positions here, I'll keep it clean. You have nothing to be sorry for. Furthermore, you never have to apologize to me. Ever."

"What if I do something wrong?"

"Fix it. But don't apologize."

"Ever?"

"Ever."

"Why?"

"Not apologizing doesn't mean avoiding accountability. It's a reminder to take opportunities to learn and grow. You can be mindful of feedback but unwilling to compromise values or well-being without hesitation too."

"You've thought a lot about this?"

"I've thought a lot about everything. Doesn't mean you have to agree with me."

Pia flattened her full lips, thinking. "I'm not sure about this. But duly noted either way. Except..." She bit her lip.

Fuck.

Me.

"What if I am sorry. I just... don't say it?"

"Give me an example."

"Like peeking into your room."

"Bad example. There's nothing to be sorry for. I'd peek at yours too."

"You would?" She blinked up at me, and so help me God, I wanted to kiss her.

"Yes, I would. Try again," I said, anxious to be away from the bedroom talk.

"What if I screwed up a reservation? Double-booked a room. And the guests were not willing to accept any compensation and threatened to leave bad reviews?"

"I'd tell them to get fucked."

Pia laughed. "You know what, maybe we should revise the duties flowchart so you aren't dealing with any guests, ever."

Smiling, I had to admit that was not such a bad plan. "Maybe I'd be more tactful than that," I admitted. "But instead of apologizing, you could say, 'I would like to fix this error.'"

"But isn't that apologizing?"

"No, it's you taking ownership without any remorse."

"Hmmm. Semantics, I think."

"To you, maybe."

"You're a hard man, Mason. Has anyone ever told you that?"

"Many people."

"I'll learn your weakness yet." With that, Pia stalked off to the bathroom, muttering something about kittens.

You are my weakness.

A scary fucking thought indeed.

17
PIA

"Ooh, this place is so nice," Sophia said, echoing my sentiments as we walked into the restaurant. The interior was cozy and inviting, perfectly capturing the essence of Italy. With the warm glow of pendant lights and smell of wood-fired pizza and freshly baked bread, Bella Luna was already a winner. As long as the food was good.

"Very clean, too." Mom led Sophia and me to the hostess stand.

"Of course you'd notice that." Sophia rolled her eyes at me.

"Reservation for five under Russo," I said. "We have two more joining us."

"Sure thing, right this way," she said, grabbing

five menus and leading us to a booth not far from the pizza oven. I hadn't planned on getting pizza, but that smell might have sealed the deal.

"Your waitress will be right with you."

"Excellent customer engagement and"—Mom opened her menu as we sat—"menu presentation."

"You can take a woman out of her restaurant, but you can't take the restaurant out of the woman," my sister said as five waters were poured for us.

"That makes no sense," I said, trying not to look at the door. We'd left mid-afternoon to walk around town and shop, so the guys were meeting us here.

"Yes it does."

"No," I said, distracted, "it doesn't."

"You know what else makes no sense? You staring at the door but pretending not to have a crush on your boss."

"Sophia," my mother chastised. "Enough teasing your sister."

"I'm not teasing her. Just telling the truth. It's so obvious."

Last night I refused to talk about Mason, but Sophia had been relentless about him all day. If it were that obvious to her after just one weekend, there was zero chance Parker and Beck hadn't noticed as well.

And then there was Mason. After the bedroom incident, I was certain he knew as well. And maybe even returned my interest.

There's a lot of ways I could respond to that, but being respectful of our positions here, I'll keep it clean. You have nothing to be sorry for.

I'd said the words so many times in my head, I knew them word for word. Maybe I was projecting my own feelings. Or maybe it was wishful thinking. Or maybe not, and Mason's words meant exactly what I thought they did.

The door opened. Parker and Mason walked inside.

When I'd seen him last, Mason had been covered in paint splatters. Not anymore. Wearing navy pants and a white button-down with a camel sport coat, he was a walking billboard for the phrase "cleaned up nicely."

More than nicely.

Before he caught me staring, I buried my face in the menu.

"Oh boy," Mom said. "I wish I could stay beyond tomorrow. Looks like things are going to get interesting in Cedar Falls."

"Great," I said just as the guys got to our table. "Now you too. Traitor."

Mom didn't appear at all guilty for teasing me herself even though she'd told Sophia a minute ago to knock it off.

"Mind if I sit with you?" Parker asked my mother.

"Not at all."

He slid into the booth next to her as Mason assessed the situation. Mom and Parker on one side of the booth, Sophia and me on the other. There was room for him in both spots.

Our eyes met.

Maybe he read my silent "sit with me" or did it of his own accord, but for whatever reason, he sat next to me.

Be careful what you wish for, Pia.

As the conversation swirled around me, I somehow managed to order a wine and pretend, for a few minutes anyway, not to notice how good Mason smelled. Or the fact that, if I moved my right leg even the slightest bit, we'd be touching.

"I'm glad you're enjoying our little town," Parker said as Sophia regaled him with our afternoon's adventures.

"Little being the operative word," Sophia said. "I can't imagine what the dating pool is like in a town this size."

I was going to kill her.

"Small," Parker said. "Very small."

"How many graduated in your high school class?" my mother asked as our drinks came and we paused to place our orders.

"Oh, I'm not actually from here. I met this guy"—Parker indicated Mason—"in college."

"How did you end up here?" Sophia asked.

"Beck was looking for a roommate. I was a business major in college and always knew I wanted to work for myself but wasn't sure of the industry. My dad owns a car dealership, and if I went back home he'd be all over me to work there. So I came here, got into construction, which I've always enjoyed, and am biding my time until I can start my own company."

"Basically," Mason added, "he wasn't ready to leave college so he and Beck came back here for round two."

"And that," Parker admitted.

My mother, true to her nature, asked Parker and Mason about a billion questions. After we ordered and got our food, I was just beginning to breathe and act like a normal human being when Mason shifted in his seat. His leg now touched mine. Subtly. And barely. But definitely touching.

I should have pulled away. Instead, I let my leg

relax into his. He probably wouldn't even notice. We stayed that way through dinner.

"So Pia's doing a good job so far?" my mother asked. "I heard you two were off to a rocky start."

I groaned. "Mom, please."

"It's okay." Mason's hands wrapped around his beer bottle. *I should absolutely not concentrate on his fingers or imagine what they could do to me.* As he lifted the bottle to his lips, I snuck a peek at his face, something I'd mostly avoided doing since our legs began to touch.

He took a sip, looked me straight in the eyes, and then glanced under the table. It was so quick, I couldn't imagine anyone else noticing.

But I had.

"I apologize for the way I treated your daughter," he said. "When she first came—"

"You'd just buried your father," my mother said gently.

"I thought you didn't believe in apologizing?" I asked, sincerely curious. I'd thought about our conversation throughout my shower. More or less. Okay, mostly I'd thought about Mason, but about that conversation too.

"I believe in rectifying wrongs, but you're right. Usually apologies are unnecessary if we see them as an opportunity to learn from our mistakes. But in this case, I am truly sorry." His words were as softly spoken as I'd ever heard him before.

"Well, that's a new one," Parker said.

"To answer your original question..." Mason ignored Parker and turned his attention to Mom. "She's doing a phenomenal job. Pia was meant to work in this field."

"She was brought up in our restaurant, as I'm sure she told you. And she was always good with the customers. Though her dad and I were surprised she didn't want to work at our place, I agree, it's a perfect fit for her."

"Um," I interjected as our food arrived. "I am right here."

"Oh look," Sophia teased. "There you are."

Well into the meal, my eggplant pizza even better tasting than it smelled, and after my mother regaled Mason with childhood Pia stories, I'd almost forgotten Mason and I were so close our legs touched.

Almost.

Until he leaned into me to snag the small bowl of grated cheese. "Pardon my reach," he said.

I tried not to inhale.

Tried not to notice our legs were now flush up against each other.

Tried to swallow my pizza. Breathe normally. The basics.

Somehow, I managed to get through the meal. And when my mother said she was ready to go to the inn—no pub for her—I'd almost volunteered to take her back and keep my butt there. I trusted the guys to take care of Soph, who was ready for a night out.

But Mason beat me to it.

"I'll take you," he said to Mom. And if that wasn't enough, when we asked the waiter for the check, she said it was taken care of as she handed Mason his credit card.

When had he managed that?

"Thank you," Mom said, Sophia echoing the sentiment.

"It's the least I could do for giving her to Heritage Hill," he said to my mom, standing.

"You're awfully complimentary tonight," I teased him, following. "And thank you."

"You're welcome."

"Looks like you ladies are mine," Parker said, linking elbows with both me and Sophia. "See you there," he called to Mason, whisking us away. Mom waved as the three of us made our way up the street, the sight of her with Mason stirring something inside me that shouldn't be there. A feeling of domesticity, as if we were together and he was taking care of his mother-in-law.

What an absolutely absurd thought.

I turned around again, for one last look, but they'd walked in the opposite direction and were already gone.

18
MASON

Tonight, there would be no sidebar conversations.

No dancing.

As I walked into O'Malley's, I summoned the discipline that had been instilled during my army days and steeled myself to have more self-control than I'd had at dinner. At any time, I could have moved away, but instead I toyed with trouble, punishing myself by testing boundaries.

Dad would love her.

How many times had that thought intruded this week as I'd watched Pia interact with guests or offer advice on the renovations? He would never know what a coup de grâce it had been to hire her. Also for the hundredth time, I wondered what he'd say about my current predicament. Though Dad would love nothing more than for me to take over Heritage Hill, he also knew the reason why I became a cop in the first place. He'd agree that screwing up my pension was a bad idea. In the end, it probably didn't matter since I was too stubborn to listen to my father, or anyone for that matter, when it came to advice in general.

There was just one person who could decide which direction my life should head, and his judgment was clouded by a five-foot-two-inch, dark-haired bombshell who was currently holding court at the bar. She and her sister sat side by side, Parker next to them, Beck showing off his drink-making skills, and a guy I didn't recognize standing way too fucking close to Pia.

I angled my way between Pia and the stranger. Since there were no empty bar stools, I stood beside her at the bar.

"Just tryin' to get a beer, man," the guy said, now behind me.

That might be so, but he'd been too close. Even I could see all the way across the room the way he leered at her.

"Whatdya need?" I asked him.

"Yuengling."

"Beck," I called to my friend. "Yuengling bottle and my usual."

Pia watched as I handed the guy a drink so he'd bug off.

"Who was that?" she asked.

"No idea. Tourist."

"You say that as if it's a bad thing." She twisted her bar stool to face me. "You do realize your entire business is centered around tourists?"

I shrugged. Tourists were fine. Ones that looked like that and stood too close to Pia were another story entirely. But I couldn't say that, so instead I sipped my beer and watched Beck try to impress Sophia. The guy really was a piece of work.

"Why so grumpy all of a sudden?"

Again, we were way too close. If I took one more step toward her, I'd basically be sitting on Pia's lap.

"I'm not grumpy."

"You kind of are."

"I don't mean to be."

"What's wrong?"

A loaded question if I ever heard one.

"Nothing's wrong."

She looked at me so expectantly, as if I was supposed to change my mind and tell her more. To be fair, something *was* wrong. But there was no fucking way I could admit that to her.

"Mason?"

"Pia?"

"I think we should talk about this."

"About what?"

She gave me a look that called bullshit on me pretending I had no clue what was going on. Parker and Sophia laughed at something Beck said. Music blared. People carried on their conversations all around us.

But for me, at this moment, there was only Pia looking up at me, waiting. She'd fired the first shot and it was up to me to respond.

"You know exactly what."

I took a deep breath and tried not to stare at Pia's lips as we talked. A storm brewed in her eyes. Not just a storm, a hurricane that was about to be unleashed. Pia had gone from timid to fiery so quickly that I almost smiled.

So my little Pia had a temper, did she?

Discipline, Mason.

On the other hand, taunting wasn't flirting. I just couldn't let this one go.

"Do I? Let me think. Is it about the paint color in

the reception room? It's only a shade darker than the original one but they didn't have—"

"No." Her eyes narrowed. "I'm not talking about the paint color."

"Oh. I see." Pretending to think about it more, I took a sip of beer and caught Parker's eye. He seemed amused, and I was fairly certain I knew the cause. "Is it about Esther's raise?"

"Mason." Her tone was sharper than usual. I really should stop.

"No? I know. The couple from Maryland. I took care of his refund already, but he did say you spoke to him as well."

She was ready to kill me.

Teasing her might not have been crossing the line, but what I was about to say definitely was. Leaning toward her, resisting the urge to tuck errant strands of Pia's hair behind her ears to be sure she could hear me above the noise, I whispered to her.

"Are we talking about the intense chemistry between us that had me wanting to toss you on my bed this morning, not giving a fuck if I was your boss?"

I stood back and didn't need to wait very long for her reaction. The storm had passed. In its wake, a completely shocked and very turned-on Pia stared at me.

"What are you two talking about over there?" Sophia asked at the very worst possible time. As much as I wanted to ignore her, and the guys, and everyone who wasn't Pia, I'd probably done enough damage for one night. Moving closer to the bar, and farther away from Pia, I raised my glass.

"Caught," I said, diverting attention away from Pia's still very-surprised expression. "We were talking about you."

"And how I am the favorite daughter?"

"You have that in common. Parker thinks he's the favorite son."

"Because I am," Parker said.

Having successfully diverted attention away from Pia's and my very private discussion, the sidebar conversation I'd not planned to have, I went back to being an observer. If I'd had this little discipline with my unit, I would have ended up dead or putting somebody in danger.

You are in danger, buddy. Big time.

Two drinks later, when a stool opened up next to Sophia, I took it, having managed not to engage with Pia after I blew my plan to hell with that comment.

"You are as broody as my sister said you were."

"And you're as outspoken," I shot back.

"Pia said I was outspoken?" Sophia pouted more than her sister but had a lot of similar mannerisms.

"Nah, just a good guess."

"I'll choose not to be insulted because it's true."

"Good, because it wasn't meant as an insult. One of the best women I ever knew was as outspoken as they come."

"Who's that?"

Already regretting having said it, not wanting questions, I had no choice but to answer. "My mother."

"Pia told me she died when you were young?"

"Eleven," I said. "Breast cancer."

And now Dad was gone too.

"I'm so sorry."

"Nothing to be sorry for," I said as Beck came over to us. "That's life."

"You two are much too somber," he said, putting shot glasses in front of us, then Parker and Pia. After filling four of them, plus one for himself, Beck raised his own into the air. "To outspoken women everywhere, may they never be silenced."

I caught Sophia's surprised expression just before downing the shot. Whether she was surprised he overheard us—Beck was actually a good listener, especially behind the bar—or his sentiment, I couldn't be sure.

"What was that all about?" Parker asked from my right.

When I looked over at him, I noticed Pia was gone. Turning around in my seat, I scanned the bar. Nothing.

"Bathroom," Parker said.

I ignored that as if I hadn't been looking for her. "Beck overheard Sophia and me talking."

"Ahh, seems like he's moved onto another conversation."

Across the bar, Beck's elbows rested on the bar as he listened to something two women were saying. Tourists, most likely, since I'd never seen them before. The dirty blonde was Beck's type, and I wouldn't be surprised if he ended up with her tonight.

She was coming back.

I should have continued to give my attention to Sophia. Or Beck or Parker. Instead, I watched Pia make her way through the crowd back to the bar. I watched the looks she got from men, and even women. I watched as her attention turned directly onto me, and Pia's entire body language changed.

Before, she'd been relaxed, but now she was on high alert.

By the time she sat, Pia was wound as tightly as me.

Something had to give. There was no fucking way I could sit here like this and pretend I didn't want to spend the night learning how Pia liked to be kissed, to be touched.

Fuck.

I stood up, tossed some bills on the bar and said, "Parker, you'll see the ladies back?"

All three of them looked at me with the same "What the hell?" expression. Didn't matter. I'd done enough damage for one night.

"Sure."

"Calling it a night," I said to all three. "Catch you tomorrow."

Some might call me a coward for hightailing it out of there. I preferred to think of it as self-preservation. As I made my way down the street and beyond the town square downhill toward the lake, my mind began to clear. There was a simple fix to my Pia problem. I just couldn't be trusted to be with her socially. No more drinking or dinners or O'Malley's. Work and that was it.

And certainly no more inviting her to stay down the hall from me.

Before they got back, I took a quick shower, considered rubbing one off after hours of an on-again-off-again hard-on, but decided to hit the sack instead. They could come back from the bar anytime, and if I saw Pia tonight, I was pretty certain all of my platitudes about what would or wouldn't happen between us would crumble to pieces.

All went well, no Pia in the hallway. Her bedroom door, empty. Until ten minutes later, courtesy of me being wide awake, I noticed my phone light up. Grabbing it, I stared at the text from Pia, trying to decide if I should text her back or pretend I was already asleep.

> Can we talk?

Three little words, but so fucking dangerous given the fact that she would be sleeping down the hall from me.

I couldn't leave her hanging.

> Sure. Where are you?

> Right outside your door.

19

PIA

Are we talking about the intense chemistry between us that had me wanting to toss you on my bed this morning, not giving a fuck if I was your boss?

I hadn't been able to think about anything else for the rest of the night.

That was exactly what I'd wanted to talk about, figuring to clear the air and address the elephant in the room. Because he took up more and more space in my mind every day. Tonight it had gotten to the point that even breathing normally had become difficult around him.

Not giving a fuck if I was your boss...

With every step toward the house, the urge not to let it drop became stronger, especially strange since

I'd done a great job of avoiding eye contact with him since he'd said that to me. Of course, it had been pretty easy when he took off, surprising me less than my companions.

By the time I passed his bedroom, my fingers itched to text him. The second I hit send, I'd wanted to take it back. Sort of.

The door opened.

He wore boxers and a T-shirt and an expression that was easy to read.

"I agree we should talk," he said, his voice low and husky. "But now probably isn't a good time."

Of course it wasn't. What had I been thinking? "You're right," I said, taking a step back.

With a sound in his throat that was part groan and part guttural growl, Mason's hand shot out and grabbed my arm, stopping me from backing away any farther.

He pulled me into his room, slammed the door closed and pushed me up against it. Surely he could hear my heart hammering as he grabbed both of my wrists and pinned them above my head. The authority with which he moved... his intentions, which were quite clear... seeing Mason lose control, something he did rarely... It was all too much.

"Mason."

The word sounded strangled to my own ears. It was desperate and pleading but filled with pent-up longing and a need to know what a kiss from this man would be like.

He filled the remaining space between us with his body, Mason's chest now touching mine. His hand gripped my wrists so easily that, even if I tugged to pull them away—which I didn't—they wouldn't budge. So much power and strength...

"Tell me to stop, Pia."

As if I'd do such a thing. I met his eyes, defiant.

"I am your boss. This isn't right."

It felt right to me. My chin lifted, but I said nothing.

"Pia," he warned, and I could tell it would be my last warning.

Good.

Mason's other hand moved to my face. Gripping my chin with his strong fingers, he held me in place. He wanted to dominate me?

Fine.

Kiss me?

More than fine.

But if Mason wanted me to stop this, he was in for a rude awakening. Every nerve ending in my body was ready for this kiss.

My lips parted.

Mason's head descended, both of his hands holding tight. The first touch of his lips was softer than I'd expected. Immediately I opened for him and Mason took advantage, his tongue swooping inside. Pressing harder, opening deeper, the kiss went from gentle to demanding almost immediately.

I did pull my wrists from his grip then, wanting to touch him, to get closer. Mason's hand not only held firm, but his other hand joined the party. I was well and truly pinned to the door as his lips continued their sensual assault. This kiss was everything I'd imagined, and so much more. It was as if our mouths were made for each other, Mason's head slanting for even better access.

I wanted to touch him so badly.

This time, when I pulled my wrists he let them go, my arms immediately encircling his shoulders. I pulled him closer. Or maybe he pulled me closer, his hand wrapping around my back. Our bodies pressed together as the kiss spiraled more and more out of control.

After what felt like days, or only a few minutes, Mason pulled back.

"Pia." He looked down at me with an expression I'd never seen on him before. It was pure, unbridled passion. Desire. Maybe even need. "If you knew how much I wanted to do that every fucking time we're together."

"I do know." Because I wanted it too.

"Like I said at the bar, I'd give my right arm to carry you over to my bed and spend the night making love to you over and over again until you couldn't walk tomorrow."

My core clenched at his words.

"I want to be inside you so fucking badly, especially after that kiss."

"But?"

Not only was there a *but* in his words, but Mason's grip was no longer as tight on me as before.

"But I promised myself not to touch you."

I untangled my arms from his neck and stepped back. This time, he let me.

"What are you saying?" I asked, the dumbest question ever. It was clear what Mason was saying, but my ears refused to believe it. Not after that kiss.

"I'm saying this shouldn't have happened. I'm your boss. It's not right."

"Maybe not," I conceded, "but you can't deny there's something between us."

"Are you fucking kidding me?" His tone was softer than his words. "Of course there's something between us. I've never wanted a woman so badly in my life."

I wasn't sure if I believed that, completely, but it was still nice to hear, especially since he was basically turning me away.

"I get what you're saying." I tried not to notice Mason through his boxers. "And I agree that it does complicate things."

"Big time."

"But I wonder if it's something more than that?"

"Like what?"

"I don't know. I just get the sense…" I stopped. Convincing someone of my worth was not only a waste of time, but it was degrading. And I wouldn't do that to myself. Not again. "Never mind. This was a mistake."

"Pia," he said. "The last thing I want to do is put you in an awkward position. I have no idea what's going to happen with the inn, or what direction I'm taking."

"What do you mean?" Now it was my turn to be confused.

He took a deep breath. "My leave is only thirty working days. When that's up, I have big decisions to make, as you know. There was always the possibility I would still sell."

"I know. But I'm not sure what that has to do with us."

"There are just too many question marks."

As in, he could be leaving. "I get it," I said, heading to the door and opening it.

"Pia." He stopped me. How could he have had me pinned against the door five minutes ago, kissing me like I'd never been kissed, but was now rejecting me so easily? Like it was nothing. Mason's expression was a mask of indifference, so different than it had been just a few moments before.

Rangers are as tenacious as they are disciplined.

The more I read about them, the more I began to understand Mason. The man who watched me walk out his bedroom door was all Ranger. I should have listened to him when he told me he was nothing like his father. "Less nice" was putting it mildly.

"It's fine," I said, knowing it was anything but. "This was a mistake." I repeated his words. "I'm sorry I texted you."

As I was about to close the door, Mason stopped me.

"Pia."

I looked up into the eyes of the man I'd been kissing so passionately just a few minutes earlier. "Remember, never apologize to me. Especially when you haven't done anything wrong. I pulled you into my room. I kissed you. You understand?"

I nodded, just wanting to leave. "Goodnight, Mason."

"Goodnight, Pia."

It took everything I had not to run down the hall to my bedroom and slam the door. I wasn't a child, and maybe I also wasn't as disciplined as Mason, but I could control my emotions too. Or at least I thought I could, since the second I opened and closed the door, tears began to well in my stupid eyes.

I wanted him. And he wanted me, too.

And that was precisely the problem.

20

MASON

"You look like shit."

Pia and her family had left earlier, along with our last weekend guest. And though I tried to tell Parker I could paint without him, that he should take the day off, he stubbornly refused to listen. Consequently, the two of us used the empty inn time to knock down the wall between the reception area and main dining room to make a bigger space for potential parties. Though I still wasn't sure about weddings, Pia's ideas on potential special events had a lot of merit.

"Thanks," I said as we cleaned, the wall now completely demolished.

"You didn't sleep?" Parker correctly guessed.

"Not well," I admitted, grabbing two waters from the cooler and tossing one to Parker. Sitting on one of the covered chairs in the corner, I took a long swig.

"Talk to me."

Of all the guys, Parker was the one I'd always opened up to most. Unlike Cole and Beck, he usually went easy on the advice unless I asked for it.

"I kissed Pia last night."

"Whoa." Parker sat down on the cooler. Clearly he hadn't been expecting that. "When?"

"When you guys came back. It's been pretty obvious there's something between us—"

He laughed. "No shit. Really?"

I ignored that.

"I may have said something to her at the bar that precipitated her texting me when she got back, wanting to talk."

"What'd ya say?"

"Something about me wanting to toss her onto my bed earlier in the day when we accidentally found ourselves in my bedroom."

Parker oozed skepticism, likely because of the "accidentally" part.

"Anyway, she texted me. We kissed. But I stopped it there. And then we hardly spoke this morning.

Which is exactly the problem. We can't fool around and work together. I should never have done it."

Parker didn't say anything. Typical of him. So I prompted him. "What do you think?"

"You want my opinion?"

"Yeah. I do."

"I think you're beating yourself up for a lack of discipline, but this isn't the army. You're not violating OPSEC. Yeah, you're her boss. And yeah, it might get complicated if you decide to stay and the two of you have to work together. Or equally as complicated if things work out, but you go back to the city. But it's not a life-or-death matter, not in the sense you're trained to think like. You're both adults and can have an adult conversation about the consequences of getting together. That there's something between you is an understatement, big time. If it were me, I'd consider exploring it. But it's not me, so I get your hesitation. But sometimes, in the real world, you have to break protocol."

"Breaking protocol can get you killed."

"Or get your heart broken."

"Almost just as bad."

"Jesus," Beck said, coming in with supplies. "It's like a funeral in here. What the hell?"

"Mason kissed Pia," Parker said. There was

zero chance Beck wouldn't find out, and I'd known it the second I told Parker. For better or worse, there were no secrets between this group of guys.

"Oh, shit."

"That's what I said." Parker stood, taking the bag from Beck.

"So what's the problem?"

"He's beating himself up about it. Boss man and all."

Parker had such a way with words. "I'm sitting right here."

"Great, then talk," Beck said, shooing Parker off the cooler and grabbing a water.

"There's nothing to talk about. It happened. Won't happen again. Let's get to work."

As if that was going to be the end of it.

"Not so fast. Why won't it happen again?"

"Besides the obvious?"

"Yeah, sure. Besides the obvious."

I was done with this discussion. "Never mind. Let's get to work. You guys sure you want to spend your Sunday—"

"Yes, we do. Now shut the hell up and let's finish this."

It wasn't until the wall was gone, the debris and

dust cleared and the three of us were at the kitchen table with beers that Pia's name came up again.

"So what's the plan?" Beck asked. "Just pretend nothing happened?"

"Great question," I said. "I have no fucking clue."

"You don't know how to deal with Pia because you have no idea what's next," Parker said. "And that's the bigger problem."

Obviously, he was right.

"There's just so much to consider," I said, having thought about little else, besides the fact that Dad would never come walking into this kitchen again.

And Pia. I'd thought a lot about Pia.

"Alright." Beck jumped up from his stool. "Let's do it."

"What are we doing?" Parker asked as Beck started opening and closing drawers.

"What the hell are you looking for?" I asked.

"Ahh, here we go." He pulled out a pad and pen from the junk drawer. One that I cleaned out multiple times but Dad always seemed to find a way to clutter up again.

Now I'd be keeping it just as it was.

Beck drew a line down the middle. He put the word "cop" on one side and "HH" on the other.

"Are you serious?" I asked.

Parker looked like he was going to crack up any second.

"One good thing about being a cop. Go."

"Beck—"

"Would you just amuse me, please?"

"You're amusing, alright," Parker said, getting himself another beer.

"Or a positive about running Heritage Hill," Beck said. "Either one. Go."

I hated shit like this. But knowing Beck, it was either amuse him for a few minutes or listen to him soapbox all night.

"There's a lot I like about being a cop," I relented.

"Alright, give me something you don't like."

"Also easy to do. Public opinion of us isn't good and not improving."

Beck wrote that down. "What else?"

"Perps suing you for everything. Department not backing us like they used to," I said as he continued to write. "Mandatory overtime. The city itself isn't really for me. And not having a hook will make it hard to move up the ladder."

"Anything else you don't like?"

"Plenty," I said, taking a swing of beer. "But those are the biggies."

"Alright, now Heritage. What do you dislike about running this place?"

I thought about that for a second. "I never really saw myself as a people person."

"Agreed," Parker shot out, for shits and giggles I assumed.

"But Pia is taking over some of the guest interactions. Lemme think."

I didn't mind Cedar Falls. I actually liked it better than the city. And the guys were here. "No Cole," I said.

"Don't write that down," Parker said to Beck. "He clearly forgot to say no me and you in the city, so those two cancel each other out."

I rolled my eyes.

"No pension," I said. "The uncertainty. Although maybe that's not really a negative since I have more control over my salary, even if it's not guaranteed. If we play our cards right, the payday will put the force to shame."

His pen hovered. "Do I write it down?"

"Yeah," Parker said, as if we were asking these questions about him. "Uncertainty is a negative. Mason's not great with that."

Jesus fucking Christ. The pair of them.

"What else?" Beck asked.

"None of it matters," I said, having thought of this laundry list before. "It comes down to choosing between carrying on my father's legacy or honoring my mother's."

That shut both of them up.

I didn't need to explain. It was no secret that helping people had been a dream of mine since my mother died. It wasn't a pipe dream either. That, or the army. I'd done both. The former was rewarding as hell, even if some of the second- and third-order effects were shitty. And the latter? I still missed it.

"Not to be glib," Beck said finally, as if that wasn't his middle name, "but I think those cancel each other out."

I glared at him.

"I'm serious. Neither are about you. I'm pretty sure Papa Bennett would be proud of whatever you decided to do as long as it made you happy."

"Damn." Parker shook his head. "Sometimes you surprise me, Beckham."

He didn't comment on the use of his full name. "I can be deep," Beck responded. "I just hide it well."

"Really fucking well," I agreed.

Just like that, the heavy tone lifted and the guys started ribbing me again. Probably sensing there wasn't much more to pull from me, they let the matter of my future drop. Even so, I wasn't done thinking about it. What the guys had said. And beyond that, the things I hadn't added to the list.

Like Pia.

On one hand, not having her around would be a negative of going back to the city. Despite the fact that I'd sent her away last night, I was also counting the minutes until she came back tomorrow. But she was a negative in the HH column too, because being here, and knowing I should stay away from her, was fucking torture.

Which brought me full circle. Except...

The left side of Beck's paper was looking mighty empty. Could I really see myself not being a cop? If I left the NYPD, that would be the end of the road. It was all or nothing.

Kind of like the Pia situation.

I either said "fuck it" and had that adult talk with her about us. Or I toed the line, tried like hell to ignore her as anything but my employee. And the more I thought about it, that second idea seemed absurd.

"We need to talk," I said, only realizing I did so out loud when the guys looked at me.

"Huh?" Beck asked.

"Me and Pia. We need to talk. To have that adult conversation."

"Oh yeah," Beck said in a "frat boy" tone. He made a "quote, unquote" gesture with his hands. "Talk. Is that what the kids are calling it these days?"

More maturely, Parker caught my eye. "I think that's a good idea."

So did I.

"Nothing like talking myself out of my own moral code," I said, half-disgusted, but also excited about the possibilities.

"Trust your instincts, Mace," Parker said. "They got you to Ranger School. Kept you alive overseas. You've got a good head on your shoulders. Use it."

Though he didn't say it, Parker's words somehow felt like an argument for being with Pia.

"You just want to sweeten the pact pot," I teased him.

"Listen, we all know the rules. You either abide by them or pay the piper."

"Who needs another beer?" Beck asked, heading to the fridge. I lifted my arm up. Might as well get good and toasted while the inn was empty. Tomorrow was going to be one hell of a day, no matter how it went with Pia.

Halfway through another beer, I wondered what

Pia was thinking. What she was doing. Fuck it. Why wait until tomorrow? I picked up my phone.

"He has that look," Beck said.

I ignored him.

Sent the text.

> Where are you?

Took another swig of beer.

Waited.

Looked at my phone.

Finally, an agonizing five minutes later, she texted back.

> I'm home. Why?

> Can I come over? We need to talk.

Another wait, though this one wasn't as long.

And it was just one word.

> Sure.

21

PIA

Since my apartment wasn't huge, I'd been able to pace the length of it at least four dozen times since Mason texted.

The last thing in the world I expected was for him to ask to come over. After last night, we'd hardly spoken. Fleeing the inn the first chance I got, which hadn't gone unnoticed by my sister, I had said goodbye to my mother and Sophia and spent the rest of the day trying to recalibrate.

As I waited for him now, the same thoughts that had run through my head all afternoon flitted by again and again. He liked me. But not enough. I liked him, probably too much. He might not be staying, and for that matter, I might not either. So much uncertainty, but I'd already decided not to worry about things I couldn't control. I came here to do my best possible work and turn Heritage Hill around, and that was what I would do.

Except, the new owner had my head spinning nearly twenty-four seven.

And that kiss? There was zero chance I'd be able to get that out of my head anytime soon. I looked down at my phone for the hundredth time since he'd first texted, just as a knock at my door nearly made me drop the phone.

I thought about changing but didn't want to look like I'd tried too hard, so leggings and an oversized sweatshirt was how I'd kept it. With a French vanilla candle burning in the living room and the lights down low, as I liked them, it looked like I was planning a seduction in here.

I wasn't. Mostly. Mason had made it clear the boss/employee line was one he didn't want to cross. So then what was the talk about? Clearing the air between us so it wasn't awkward? Might be a bit late for that.

I opened the door. A jeans and sweater-wearing Mason with just enough scruff to make him look even more menacing—and sexy—than usual filled the doorframe completely.

"Come on in," I said, trying to sound casual. "Can I get you a drink?"

"Sure." He closed the door behind him. "So this is your abode?"

"It's small," I said, heading to the kitchen. "And needs more decorating. But it's convenient. Maybe a little too convenient with the coffee shop downstairs. I know you don't drink wine but—"

"I do," he said. "Here and there. I'll take whatever you're drinking."

Grabbing a second glass, I handed him a wine. "I had no idea you liked red wine."

He took a sip. "There's a lot about each other we don't know."

"True." I took my own glass and tried to play it cool. Was likely failing. Why did my kitchen seem so much smaller with him in it? Without a word, I headed to the living room and sat on the only couch. Mason sat on the armchair and, unlike me, appeared totally relaxed. Not a care in the world. "So?"

"So," he said, putting his glass on the table between us. "I want to know more."

Blinking, I waited to see if he would elaborate.

"I want to know everything there is to know about you. Why do you care about the coffee shop being downstairs as if your ass wouldn't perfectly fit in my hands no matter how many cinnamon buns you ate."

Wait a minute. Did he literally just say that?

"Why did you let your asshole boss get the best of you? Why did you really take this job? All of it. But only after I spend the night learning every curve of that luscious body of yours. If you want that too."

To say I was speechless was an understatement.

"And if you don't... if you think our positions will make it impossible to explore this thing between us, I will be the picture of propriety."

I put my wine down.

"Mason, I have no idea what to say. This isn't at all what I expected."

He leaned forward, still awfully casual, elbows resting on his knees as if he hadn't just said he wanted to learn every curve of my body. "What did you think I was going to say?"

"That things didn't need to be awkward between us. Stuff like that."

He didn't say another word. I'd gotten to know him a bit. It was like Mason only had so many words, so he used them carefully. And he'd certainly made his point clear.

The ball was in my court, so to speak. "It's complicated, for sure."

"It is," he said.

"And will likely even get more so if we explore this."

"Agreed."

"But you want to anyway? I know the whole boss thing is a monkey wrench for you."

"It is," he admitted. "But I'm going with my gut on this one."

"And what does your gut tell you?"

He stood up, closed the space between us and sat on the couch next to me. Reaching out his hand, Mason cupped my cheek. His thumb caressed it, jumbling my thoughts.

"That I've never wanted to get to know a woman more than you."

I swallowed. "Get to know me, as in...?"

"As in, all of it."

Words escaped me. So instead, I parted my lips in response, knowing already what I would say if speaking were actually possible.

His thumb inched toward my mouth. I opened

wider. When his thumb got close enough, I darted my tongue out to touch it. Tease it.

Mason groaned.

I leaned into him, taking his entire thumb into my mouth. And I sucked. Used my tongue to show him what it would be like. What he could look forward to.

"Pia." His voice was almost hoarse.

I loved it.

Pulling his thumb from me, Mason replaced it with his mouth. His lips crashed onto mine, immediately relentless. His tongue and lips in a perfectly balanced dance that had me grasping at his sweater, wanting so much more this time.

Clearly, he did too. Tugging on my sweatshirt, he tore it off in a heartbeat, barely pausing the kiss. While Mason's hands roamed everywhere—my shoulders and back, to my chest, cupping both breasts through the lace fabric of my bra—I was just as explorative. I lifted his sweater, and Mason finished the job as he stood, then reached for me. I was pretty sure he said something, but I was too busy staring at more lines than I'd ever seen on a man in real life, except the first time I'd seen him without a shirt. He was absolutely shredded, all Army Ranger.

Or cop. Or whatever had him working out hard enough to achieve—that.

"You're sure about this?"

"No. But I want it anyway."

What I really wanted was to touch him, so I indulged in the urge. "Do you go to a gym?"

"No," he said, reaching around my back. "I have some weights in the basement of the inn."

"Some weights?" I asked, tracing the lines of his abs as my bra strap popped free.

"Yeah." Mason stared and then immediately cupped both breasts as if they were fine pieces of china. "Fuck me, you have magnificent tits." His eyes lifted up to mine, an apology in them even though Mason didn't apologize.

"I'm okay with it," I said as his thumbs circled my nipples. "I don't mind at all."

He came closer, obliterating any distance between us. "What don't you mind, Pia?" he asked, continuing to rub my nipples as my hands moved to his arms.

"The word you used."

He smiled. I guessed someone liked me being suddenly shy. "Tits?"

I nodded.

"Are you telling me you want me to talk dirty,

Pia?"

Mortified, since I'd never told any previous man such a thing, I looked down to where he continued to fondle me, quite expertly, I might add.

"Pia?"

I looked back up.

"Tell me. Say it."

Nodding, I said, "Yes. I want you to talk dirty, Mason."

"How dirty?" he said as one of his hands slid down the waistband of my leggings.

"Very," I admitted.

His hand slipped lower and lower, Mason never taking his eyes from mine.

"And what should I do as I talk very dirty to you, sweet Pia?" As if I could answer with his fingers dipping even lower. "Should I slip one of my fingers inside, to see if you're wet for me?"

He didn't wait for an answer. "Mmm, so fucking wet. Maybe another finger, for good measure?"

Clearly he didn't want an answer but was simply following my lead.

"Mason," I groaned as his fingers began to move.

"Should I talk about how fucking much I've wanted to do this? To make you so wet for me that you would say my name just like that. Or if I'm being honest," he said, continuing the sweet torture, "even louder. I want you to... call. My. Name."

He was going to actually give me an orgasm this way. Sitting on my living room couch, his hands down my pants.

Unbelievable.

"Mason," I said, louder.

"Not good enough," he whispered, this time directly into my ear. "Guess I'll just have to play with your clit too."

His words, coupled with the fact that his thumb did exactly as he promised, meant Mason got exactly what he wished.

"Mason," I cried, unable to hold back as the most easily wrought orgasm of my life took over my body.

"That's it. Come all over my fingers."

His words only intensified the throbbing between my legs. That and having wanted Mason to touch me since we met.

"Oh my God," I said as the pulses ebbed. Except, I didn't have time for an afterglow. Mason was already tugging down my pants. His kiss was so intense that I swear, if I wasn't so busy unbuttoning and unzipping Mason's jeans, I probably could have had another orgasm.

The second my hand found him, Mason's intake

of breath was all the reward I needed. When I began to stroke him, the fact that he began to lose control—the man who was always, always, in control—made me want to please him even more.

Mason broke off our kiss and helped me out by standing, removing his jeans and underwear, as I did the same and fully ditched my own.

"Fuck, Pia. Look at you."

"Look at me?" I glanced down. He was hard, huge and so ready for me. "You're like a sculpture, Mason. Oh," I added. "I'm on the pill."

It was as if the floodgates had been opened. He pulled me toward him, grabbed both ass cheeks with his hands, and squeezed. His mouth covered mine as I pulled him close, our movements almost frantic.

How he got me to the couch, I wasn't sure. But as my head hit the pillow and I watched Mason use his knee to separate my legs, it hit me for the first time, somehow.

"We're doing this," I blurted as Mason's fingers once again slipped inside me.

"This?" he asked, almost smiling. "In the interest of talking as dirty as my sweet Pia requested," he said, a second finger joining the first as my hips lifted to meet him, "let's call it what it is."

Kneeling between my legs, with his dick so hard

I couldn't stop staring, Mason licked his lips as he continued to work magic between my legs. "I'm going to fuck you so damn hard, Pia, that when you scream my name this time it will make that last one sound like a kitten's meow."

Oh my God.

Just like that, his fingers were gone. Moving over me, he braced himself between my legs. I reached down to guide him into me, unable to wait any longer. "Please," I said, bringing the tip of him to me. "Mason, please."

"Tell. Me."

"Oh God, no. Just do it. Please."

"Do what, Pia?"

This was hard Mason. Ranger Mason. He would never relent.

"Fuck me, Mason," I said.

And so he did. Thrusting into my absolutely drenching wetness—probably as wet as I'd ever been in my life—he buried himself full hilt. Grabbing onto his shoulders, when Mason's lips found mine, I held on for dear life. He wasn't gentle, but I didn't need him to be. I needed the man who knew what he wanted, and at this moment, Mason wanted me.

I met every thrust, my hips swaying in perfect

rhythm to his as Mason's thumb found my clit and began to press and circle it. I wanted to call out, but his tongue mimicked our movements down below. No, not mimicked, anticipated. It was as if he was giving me a preview of every thrust.

My nails dug into him.

Lifting his head, Mason looked into my eyes, and I couldn't decide which was hotter, his kisses or his stare. So intense.

With one thrust, so deep that the pleasure-pain line came close to being crossed, he paused.

"Are you gonna come for me again, sweet Pia?"

I tried to move my hips, but Mason wasn't having any of it.

"Yes," I said, trying again.

"You're gonna call my name?"

"I am. Please, Mason."

"Say it."

"Mason." He moved, finally.

"Again."

"Mason," I said, over and over as he thrust and used his thumb to bring me so close. "Mason," I called, louder this time. Knowing he liked it. Wanting to please him. Wanting to find that ultimate pleasure again.

"Fuck, Mason. Yes."

"That's it," he said, unrelenting. "Come all over my dick this time, just like you did my fingers."

His words. His expression.

"Mason, I'm gonna come. So hard."

"Good. That's it. Come on, Pia."

Every muscle in my body tensed and then I absolutely exploded. Taking away his hand, Mason buried himself so deeply inside me that I couldn't tell where one of us started and the other finished.

His head tilted back as I continued to call his name. Mason made the most incredible low, sexy sound in his throat as he, presumably, came too.

"Fuck," he said, not moving as my orgasm began to subside. "Jesus fucking Christ, Pia. I don't know what the hell that was, but it felt really fucking good."

He didn't move just yet, and I didn't want him to. I pulled Mason on top of me, wanting him to stay just a little bit longer.

"There've been a lot of fucks flying around here tonight."

"Mmm." He held himself up, so as not to crush me, but still I could feel Mason's hard chest against my own as he did, unfortunately, pull out. "There could be more."

Neither of us moved. Or spoke.

I'd just had sex with Mason Bennett. My boss. And it was really, really, really good.

"Count me in," I said with a smile, wondering if I'd ever be able to get enough of him.

In response, Mason lowered his head and kissed me, the silent promise of more where that had come from ensuring it would be a long night ahead.

22

MASON

"Can I come in?"

Tearing myself away from Pia early this morning had been hard. Seeing her now behind that desk and keeping my hands off her was going to be even harder.

"Of course."

She didn't look at all as if we'd been up half the night, me making good on my promise to learn every curve of her body. My blue-eyed manager was as passionate in the bedroom as she was competent at her job.

I closed the door.

"We should probably talk."

I'd left in the wee hours of the morning, Pia half-asleep, saying we'd talk later. Thankfully we didn't have any guests at the moment, and while I had to get downstairs to finish the wall with Beck before tomorrow, that could wait.

"What's this?" she asked as I put a plate in front of her.

"Courtesy of Esther. She's trying out a new scrambled egg casserole recipe."

When we didn't have guests, Esther cooked breakfast for my father anyway, and now me, since it gave her something to do. A retired schoolteacher, Esther hated being idle.

Another reason to keep Heritage Hill. She was like family and likely would be out of a job if I sold.

"Thanks," Pia said, scooting her chair closer to the desk. "I almost never eat breakfast."

"No? It's my favorite meal of the day."

"I like it," she said, popping a forkful of egg casserole into her mouth. "Just don't usually make time for it. Sometimes I take a granola bar or something with me, but that's not as good as this. What's in it?"

"Esther never reveals her secrets in the kitchen, so..." I shrugged. Watching her lips part, the pink gloss slowly disappearing, it hit me like a ton of bricks.

Things would never be the same. Not here, at Heritage Hill. Or between Pia and me. Whether that was a good or bad thing was yet to be determined.

"Speaking of secrets," Pia said between bites. "Do the guys know?"

"Not yet. Do you not want me to tell them?"

"Doesn't bother me, I'm just preparing for some major ribbing from Beck."

"You know him well." Beck would be incorrigible when he found out, especially to me. Hopefully he'd go easy on Pia. "So..." she said, clearly wanting to tell me something.

"Say it. Don't be shy around me ever, Pia. Unlike Esther"—I smiled—"you can give up all your secrets, and they'll be safe with me."

She nearly choked. Pia reaching for her coffee to wash down a bite of eggs was charming for some reason.

"You'll be the death of me, Mason."

"How so?" I leaned back in my chair.

"You know exactly how so. And speaking of secrets, I'm not the one who keeps them."

"Are you insinuating I keep secrets?"

She laughed. "You are the most secretive person I know."

"Ask me anything," I said, knowing we both had to get to work but not wanting to leave her yet.

Pia took a bite of toast and watched me, skeptical. While it was true I didn't readily volunteer information, there wasn't much to hide. I was a pretty simple guy.

"Favorite color?"

"Green."

"Food?"

"Burger and fries."

"Best memory?"

That was a bit harder. "My father, teaching me to fish," I said.

"Worst memory?"

Pia wasn't messing around. "You went from favorite color to that awfully quick."

She finished the eggs but said nothing, waiting.

"Fine. Holding my mother's hand in the hospital, knowing she wasn't coming home with us this time."

Immediately, Pia's eyes welled up. She had enough emotion for both of us.

"It's okay. It was a long time ago."

But my dad, not so much. And that still stung. At

least being in his office was getting easier and easier every day.

"I'm surprised you answered, honestly."

"Told you. I'm an open book."

"Haha, sure you are. Only if I pry answers from you."

I leaned forward. "Here's one you don't have to pry from me. I like you, a lot. Last night was incredible, and I've thought of tossing every single item on this desk onto the floor to fuck you on top of it nearly every second since I walked in the door."

Pia finished eating, picked up her plate and swiveled in her chair. She placed it on the bookshelf counter behind her, spun around and then did the same with her laptop, tossing the charging cable to the floor.

"What's stopping you?"

Fuck me. This woman.

I stood up and swiped every paper, journal and other item on the desk to the floor in one clean sweep. Then, stalking around the desk to her, I grabbed Pia and kissed her.

Hard.

Her head bent sideways to give me better access as my tongue tangled with hers. Unlike the last time, I had no desire to go slow. To make love to her. I wanted to be inside Pia as badly as I ever wanted anything in my life.

Picking her up and putting her on the edge of the desk, I bent down. Without saying a word, Pia watched as I removed each of her flats, one shoe at a time. Picking her back up, I made quick work of her pants. This time Pia didn't wait for me and instead hopped up onto the desk.

I had my own jeans and underwear down in no time flat just as Pia provocatively spread her legs, giving me a perfect view. "You show me that pussy," I said, closing the distance between us, "and I'm going to absolutely take advantage. I hope you know that."

"Promise?"

Groaning, I bent down in front of her, smiling at Pia's look of surprise, as if I'd take her without making sure she was ready for me. Holding her legs open with each of my hands, I tasted her for the first time. Somehow we'd never got to this last night, but as I licked and listened to her soft moans, I wished we had.

As she was clearly enjoying the attention, I gave her more. I gave her everything. My lips, my tongue, my fingers. It was only when her legs began to quiver, Pia calling my name just like I'd asked her to, that I stood up.

Licking my lips, making sure Pia knew how good she tasted, I guided myself into her.

"You're unbelievable," she said, holding on to my shoulders.

"We're just getting started, sweet Pia." Fully inside her, the angle perfect, I buried myself even deeper.

"I want to kiss you," I said, knowing she liked when I talked during sex. "But I want to watch those incredible blue eyes as I fuck you even more."

"Mason, we... I..."

I circled her clit with my thumb, thrusting in and out with increasing intensity. I didn't hold back, and Pia didn't seem to mind a bit.

The opposite, actually.

"Come for me, sweet Pia. Call my name as you come all over me, sweetheart."

That did it. As she tensed, I pulled my hand away and thrust balls deep. I came with her, my eyes never leaving Pia's. It was as if more than just our bodies were connected as I came as hard as I'd asked Pia to. My legs shook as Pia's arms wrapped around my shoulders, the two of us breaking eye contact for the first time.

I held her there, not wanting to let go.

Not now. Maybe not ever.

If that scary fucking thought didn't have me pulling away, a knock at the door would anyway. "Mason, you in there? Someone's here to see you."

Someone? That was specific.

"Give me a second," I called back, reluctantly pulling out of Pia. "I guess his timing could have been worse."

She smiled. "So much for our talk," Pia said as we both hurried back into our clothes.

"Let's talk tonight. Stay late and have dinner. I'll wrap up with Beck early and cook for you."

"You cook?"

"Esther taught me a thing or two. But don't expect anything gourmet."

"Alright. Tell me what to get at the store. I'd planned to take a lunch break in town anyway since I'm out of wine. Figured I would say hello to Emilio."

"I'll text a list. Any allergies? Foods you don't like?"

"I'm not a huge fish eater and hate mushrooms. Pretty much everything else is fair game."

"Got it." I leaned forward and kissed her as Beck knocked again.

I strode toward the door and opened it, giving my friend a peek inside at the wreckage. It probably didn't help that I was also tucking in my shirt.

He whistled. "This is an interesting development."

"Fuck off," I said, passing him. "Who's here, anyway?"

"That's for me to know," Beck said in a conspiratorial tone. "And for you to find out."

23

PIA

Blinking, I sat back in my seat and tried to focus, but the computer screen wasn't cooperating. Or my brain wasn't cooperating. Either way, it seemed like as good a time as any for a break. Just as I gathered up my things, a text came through from Delaney.

> I know it's last minute, but any chance you can do lunch?

I actually hadn't thought of lunch. Wonder why?

Chuckling at my own joke, a vision of half-naked Mason standing just about where I was seated right now as he absolutely dominated me, I texted her back and grabbed my purse.

On the way out, I popped into the reception room where Mason and Beck were painting. "Wow," I said, not having seen it earlier. "It looks completely different."

Mason stopped painting and turned around. "Taking out a wall, new floor, new color… that'll do it. What do you think?"

"I love it," I said as he put the brush on top of a paint can.

"Hey, Pia," Beck said without stopping.

"Hi, Beck."

I thought that would be the end of it, Beck uncharacteristically quiet, until Mason took my arm and started leading me to the kitchen.

"I guess we weren't meant to be." Beck sighed dramatically. "It could have been amazing."

Smiling, I called back, "I love you, Beck."

"Love you more," he said, teasing.

Mason backed me up to the island. When I couldn't move anymore, he took advantage, grabbing my hands and pinning them to the countertop on each side of me.

"So you love Beck, huh?"

Although his tone was as teasing as mine had been to Beck, Mason's eyes flashed in a way that told me there was a slight serious side to him too.

"In a brother-sister sort of way, yes."

He closed the space between us. "I'm glad," he said, his face just inches from mine.

"That I love Beck?"

"That you think of him like a brother."

"Why?" I prompted.

"Because I'm a one-woman kind of guy."

Before I could respond, he kissed me. My mouth opened for him, the now familiar taste and feel of his tongue as it tangled with mine a heady aphrodisiac. I couldn't touch him, my hands still pinned as they were, so I put all of the longing he summoned into the kiss.

"Fuck," Mason said when he finally pulled away. "We are screwed, Pia. Do you realize that?"

"Actually, that was earlier. I still can't believe"—I lowered my voice—"that we had sex on my desk."

Mason peered around me toward the island. When his eyes met mine again, he didn't have to say a word.

"A bit more complicated, don't you think?" I asked.

"Nah. Beck's working tonight."

"And Parker?"

"Will be told to stay away."

Mason pushed my hair back, leaned down and

touched his lips to my neck. I bent it to give him better access.

"So when you say you're making me dinner, what you really mean is making me come on yet another table."

Mason gently bit my earlobe before whispering, "I'm going to make you come on every table, in every room, in this entire inn, Pia. That's a promise."

I swallowed just before he kissed me. Knowing it wouldn't last long, I reveled in every second until Mason stopped.

"Hate to do it," he said, letting go of my hands, "but I have to get back if I'm going to finish up early."

"And I have a lunch date," I said just as Mason started to back away.

"Oh yeah?"

Maybe I should not have put it quite like that. Mason's expression wasn't jealous, exactly, but it wasn't neutral either. A guy like him, with so much discipline... no way he was the jealous type.

"Yep. With Delaney. A last-minute thing."

He stared at me for an extra few seconds and then said, "We're definitely gonna need to talk tonight."

"About..." I waved my hand to indicate the two of us. "This?"

"Yeah." His lips tugged upward. "About this." He mimicked my hand movements.

"I look forward to it."

"As do I," he said, heading back to Beck. "And the island christening," Mason called, his voice carrying back to me. Hopefully, Beck didn't hear that.

Taking a few deep breaths, I got myself back under control. To think less than twenty-four hours ago we hadn't so much as touched, unless our legs at dinner counted, and now... well, things were different.

And more complicated too.

***

The Yellow Deli was in the main town square, catty corner from my apartment. I loved that they sourced ingredients locally, and the bright yellow and white interior put a smile on my face as I walked inside to find Delaney already sitting.

Or maybe that smile was from something else.

"Hey there," I said, sitting. "How's it going?"

"It's going. Already ordered you a diet. Why did we pick somewhere without cocktails?"

"I like the way you think," I said. "And wondered the same thing."

A waitress brought our drinks, two diet sodas, as I opened the menu.

"So how's it going down the hill?"

"Great," I said, scanning the menu. "It's a little tricky to renovate with guests, but since we were close with Mason's dad, we didn't want to disrupt the schedule any more than we needed to. So it's mostly soft renovations for now, but it's looking good. I could definitely use your help one of these days making a list of potential local partners. I could ask Mason, but I'd like a woman's perspective with some of the winery contacts."

"Oohhh, that sounds like fun. Let's get a driver and do a proper wine tour."

Delaney's bubbly nature was rubbing off on me. I couldn't quit grinning. "Only for the sake of work."

"Of course."

"What else? Has Mason chilled out? Any word on him staying?"

I'd known it would come up and debated telling her. On one hand, I didn't know Delaney all that well yet. On the other hand, I was bursting to talk to someone who actually knew him.

"Sooo..."

"Are you ready to order?"

Delaney's eyes were like saucers. I guessed I'd

put enough intrigue into my tone, but she had to wait until she finished ordering sandwiches before getting the story.

"Oh my God, tell me," she said, the second the waitress walked away. "You and Mason?"

I nodded.

"I knew it. The way he looked at you that night at the Big Easy. I just knew it."

"It's a very recent development."

"How recent?"

"Last night."

"Oh, snap. That *is* recent. Tell me everything."

"Well, it got to the point that it was impossible to ignore. My mom and sister came in for the weekend to surprise me, and since the apartment is so small, Mason offered for us to stay at the inn."

Her jaw dropped, so I added, "Nothing happened there. Except for a brief conversation in his bedroom and two very long nights knowing he was sleeping right down the hall. Oh, and maybe one kiss."

"Oh my God, I wish I had popcorn for this."

Smiling, I thought about last night. "I asked if we could talk and he basically called out the attraction between us. One thing led to another and... he came to my apartment."

"And? You cannot possibly stop there."

"And... all I can say is that if I look like shit today, there's a reason for it."

"First of all, you don't look like shit. Just the opposite. Second of all, holy crap."

"Yeah, I know. We really need to talk though because I had no idea how to act at work today. If we were going to keep it from the boys—"

"The boys." She laughed. "I love how you refer to Beck as a boy. Since he kind of is still."

"I actually adore him. And Parker, who you have to meet someday." The waitress returned with our lunch, but I was too wrapped up in my story to eat. "Anyway, he came to my office this morning, and I had no idea what to expect. He was really hung up on the idea that he's my boss, which, to be fair, does complicate things a bit."

"So what happened? I can see you grinning like the cat who ate the canary so..."

I simply could not stop smiling. "I guess the workplace is not off-limits."

"No you didn't?"

I nodded.

"In your office?"

"On the desk," I admitted as our food was brought to us. I hadn't planned to reveal so much, but Delaney's expressions were killing me.

"I can't even," she said, taking a bite of her tuna sandwich. "That's hot."

"Agreed, but we really do need that talk. He's making me dinner tonight."

Delaney took a sip of her drink as I finally dug into lunch.

"For what it's worth, I thought there were some serious vibes between the two of you, so I'm not surprised. It was inevitable, in my opinion. Secondly, talk about complicated. Not only the boss thing, but I thought you said he might be selling and heading back to the city?"

"I honestly have no idea what he's thinking there. But I'm really liking the job, and Cedar Falls, so I'm hoping that's a part of our discussion. I've been thinking a lot about this and wonder if he'd consider not selling and letting me oversee the renovations if he goes back. That way he can stay the owner, which I know a part of him wants to do for his dad."

"So you would be the innkeeper and manager? Seems like a tall order."

"It would be," I admitted between bites. "But it's possible. His father did it for years."

"Possible, sure. But he lived and breathed Heritage Hill. Are you ready for that kind of commitment? And what about Mason? He just goes back and the two of you..."

That was a big question mark, for sure. "I don't know. It's too early to be thinking like that. We're just having fun for now. I'm trying really hard not to have expectations since they're usually a major source of disappointment."

Delaney peered up at me as she took another tuna sandwich bite. When she finished chewing, she said, "Agreed."

"So tell me about you. What's up with the boyfriend?"

We chatted for a while, and though Delaney was off for the day, a mix-up in the schedule accounting for her last-minute text, I still had to get to the grocery store and wine store. We finished lunch, paid and walked out into the crisp fall air.

"I really do like this place," I said. Its grassy square with gazebo centerpiece gave it a quintessential small-town vibe.

"I honestly never thought I'd come back. But as they say, greener pastures and all that. I'm actually glad I didn't stay. It's easier to appreciate now."

"I bet."

Hugging, we parted, and I walked to the wine store thinking to get some bottles to drop off at my apartment before heading to the grocery store and then back to Heritage Hill. At least, that was the plan, until I saw Mason clear across the square.

In an embrace.

With a woman.

24

MASON

"How'd you do?"

Beck had just finished reinstalling the new baseboard when I came back with more nails. "Good. But I swore Parker just got some. No idea where they went."

Grabbing a water from the cooler, he looked around the room. "You've got me for an hour or so before I have to wrap up. Early shift tonight."

I sat down on the cooler and tossed the bag of supplies next to it as Beck took a break.

"I've got this. Go do what you need to do."

"I'm good."

"Thanks, man. I appreciate you helping out."

"And I appreciate the entertainment."

"I assume you're referring to Pia?"

"Jackpot."

"Let's get back to work," I said.

"Not so fast. You've been tight-lipped since this morning."

"With good reason."

"Mace."

"Beck."

"Come on," he said. "Kindergarten, buddy."

Since Ranger training, I considered myself impervious to any kind of manipulation tactics, but there seemed to be an exception. His name was Beck Claymont, who refused to take a dime off his richer-than-Croesus father and was currently helping me renovate the inn for the cost of breakfast and board. What a winner.

"Fine. But you're not getting details."

"I know, I know. You're not a kiss and tell guy. Gimme something."

"We got together last night."

"And this morning, from what I could tell. Well done on trashing your father's old office."

Unfortunately I'd thought of that only after the fact. But I didn't think Dad would have minded. "He'd have loved Pia."

"What's not to love? The woman is smart. Beautiful. Only downside I can see is that she seems to think highly of you. I tried to talk her out of it but—"

"Hey, asshole. That's enough."

"Kidding, obviously. I consider Pia a friend."

"She said the same thing about you."

"See? The woman also has good taste." He made a face. "Usually."

I swear Beck couldn't be serious for three seconds if his life depended on it.

"So now what?"

"With Pia?"

Beck rolled his eyes. "No, with the baseboard. Of course with Pia."

"I dunno. I'm making her dinner tonight. We definitely need to talk."

"Good start. What are you going to say?"

I shrugged. "That I can't get into anything serious. Not without knowing where I'll land in a few weeks. I'm meeting with Paul Baker on Friday."

"Still thinking of selling?"

Frowning, I tried to sort out my current thoughts aloud. "I have to at least hear his offer. I can't imagine walking away from a pension, or Heritage Hill. With you guys here, and Esther—"

"And Pia."

"Right. And Pia." Banking on the fact that Beck

knew my father better than any of the guys, and the hope that he could manage a serious conversation, I asked the question I'd been wondering these past few days.

"What do you think Papa Bennett would tell me to do?"

Beck grabbed the bill of his hat, squeezing it. His tell. It meant he was unsure. Not surprising since it was a major life decision, and no one, including Beck, could tell me what Dad would say. It was a stupid question.

"Never mind," I said, standing.

"Wait." He circled his neck, another of Beck's nervous habits. If there was a person alive with undiagnosed ADHD, it was Beck. "This might be a cop-out, but I don't think he'd give you a straight response. He'd ask questions. Like... Mason." Beck used his Papa Bennett voice. "What's most important to you? Time? Money? Relationships? Quality of life? Decide that and the answer will come easier."

That did sound remarkably like my father.

"You're a piece of work."

"I also think he'd remind you I'm unlikely to ever leave Cedar Falls, which is a major plus in the 'stay here' category."

"You think so?"

"I know so."

Smiling, I pulled a box of nails from the bag. "Thanks," I said, effectively ending the conversation. "Oh, by the way, I saw your Aunt Ginny when I went into town. She mentioned your mom was on a girls trip in Aruba?"

"Sure," he said. "Girls trip."

"You don't sound convinced."

He sighed. "Last time I saw Dad was in late August, strolling down Shethar Street not even bothering to hide his new mistress. My guess is Mom found out, hence, girls trip." He put the last phrase in quotes.

"You haven't talked to her?"

"I did, just last week. But she didn't say anything about a trip so..." He shrugged, like it was no big deal. But I knew otherwise.

"Hey there."

My head whipped around to the entranceway. "Pia," I said, stupidly. I could execute a perfect ambush, but one look at Pia and I was grasping for words like a raw recruit.

"Mason," she said back as I belatedly realized her arms were full of bags.

"Let me grab those," I said to Beck. "Be right back."

"No problem. I'll just be here working if you want to join me."

Pia stifled a smile.

"Thanks," she said as I grabbed her bags and brought them to the kitchen. I began to put the things away. "I'd help, but I don't know where anything goes."

"I got it. Thanks for grabbing these. I ended up having to go into town anyway but figured you'd gone already. I should have texted you."

When Pia didn't say anything, I shoved chicken into the fridge, closed it, and glanced back at her. She had an odd expression on her face.

"What's up?"

"Nothing," she said, her voice unnaturally high. Something was up.

"No?"

"Nope. It's just... I did see you in town."

I grabbed the box of angel hair pasta and put it away. "You did? Why didn't you say anything?"

"You were..."

I couldn't read her expression, but something was off. I stopped putting away the groceries.

"I was?"

"With someone."

It took me a second to figure out what she meant.

Beck's aunt. She was his mother's youngest sister and had Beck's good looks. I tried not to smile. Pia was jealous. For some reason, that was hot to me.

Sidling up to her, amazed we were in a place that I could now touch her as I'd wanted to do from almost the moment we met, I reached around to the back of her neck.

"That was Beck's aunt." To drive the point home, I brought her face to mine and kissed her, hard. When her mouth opened for me, I immediately captured her tongue, promising her, without words, tonight would be more than dinner and a talk.

As quickly as the kiss began, it ended.

That felt like a good place to leave it.

"Dinner's at six."

I was certain Beck's strange look when I left the kitchen and re-joined him was because of the way I grinned from ear to ear as if I were him, or Parker.

Just a few more hours, and I'd be with her again. Why did that suddenly feel like forever?

25

PIA

I'd originally planned on heading down right from work, but by four o'clock I was getting restless. So instead, I packed up my things and left. There was no sign of Mason, or Beck, but the reception room looked amazing. I couldn't wait to see all of the renovations when they were completed.

If I was still at Heritage Hill.

After taking a shower and changing into jeans and a cream sweater, something occurred to me. Before heading out, I grabbed my phone and texted Mason.

> Am home, about to leave.

> I noticed. Thought maybe you changed your mind.

> Nope. But... should I bring anything?

> Such as?

I almost chickened out. Said something like, "A bottle of wine." But I didn't come to Cedar Falls to sit by the wayside and let things happen to me. I came here to prove I could be the master of my own destiny. The captain of my own ship.

Okay, enough cheesy analogies.

> An overnight bag.

I held my breath as I watched the text bubbles, and finally Mason's message came through.

> Abso-fucking-lutely.

Smiling, I tossed some things in a bag and headed back through town. Since I had never gotten to grab wine yesterday, seeing Mason with Beck's aunt derailing my plans, I popped into Casa Di Vino, glad to see Emilio was there.

"*Buongiorno*, Emilio," I said, walking into the shop.

"*Buongiorno*, Pia Russo," he said, waving enthusiastically. "*Come stai?*"

"*Molto bene, grazie*," I said.

"What can I get for you?"

"Just a bottle of red for a special occasion. You pick."

"Ahh, special occasion?" he asked suggestively, heading out from behind the register toward the red wine aisle.

Damn. I shouldn't have said that. I didn't want to lie but I also didn't want to make a big deal of Mason and me. Since there really was no Mason and me, yet. Would I like there to be? That was a dangerous question given our circumstances, and one best left unasked.

"Just dinner with the boss," I said. "Celebrating the progress at Heritage Hill."

At least it was mostly true. And we could be celebrating since we'd gotten a lot done in a short time. I'd been on fire all day, finalizing long-term plans that I knew would turn Heritage Hill around.

"How about this one," he asked, pulling a wine off the shelf. "Il Tempo Ritrovato, a red blend. It's one of my favorites."

I took the bottle from him. "*Tempo* is time. I don't know *ritrovato*."

"Time rediscovered. It's a three-year-old vintage that is..." He pressed his fingers to his lips in a chef's kiss.

"I'll take it."

"How is the boss?" Emilio asked, ringing me out.

"Doing well, all things considered," I said, paying for the wine.

"I'm glad to hear it. His father's death was such a shock to everyone. Thomas was always running around town, fit as a fiddle."

I didn't know his dad was a runner. "It's terrible," I agreed. "I'm not sure what's worse. Knowing someone you love is going to pass or having it happen so suddenly, there is no time for goodbyes."

Emilio sighed. "Well, Mason would know better than anyone. He lost his mother, as I'm sure you know, to a long battle with cancer. Although he was still young and might not remember it."

"He remembers," I said quietly. "At least some of it."

The sadness in Emilio's eyes was so unlike him. "She was a beautiful woman, Margaret Bennett. Inside and out. Thomas never recovered from her loss."

I cocked my head to the side. "No?" I asked, trying to keep it casual sounding but wanting to know more too.

"No." Emilio shook his head. "Never remarried."

That I knew.

"Carried a torch for her until the day he died." Sighing, he seemed to snap out of the melancholy mood. "Poor kid. Losing two parents so young."

And without siblings, too. I wondered if his mom was too sick to have another? I supposed it didn't matter, but the thought of losing my mom and dad, and not having my sisters to help cope or to be there with me...

"What about extended family?" I asked, realizing he didn't talk of aunts and uncles or cousins.

"You'll have to ask him, but I think his mother was an only child as well. His father had one brother who I met at the funeral. Lives in California, I think."

Poor kid indeed. No wonder he was so close with Beck, Parker and Cole. They were, for all intents and purposes, like his brothers.

"Well." I held up the wine. "Thanks for your help with this."

"Anytime, Signorina Pia. I hope you enjoy it, and your celebration."

I was pretty certain I would. "*Grazie. Ciao,* Emilio," I said, leaving the store.

"*Ciao ciao,*" he said, waving.

As I made my way down to the inn—the few blocks' walk away from the main square and toward the lake was one I could do in my sleep now—I was amazed at how quickly I'd acclimated to Cedar Falls. I'd always heard the east coast and west coast were so different, and while this town was much smaller than where I grew up, it wasn't foreign at all. The people had been welcoming—with the exception of Mason—and I could absolutely see myself settling here.

Maybe it was making a friend on that first day. Or little things like Emilio's Italian that reminded me of my family. Or likely, my boss. The one that had kicked me to the curb on that first day but had since become much more. I didn't know where things would go with him, but I did know two things for certain. One, that Heritage Hill was going to become an award-winning inn, and Richard Sterling and his good ol' boys club could shove it.

And two... it was going to be an interesting night.

26

MASON

It was impossible not to think of my father as I cooked as the smell of garlic wafted through the kitchen. One that was suddenly occupied by Parker, who said he was heading to O'Malley's for the night.

"Smells good. Maybe I'll join you and Pia for dinner before I head out."

"Funny," I said, my phone lighting up.

> On my way.

I gave Pia's text a thumbs up and turned on the water to boil pasta.

"Time for you to bounce, hotshot," I said as Parker opened the silverware drawer.

"I will. Just have to test this out." Putting his fork in the pan, he cut off a piece of chicken scampi and took a bite. "Not bad. Just like the big guy."

"He was one hell of a cook, wasn't he?"

"The best. He'd even put my mom to shame, but don't tell her I said that."

"Pretty sure I won't since she's in Rochester, and I never see her."

"Speaking of Rochester, when the indoor renovations are done, I'm gonna head there for a weekend. She's been after me to visit and won't wait till Thanksgiving."

"Go anytime. I've got things under control here."

By now, Parker had gotten a plate out, pulled the rest of the piece of chicken onto it and was eating at the island.

"For now. Your leave clock is ticking. I heard you have a meeting with Paul Baker on Friday. You seriously considering selling the place? Seems to me you've got a solid plan for it."

"I figured I'd at least hear his offer and go from there. Any of the improvements we make will only increase its value."

Parker was quiet while he ate. Emptying the box of angel hair into the pot of boiling water, I tried not to think about it. Which was impossible, of course.

The end of my leave was like a sword of Damocles hanging over my head. Every day it came closer, my life path seemed more and more uncertain.

And then there was Pia.

"Hey, guys."

Speak of the devil.

Parker raised a hand in greeting, having just taken a mouthful of chicken. I tried to finish the meal without staring at her like a lovesick teen. Not an easy task. She looked amazing. Jeans. Black booties. A black, low-cut shirt that made it next to impossible not to stare at her incredible tits and imagine myself cupping them, my head leaning down to take each one into my mouth, hardening her nipples while—

"The water." Pia gestured to my pasta pot. Shit. I turned down the heat, took a deep breath and tried again.

"Hey, Pia. Don't mind Parker. He was just leaving."

"Chicken's great," Parker said, putting his dish in the sink. Then to me, he whispered, "Get those bills ready to pay up. You're going down, buddy."

"No chance," I said quietly.

I might be losing the battle, but I could never lose the war. If I was dumb enough to fall in love then I'd have to accept the possibility of the kind of lifelong heartbreak Dad suffered.

No. Fucking. Way.

"Get the hell out of here," I said.

"There's a reason he was made sergeant in the army," Parker said to Pia. "Have a good dinner."

"See you," she said, laughing. "So, a sergeant, huh?" she asked, opening drawers. "That explains a lot."

"Uh huh. Whatcha looking for?"

"A wine opener. Brought a special bottle from Emilio's."

"In there." I indicated a drawer. "You didn't have to do that. We have plenty of wine."

"But are they special?"

Not as special as you.

The line rolled through my mind, unspoken. Not because it wasn't true, but because it was.

"Obviously not," I said, straining the pasta and plating our meals. "Island or dining room?"

"Island," she said, turning the lights down slightly and cleaning the counter.

"My father used to always say 'clean as you go.' I never realized until a few years ago that came from the army, where he was a cook."

"Your father was a cook in the army? I had no idea."

Finishing up, I joined her, picking up my now-filled wine glass. "There's lots you don't know about me, Miss Pia Russo."

"Well, you said you wanted to know everything about me. Same goes for you. Tell me more."

We ate, drank wine and started from the beginning. I told her about early days, when my mother was still alive, and Pia regaled me with stories of her sisters' antics. We talked about middle school, high school and college. Even exes.

The thought of Pia with any guy wasn't a happy one, and I didn't normally consider myself a jealous person.

"So what did you do to the principal guy to get back at him?"

Pia had told me about a guy she particularly liked, and said getting back at him after he cheated was one of her favorite guilty-pleasure memories.

"I was lucky enough to be invited to a fourth of July party I knew he'd be at. Wore my white bikini, which I knew he adored. I happened to be in really good shape at the time, and was totally over him by then, so it was easy to say 'thanks but no thanks' when he tried to rekindle."

"Okay," I said, taking a sip of wine. "Lots to unpack. First of all, you're in really good shape now. Second, I didn't know my sweet Pia had a little vengeful streak. And third of all, please tell me you still have this white bikini."

"Unfortunately, I don't. That was a few years ago. And I don't consider myself vengeful usually but..." She smirked. "I guess, guilty as charged in this case."

As we finished eating, I'd planned to just grab Pia's plate, but when I stood close enough to her that I could smell her perfume, I leaned down to kiss her instead. She tasted like garlic, wine and promise. When she kissed me back as if she'd been waiting for that, I reached around the back of her neck and pulled her closer. We'd nearly polished off the bottle of wine she brought, but that didn't affect me nearly as much as this kiss.

"Mmm," I murmured, standing up and taking my stool again. "Any more of that and we'll never get to our talk."

"Ahh, the big talk."

"The big talk," I repeated. "I'm more concerned with you than me, Pia. I don't want this to ever be awkward for you."

"Dating the boss man and all," she teased.

"Exactly."

Pia picked up her wine glass. "I know you're my boss, but in a lot of ways we feel more like partners. I honestly don't think it'll be awkward. But lots of things can happen."

"Which is my concern. So let's talk about them."

"You make this sound very methodical, like a mission or something."

"Occupational hazard," I admitted.

"It's fine. Let's do it. Then I would like you to make good on your promise about christening the inn, please."

She said it so sweetly and understatedly that it took a second for Pia's words to sink in. As they did, thoughts of our talk went right out the door. But when I tried to stand back up, Pia held up her hand.

"My bad. Shouldn't have said that. Business first."

Imagining ripping Pia's clothes off and finding one of many, many rooms to christen wasn't going a long way to a business-first discussion.

"Seriously." Pia's smile reached all the way up to her eyes. "I shouldn't have said that."

"You really should have, though."

"Lots of things can happen. We're talking about them. Go."

My dick was not going to survive this woman. Growing hard for the third time since she walked into the kitchen, I looked away and thought of puppies until Pia became concerned.

"You okay, Mason?"

"Not really, but let's do it. First of all," I said, "I could be heading back to the city in a couple of weeks."

"Which is something I wanted to talk to you about, actually. If you decide to do that, would you ever consider not selling and letting me manage Heritage Hill on my own?"

"I've already considered it. But that's a much bigger job than you signed on for."

"True," she said. "But I really do like it here and I know we could do amazing things. I'm ready for the challenge."

Pia had managed to surprise me, something very few people did. "Until we're back in the black, your compensation—"

"Could be built into future profits. I'm not looking to take more until that happens."

"You sure about that?"

"I am."

"Consider it considered," I said.

"Great."

So far, so good. Better than good, actually.

"So possibility one, I sell. But if that happens," I

added, already having decided for Friday's meeting, "you and Esther stay on as a condition of the sale. At least for a period of time that works for all of us."

Pia's brows raised. "Quite a turnaround from being fired on the spot."

"So kind of you to remind me," I said, lighting the candle on the island. Pia liked candles and always had one burning in her office. Sitting here, finishing our wine after dinner, was nice.

Really nice.

"Alright, so what else. You go back to the city. Heritage Hill, hopefully, remains in the Bennett family. That's scenario one."

When she said "remains in the Bennett family," a twisting in my gut to imagine it otherwise almost made me want to cancel the appointment Friday. How could I ever sell my dad's inn? Especially now that I had a viable alternative. Pia would be a fantastic innkeeper. Better than me, actually.

Shaking it off, I dove into scenario two. "I stay. We don't work out."

"Awk-ward," she said, laughing. "I'm kidding. Obviously that was the risk we took jumping into this. Whatever this is. We'll just have to be adults about it. If Hollywood actors can kiss their coworker exes, I'm sure we can manage, right?"

"Kiss their... never mind. That is the big risk here. But I'd like to talk about the 'whatever this is' part of your equation."

"Shoot."

"I don't share."

Clearly, she hadn't been expecting that. "As in, like a threesome?"

"As in," I clarified, "at all."

"I see."

"Is that a problem?"

She thought about it for a second. "Only inasmuch as 'sharing' implies dating other people. And if we're not dating other people..."

Pia let that one hang out to dry. But I also didn't want her to get the wrong impression. "I'm not talking about something serious between us. We can keep it casual. I can't tell what the future will bring. But in the meantime, I'm not the kind of guy to be intimate with more than one woman."

"So exclusive, but not serious."

"Exactly."

"And if you do move?"

"Obviously that changes things. I wouldn't expect either of us not to date."

"Do you have any idea how confusing all of this is, Mason?"

"Seems pretty straightforward to me."

"Seriously?"

"Seriously."

"Is there any room for negotiation?"

"Such as?"

Pia plopped her elbows on the counter, resting her chin on her hands. "Let me think."

After a few minutes, when she didn't say anything, I stood up. Moved behind her. Made good on what I'd wanted to do all through dinner as my hand reached underneath her shirt, splaying on the bare skin beneath. Inching my way up to her breasts, I covered Pia's lace bra with both hands, rubbing my thumb over her nipples.

"Still thinking?" I whispered.

"Mmhmm," she murmured, leaning into my hands.

"Any way I can help?"

She sat up so that her back touched my chest. "You're actually doing just the opposite. My brain isn't working now."

"Good," I said, pulling down the material of her bra. I could have taken an extra few seconds to unclasp it, but this would do.

"Mason, you're not playing fair."

"How about this for fair," I asked, slipping one of

my hands from under her sweater down to the button of her jeans. Making quick work of that, and the zipper, my fingers found their mark. She was already so fucking wet.

If Pia wanted to negotiate, she could do it with my hands all over her, my mouth finding her ear and telling her exactly how this night was going to go, starting with a climax on this stool and ending with me claiming her body in every goddamn room she could handle.

Not letting up until she thrust into my hand and screamed my name, I decided to start a count.

"That's one, sweet Pia. How about we talk again after a few more of those."

27

PIA

"A little early to start drinking for you, isn't it?" Beck asked as I sat at the bar.

I gave him "the look" but that didn't stop Beck.

"Someone a little on edge about the meeting today?"

"I was hoping you could take my mind off it," I said. Mason had now been with Paul Baker for nearly two hours. "Not remind me of the fact that he might be agreeing to sell Heritage Hill as we speak."

All week, we'd avoided the topic. In fact, since he'd made dinner, we hadn't talked about the future at all. Or any of the scenarios Mason had gone through, all of which, in retrospect, were a fairly accurate representation of where we stood. Even if, at the time, I hadn't liked the clinical nature of his relationship assessment, as if I were a mission to be planned.

"He's not gonna sell."

At four in the afternoon, O'Malley's was just getting going, even for a Friday, leaving Beck to hang with me a bit. I could have called my mom or sisters, or friends back home, or Delaney, but when I got restless enough sitting behind my desk, I'd come here.

To talk to Beck. Of all people.

"You don't think?"

"Nah, I don't. He told me about your proposition. Sounded to me like Mace thought it was a real viable option. Why sell if you're willing to take it over, you know?"

"True," I said. But the longer the meeting went, the less sure I became.

Beck went behind the bar, poured something and handed it to me.

"What is it?"

"Gin Gimlet."

"How did you know I liked these?"

"Lucky guess." Beck went off to serve another patron. When he came back, I was two sips in.

"Not bad," I said.

"So tell me why you're here. I know it's not to tie one on." Before I could respond, he said, "But if it is, I got you covered." He gestured to the bar behind him.

"That wasn't the plan." I lifted the limoncello. "But I'm starting out with this. It's a high-proof one."

"You're right," he said. "It is."

"My parents serve a few different brands at their restaurant. I can tell this is probably..." I took another sip. "Closer to sixty proof."

"Right on the money. The girl knows her liquor."

I laughed, looking down at my phone. Nothing.

"Turn this thing over," Beck said, unnecessarily since he did it for me. "Does he know you're here?"

"No," I said.

Beck grabbed his phone, shot off a text. "There. Now he does and will undoubtedly come as soon as he's done. Time to relax and enjoy my company."

It was impossible not to do so. "You are so different than I first thought," I admitted. "Not unlike Mason, I guess."

"I could tell you liked me right from the start."

He was teasing, and I could not in good faith keep a straight face. "You are a nut."

Beck didn't answer until he came back from serving another customer.

"Guilty as charged. So tell me why you're really here."

I shrugged.

"Oh no, you're not getting out of it that easily. You're worried, obviously. But why here? Why me?"

"Great question."

Beck spread his hands out on the bar and leaned toward me.

"Pia. Talk to me."

"Forget it. Let's talk about something else."

"No bueno. Try again."

"You are relentless."

"Among other things. And been tending bar long enough to be able to read people. This is not the Pia I've seen flitting through the inn this week like a woman on a mission. The one sneaking off into corners when she and my friend Mason don't think anyone is looking. Who has him smiling more in a week than I've seen him smile in a year. This one is nervous, and tense, and I don't think this is just about your job."

Astute man.

"Do you think he'll go back to the city?"

Crossing his arms like his prize pig just won a blue ribbon at the farm show, he grinned. "Now that's why my girl needs to down that drink and stop sipping it. Come on."

"No, Beck. I'm not doing shots."

"Yes you are. Sometimes it's good to let loose. Down it."

"Beck."

He started chanting for the handful of people who were at the bar to participate. And they did. After a few choruses of "down it," I finally took a drink, sucked it back and slammed it on the bar.

"Should the bartender really be encouraging his customers this way?"

"When the customer is you, yes. This time, I'll join. As a matter of fact..." He stepped back and called out, "Shots on me. It's Friday night, people, let's make some noise."

He was out of his mind.

Two shots and a half glass of vodka soda later, the bar began to get busy. Our talk, I assumed, was over. But Beck came over, leaned in and said, "It'll be a game-time call. Mace has wanted to be a cop most of his life. On the other hand, he hates the city, loves the inn and really likes you so... hard to say."

I was still taking in his words when a soft voice said from behind, "A little birdie told me you were here."

Like every time he was close, goose bumps spread all over me. Or at least, it felt that way. I turned my head, unsure how public he wanted to be since most of our intimacy this week had been at the inn. I'd even begun to wonder if Mason kept it that way on purpose.

His long, lingering kiss answered that question pretty firmly.

"That's enough." Beck's voice broke through the fog that was my attraction to Mason. Since we'd gotten together, it had only grown. After staying with him for the night, sleeping in my empty apartment bedroom all week had been a major letdown. "Or get a room."

"Have plenty of them," Mason said, sitting. "But I'd rather annoy you."

"Dude, if you want to pack on the PDA, be my guest. I'm just here to serve," Beck said, getting Mason a beer.

"Speaking of…" I'd always wanted to ask. "Mason said you have a business degree. Ever think of using it?"

Mason's expression said it all. Apparently this was a sore subject. At least Beck didn't take offense.

"Not really. I'm pretty happy here, especially now

that I'm not paying rent." He leaned over the bar to pat Mason on the back. "Thanks, buddy."

As Beck moved away, I waited for the hammer to drop, letting the topic of the bartender's life plans go for the moment.

Looking into his eyes, I tried not to let pleading define my gaze. I was here to prove that I was worth more than my asshole boss thought, not fall head over heels for a guy to seek his validation too.

"He drove a hard bargain."

What did that mean? I remained calm. "Oh yeah?"

"Yeah," Mason said, taking a swig of beer. "Paul came prepared. He'd done his homework, that was for sure."

I grabbed my vodka soda and took a long drink, needing the liquid courage. This did not sound good.

"Pia Russo. Are you tipsy?"

Not what I'd been expecting.

"Maybe. Someone was feeding me shots."

"Someone? What time did you get here?"

"Not sure," I said, hearing the slight slur in my voice that had given me away. "I don't handle shots well."

"And why did you come to O'Malley's in the first place?"

I lifted my chin. "Am I in trouble? Work was done for the day, none of the guests were in house and—"

"You don't have to explain."

"But you asked why I was here."

"Right. I didn't ask why you weren't at the inn."

"Mason?"

"Yes, Pia."

"Did you sell?"

His smile fell. Mason became so serious, I knew his answer before he said it. No number of shots would dull the pain of his next words because I knew, without a doubt, he had. Mason had sold the inn.

He was leaving.

"Yes, I did."

28

PIA

The immediate pit in my stomach... no, the giant hole that opened up and swallowed me, told me more about my feelings about Mason than I wanted to know at the moment.

"I'm teasing."

It took a second for his words to penetrate. When they did, I swatted him. "You just wanted to see my reaction."

"Maybe. Does that make me evil?"

"Yes, it does."

"What's the word?" Beck asked in a break between customers. It was getting busier by the minute.

"He was prepared," Mason said. "And made an

offer that was hard to refuse. I almost told him I'd sit on it but..." He turned toward me. Our eyes met. Locked. Then, to Beck, he said, "I can't sell. My father *was* Heritage Hill. And now I have a viable way to keep it, even if I go back to the force."

Even if I go back to the force.

This was good news. Why did it feel like it wasn't?

Beck reached across the bar to shake Mason's hand. "Congrats, man. That's a big decision that I know was tough to make."

"Thanks," he said, but when Beck started pouring shots, I waved my arms. "No way, not for me."

"Fair enough," he said as the pair clinked glasses to celebrate.

When he left, I shook my head. "He's out of his mind."

"You don't know the half of it. I could spend the night telling you Beck-in-college stories."

I made a face. "Not sure I want to hear most of them."

"You don't. Let's get you some food, and I'll tell you about the meeting." Mason waved down Beck. "Wings are great here, have you had them yet?"

"Nope, but I've never met a hot wing I didn't like."

"Ahh, so the girl likes it hot, does she?"

"In more ways than one," I teased back.

"Two orders," he said to Beck, who was in the process of tossing a bottle into the air. Must be a cute girl around. Looking down the bar, I found her. "Of wings. Hot and extra crispy."

"Both hot?" Beck asked. He turned to me. "Sure you don't want medium? Our hot is really hot."

"Can I ask you a serious question?" I said. Beck was like a project I was determined to work on. He could be saved, potentially. Although I wouldn't let my sisters or friends date him. "Would you ever ask a man if he wanted to downgrade his wings?"

"Downgrade. Interesting way to say it."

"Seriously, though?"

"No."

"Why not?"

Beck looked at Mason, appealing to him.

"Don't look at me," Mason said. "I didn't ask her to downgrade."

Beck sighed. "Because I've never met a man who said, 'Ooohhh, too hot.'"

I didn't know if his extravagantly waving arms or terrible woman's voice impression were worse.

"You're gonna get it," I said as Beck chuckled and walked away. "There is zero chance I can ever get him girlfriend-ready."

Mason nearly spit out his beer. "Girlfriend-ready? You're joking, right?"

I shrugged. "I like challenges."

Mason shook his head. "Even if it weren't for the pact..." He stopped.

Clearly Mason had said something he hadn't meant to. "The pact?"

"It's nothing. Just some stupid agreement we made in college."

"Mason?"

He put his hand on my knee, rubbing my leg up and down suggestively.

"That's not going to distract me."

"No?"

I placed my hand on top of his. "No."

Threading his fingers through mine, he exhaled. "It was originally Cole's idea. As shitty as Beck's parents' relationship is..." At my expression, he added, "Ask him. Beck's not shy about it. So anyways, at least everyone knows their marriage has been fucked two ways from Sunday. Cole's parents' marriage is worse for a lot of reasons, that he can tell you. Then you have Parker, whose parents have multiple divorces under their belt. And you know about my father, who pretty much never got over my mother's death."

A shadow crossed his expression at that last part. Whether he was thinking of his mom, or his dad, or the fact that his dad had never recovered from her death, I wasn't sure. But the small hint of vulnerability was so out of character for Mason, I wanted to pull him toward me and squeeze.

"For one reason or another, none of us have a high opinion of the success rate of marriage. Cole decided we should make a pact. A 'bachelor pact,' he called it. We all tossed in 250 bucks. If anyone gets engaged, it's another two fifty to the kitty. Marriage is 500. Last man standing gets the prize. But I have a feeling that money will rot since I don't see some of the guys ever marrying."

It was a lot to take in.

A bachelor pact. How sad.

"Do you?" I asked.

"See myself marrying?"

I tried not to look hopeful. Did I want to meet and marry the man of my dreams? Sure. Was that man Mason? It was way too soon for any such thoughts, so it didn't matter what his answer was.

Or so I told myself.

"No."

His answer was so confident. So immediate.

"Interesting." Except it wasn't. Not at all.

"Do you?" he asked.

Mine was just as easy. "Yes. Of course."

"Despite the fact that a majority of marriages end in divorce. Or infidelity. Or loss, eventually."

"First of all, I don't know if that's even true."

"It is."

I ignored him. "Second of all, that's like saying I'm never going to take another risk in my entire life because something can go wrong. That's not me. Didn't think it was you, either."

"There's risk and then there's calculated risk. Two different things."

"Oh, here we go. Talk to me, Sergeant Bennett." I was half-joking. But half-serious, too. His logic was flawed.

"Gladly. I—"

"Two orders of hot." Beck emphasized the word *hot*. "Wings."

Although he put them in front of us, napkins and all, Beck didn't leave. He was obviously waiting for me to take a bite. Little did he know, I was competitive as hell, and even if my mouth was on fire, I'd never let it show.

So, with an eye roll, I grabbed a wing. Took a bite. And smiled. After a second, the heat kicked in. And he was right. These were more like extra hot. My drink beckoned, but I didn't dare reach for it. Instead, I took another bite.

Both of the guys watched as I ate the wing, discarded it and picked up another. Meanwhile, my lips burned.

"Point made," Beck said, moving away.

When his back turned, I grabbed my drink.

Mason smiled knowingly. "Hot?"

"So friggin hot. Dear lord."

"No faces, Beck's turned this way."

I loved that he played along. But I didn't love this whole bachelor pact thing or the discussion it brought up. I did love the wings, though, even though they were really hot.

Though part of me wanted to go back to the marriage/risk discussion, I also wasn't interested in convincing Mason that he *wanted* to get married. You couldn't make someone want what they didn't, especially in matters of the heart.

Instead, I took it in another direction. "So besides you, who will be the last man standing? Beck?"

"Nah. He loves playing the field, but as long as

Mae O'Malley sticks around, there's a chance for him to settle down."

"Who's Mae O'Malley?"

"His boss's daughter. Grew up next door to him." Mason lowered his voice. "He's had a crush on her his entire life. Even Beck knows she's too good for him. They're friends but..." His voice trailed off.

"Does she know that he likes her?"

"Oh God, no. Beck won't even admit that he likes her himself. I think the bunch of us are damned fools. Even when we made one of the rules just for her, he still won't admit it."

I groaned. "Rules?"

Mason winced.

"Spill it, Sergeant." That was my new favorite nickname for him.

"Bachelor pact rules. There are four of them."

"And?" I waited, eating wings and really wishing I could order a glass of water. Which, of course, I couldn't. Might have to go to the ladies' room and use the sink.

"We're not supposed to talk about it with females."

"Is that so?"

"Yep. But I'll make an exception."

The butterflies in my stomach at Mason's words

needed to be drowned with some tequila. He was talking about rules for not marrying women, after all. Ridiculous.

"Lucky me."

When he finished chewing, Mason wiped his mouth, making me very aware of his lips. And where I wanted those lips. Swallowing hard, I focused on the conversation at hand.

"First, there's never stay the night. Too intimate."

"Um..." I hated to be Captain Obvious, but... "We broke that rule."

"True. But it was mostly made for Parker. He's the softie that gets attached too quickly."

Fantastic. So it didn't actually mean anything that we'd broken the rule. This conversation was doing a real number on any lingering happiness that Mason hadn't sold the inn.

"And then the one we made for Beck. Never date the neighbor."

Despite myself, I laughed. "You literally made a rule just for Beck and Mae?"

"Yep. Because we all know, without a doubt, if Mae was ever into Beck, it'd be all over."

"Why haven't I met this paragon of womanhood?"

"She's in Paris, studying under some famous

pastry chef. But word on the street is that she's coming back soon."

"Can't wait to meet her," I said, meaning it. Beck taking any woman seriously was definitely noteworthy. I wondered what Mae was like.

"And then," Mason continued, "there are the obvious rules. Never fall in love. And never say 'I do.'"

Never fall in love.

"Wow," I said, trying to be nonchalant about it. "Those are some rules."

"Like I said, just college guys being idiots."

"So you don't take it seriously? The rules and the pact?"

"Eh. I don't live and die by it, like Cole. But I get the point of them and mostly agree the pact was a good idea."

Don't latch onto one word. Do. Not. Do. It.

"Mostly?"

I did it.

"Sure, mostly."

Mason didn't seem inclined to elaborate. And to be honest, I wasn't inclined to ask additional questions. The more I heard about the pact, the less I liked it.

"Interesting," I said again, for lack of a better

word to describe the whole thing. "So tell me about the meeting."

Mason licked his lips. No wing sauce remaining there. "I can do that. Or I can take you back to my place to explore this extra hot side of you I didn't know was there."

Clenching at my core, marveling at Mason's ability to make me do that so effortlessly, I decided his plan was a solid one. "And then we'll talk about the meeting."

"Sure," he said, hand raised in the air for Beck's attention. "I can tell you about it from between your legs just before I lick"—his voice lowered—"that sweet pussy of yours like you just licked wing sauce from the corner of your mouth. Don't think I didn't notice."

Screw waiting.

"Hey Beck," I yelled across the bar. "Check, please."

Mason's low rumble of a laugh forced a smile from me, despite all that I'd learned about his future plans and college bachelor pact.

Problems for another day.

29

MASON

"Can I suggest some activities in the area?"

One of our Saturday check-in guests had just arrived. Although there was a self-check-in process—guests receiving instructions prior to arrival about their room and amenities, along with the key procedure—my father tried to greet everyone upon arrival. It wasn't always possible since he stubbornly refused to hire someone just for that purpose, and though we still used his system, Pia and I had discussed modernizing it. Hiring someone at least during the day made sense.

Especially if I went back to the city.

"Sure," the wife said. At least, I assumed they were married. Assumptions could be dangerous, though. Something I knew better than most. "We're only in town for a night and have a few wineries planned this afternoon."

"Tell me what wineries. And do you have a reservation yet for dinner?"

I talked to them for a few minutes, guided them to a different winery for their last stop and made a dinner suggestion. They left, holding hands and looking quite happy.

With no renovations on the schedule today for a change, I'd been looking forward to catching up with paperwork. And taking Pia out later tonight. It was only two hours into the paperwork that I regretted actually looking forward to it. Heritage Hill was going to need a miracle to get out of debt, and I'd turned down an incredibly generous offer last night.

"You really need an office," Parker said, coming into the kitchen.

"I had one. Gave it to Pia."

"Right." Parker pulled a soda from the fridge. "But there's plenty of places to set up another one in this place. Besides the kitchen."

"I like the kitchen."

"Suit yourself."

"Job end early?"

Parker had planned to work all day. Plus we

needed materials to start the windows—our next order of business on the punch list—hence the day off.

"Jack fucked up the kitchen cabinet order for our house. Not much left we can do without them, so..." He shrugged. "Afternoon off."

"You really need to ditch him and get something going of your own."

He waved me away. "Yeah, yeah. I'll do that when you decide on a career yourself. Heard about the sale." Sitting on a stool at the island, he cracked his knuckles... a habit of his that drove me nuts.

"One big decision at a time."

"How much?"

"One point eight."

"Million?"

"Yeah."

Parker whistled. "That's a chunk of change."

"Tell me about it."

"So what tipped your hat?"

"Honestly? Pia."

By the look on Parker's face, I realized he misunderstood. "Volunteering to take on a bigger role, I mean."

Never mind the fact that, when we weren't together, I wanted us to be. And that when we were, it felt... right. Better than right. Every time I peeled back another layer, I wanted to know more about her.

And the sex.

My fucking God. The sex.

"Uh huh."

"Seriously. Selling this place... I couldn't do it. But I don't know if I'm ready to give up my career either. Especially for this. Earlier, I talked to a couple about which winery and restaurant to choose, but if it were a month ago, right about then I'd have been on the job, responding to calls. Or ordering a Riker's Island special. Or shooting the shit with another shield."

"Or dealing with putting someone on the bus. Or worse."

He was right. Although it was harder in the beginning to watch someone who you knew wouldn't make it be loaded into an ambulance. "The fact that you know what a bus is means I talk about my job too much."

"You don't talk about anything too much. If we didn't pry it out of you, I probably wouldn't even know you were NYPD."

"Funny."

"Listen, I'm not trying to convince you one way

or another. You've got a lot on the line if you walk away from the force. I get it. But you complained about the politics of the job, and the city itself, more than you regaled us with war stories of the good deeds you always thought would make up for not being able to help your mother."

"That's not why—"

"That's exactly why. You might have been too drunk at Cassie's party to remember telling me that, but it's not something you forget. I just never needed to toss it back at you before now."

Fuck. "I said that?"

"Sure did."

"Cassie's party. That was senior year in college. And you're just telling me this now."

"Never would have told you if I didn't think it was necessary." Parker shoved the soda away. "Screw this." He went to the fridge, opened two beers and handed me one.

"I was working."

"Operative word. Was. Now you're drinking. And being honest with me about Pia. Beck and I are convinced there's something more there with her."

"You and Beck? Don't you both have something better to do with your time than dissect my love life?"

"Not really, no."

"We have an understanding," I said, knowing I'd regret telling him this.

"Can't wait to hear this one."

I told Parker about our talk. How we'd outlined all of the possibilities between us. "She gets where we're at."

"In other words, Pia's been briefed?"

I gave him a "fuck you" look.

"What? This isn't a military mission, Mace."

"No shit."

"You've got a lot to work out in a few weeks. Can't say I envy you, brother."

I thought of last night. Parker might be singing another tune if he had a woman like Pia in his bed. Her proclivity for dirty talk was matched by her enthusiasm.

"If you do go back, I can't wait for Cole to see this new Mason," he added.

I'd been staring at my beer bottle. Parker gave me a strange look. "What?" I asked. "There's no new Mason."

"Sure there is. I don't think I've seen you smile this much since..." He looked up, thinking. "Ever."

"Whatever. How about a new topic? If I do go

back, no way you're continuing the renovations without me or payment."

"Jesus. This again? You know damn well I'm not taking your money. You're saving me rent. And I like space."

"You mean you like not having to listen to the women Beck brings home."

"That too."

"Seriously though—"

"Stop." Parker looked me in the eyes. "If you aren't here, it will take longer, but the renovations will get done. I have Beck, and if I need to pay anyone to help, like when we tackle some of the bigger jobs, you can take care of that. Otherwise, I don't want to hear another thing about it."

When Parker took that tone, a rare stern one from him, I listened. "Fine. I'll come back as often as possible. If it weren't for the damned mandatory overtime, I could probably make it back every other weekend. But we'll see how it goes."

"Sounds like you're leaning toward that."

If only I really was leaning in any direction. It was a huge decision, and for once in my life, I had no idea what the fuck to do. "Who knows. What are you doing tonight?"

"No plans. Why?"

"Pia is going out with her friend Delaney. Apparently she's introducing her to some other ladies."

"No Pia tonight. Wow. I'm surprised."

I was too when she told me about her plans. But I also wasn't one of those guys who needed to be with his girlfriend twenty-four seven. Not that she was actually my girlfriend. If I went back to the city, we'd agreed we would date other people. But for now, I guess...

I shook my head. "Let's tie one on," I said.

"Mason on the loose. Count me in."

Tonight, I'd forget about all of it. That Dad was never going to walk into that kitchen door again. That I'd turned down almost two million dollars. That I had a huge life decision to make and the clock was ticking.

And that not seeing Pia tonight bothered me, even when it shouldn't.

I stood up. Took out empty beer bottles and tossed them into the trash. Not caring about the papers sprawled out all over the kitchen island, I said, "Let's start now."

30

PIA

"I love this place."

Delaney and I sat with her friend, a woman I'd heard about but never met, at the Grapevine Bistro and Bar. Overlooking the lake, about two miles from the inn, it was a place on the list of recommendations we offered but my first time visiting.

It was awesome and apparently only a few years old. Embodying cozy sophistication with its brick interior, flickering candles and barnwood accent walls showcasing local art, apparently it was also a favorite of Juliette's. The wine list offered top selections both local and global, perfectly paired by their in-house sommelier. At night, the rustic bar with twinkling string lights filling the terrace created a romantic atmosphere that we couldn't completely enjoy since it was raining.

"Same," Jules said. We'd been talking for all of three minutes when she told me to use the nickname, explaining that Juliette felt so formal to her. "How are your scallops?"

"So good," I said. "I'll admit curried cauliflower puree scared me a little, but it's so good."

"Pia likes to live on the edge," Delaney said.

"Anyone dating Mason Bennett clearly likes to roll the dice." Jules took a bite of roasted duck that looked as good as my scallops.

"Well, we're not actually dating."

Delaney gave me a pointed look.

"I mean, I guess we are. I have no idea what we're doing to be honest."

"Sounds like dating to me." Jules took a sip of wine. "But I will admit it's a complicated situation. Boss and all. And with him unsure about staying."

After introductions, we'd talked about our dating situations, Jules not hiding the fact that she wasn't a fan of Delaney's boyfriend. She was currently single but seemed fine with the fact. I had liked her immediately—Jules was the kind of confident woman that I knew would be a new friend.

"I'm trying not to think about that and be like water, just going with the flow."

"I like that." Delaney folded her napkin and placed it on the table. "Like water. If it meets a rock, it just flows around it. Adaptable."

"Exactly," I said. "That's easier said than done. At my last job, I was up for a big promotion and, long story short, the good ol' boys club screwed me. Guy who got the job was way down the ladder, worked there less than a year but... golfed with the boss."

"Oh gawd," Jules said. "That sounds about right."

"So tell me more about your writing," I said, not wanting to steal the spotlight.

"Basically, I love to murder people."

My eyes widened.

"In my books, of course. I write mystery fiction, but just for fun. Actual money comes from freelance editing, mostly."

"And teaching writing classes, and she owns her own business with all sorts of writing services," Delaney kicked in, supporting her friend.

"And that," Jules admitted.

"You sound thrilled about it," I said.

"Yeah, not so much. I'd love to focus on one thing, just writing fiction. But getting published is so freaking hard. I tried for a few years and gave up."

"Can I get you ladies anything else?" the waiter interjected. "More drinks? Dessert?"

"What do you ladies think? One more, or head back into town?"

I kept quiet. Heading into town meant, likely, running into Mason. He'd texted earlier that he was going out with Parker, so I assumed they were at O'-Malleys. But I didn't want to pressure the girls into going there just for me. And I also wanted to prove to myself I didn't need to be with Mason all the time. Pretty soon, I might not see him at all, so better get used to the fact.

The thought was like a punch to my gut. Unwelcome and entirely too painful.

"Let's head into town. I haven't been in ages," Jules said.

It was odd for me to think that she lived in Cedar Falls but never went into town. I really needed to get out more and see some of the outlying areas.

"Sounds good."

We got and paid for the check, and having called for a car to drive us, all three of us a few drinks in, Jules steered me over to one of the brick-exposed walls. Artwork from local artists hung everywhere, but the painting she pointed to of a sunset was particularly pretty.

"Check this out," she said.

I wasn't an expert at judging art by any means, but the lakeside sunset perfectly captured Keuka Lake. "It's beautiful. So realistic, almost like a photograph. But prettier."

When I noticed Delaney's expression, I finally put two and two together. Moving closer to it verified that it was, indeed, her painting. "Holy shit. I knew you said you painted, but Delaney, this is so good."

"Thanks," she said. "And they actually paid me for it, so even better."

"Delaney is so talented. Every art teacher we had in school said she was amazing."

"What can I say." Delaney shrugged. "We're just two struggling artists trying to find our way."

"Well," I said as we headed outside, "I admire both of you like crazy. I couldn't paint, or write stories, or do anything creative like that, even if you put a gun to my head."

"I don't think I could write with a gun to my head," Jules admitted. "That would be way too stressful."

We all laughed as the car pulled up. "Where are we headed?" I asked.

"O'Malley's," Delaney answered with a smile on

her face. "Figured you wouldn't mind heading there."

"Another place I haven't been in ages," Jules said. "I really need to get out more."

She didn't get it, but I did. Delaney knew full well Mason hung out there, and had probably guessed I wanted to see him. I gave her a smile and my friend winked back.

Hey, I tried. Wasn't my idea to head there, and I'd tell Mason that. Not that it mattered. I was pretty sure the "playing it cool" ship had long sailed. And most importantly, I was going to see Mason in a matter of minutes.

The butterflies in my stomach worried me. I was very likely setting myself up for a massive heartbreak, but what could I do at this point but ride the wave and hope the crashing down wasn't too hard.

* * *

"There's my girl."

Two things hit me when I saw Mason at the bar. First, he was sloshed. It was the first time I'd seen him drunk, but there was no doubt he'd been here a while. Second, being called "my girl" by a drunk "not my boyfriend" should not be giving me full-body tingles.

Didn't somebody say that expectations were the thief of joy?

"Hi there," I said as the three of us walked up to the bar. He'd been talking to someone I didn't know when we came in, but Mason's full attention was on me. Hauling me into his side, he wasn't shy about kissing me, and I wasn't shy about returning the kiss, though I did end it fairly quickly, not wanting things to be awkward in front of the girls.

"Mason, you know Delaney. And this is Juliette Porter."

Mason smiled at Delaney. Good to know he was a fun drunk. Mason seemed pretty darn happy.

"Jules," she said to Mason from behind me as I angled so the girls could get closer to the bar. "My mother knew your dad. I'm very sorry to hear of your loss."

"Thank you," Mason replied in a moment of sobriety. "Jules Porter. Hmm. You're from Cedar Falls?"

"Not originally. I moved here when my parents divorced in seventh grade. I think you were a senior at the time."

I hadn't realized Jules was that much younger than Delaney and me.

"Delaney baney," Beck called from behind the bar. "What can I get my girl and her friends?"

Suddenly the "my girl" steam was taken out of Mason's words. And now I was just being silly. What the hell was wrong with me? *Water, Pia. Be like water.*

As they ordered drinks, I gave my attention to Mason.

"You've been here a while."

"Yes, ma'am, I have. Glad you came. How was dinner?"

"Amazing. Did you say you've been there before?"

"Once or twice. Food is good. It's too bad the weather sucks," he said with a slight slur to his voice. "The lakeside patio is one of their best features."

"I bet. It was still really good. We'll have to—" I stopped, realizing we might not get the chance.

"Go there sometime?"

I nodded.

"How's next weekend?"

Because he might not be here much beyond that. "Sure," I said, trying to drum up some excitement and take my own advice about going with the flow. But at the same time, I could feel myself getting attached.

Not good.

"Works for me," I added. "So what else have you been up to tonight?"

Mason pulled me close again. "We started early at the house. There are a few things I want to talk to you about as I finish combing through Dad's books, but no work talk. Decided to get drunk. Parker's idea. Or maybe mine, not sure. You probably noticed I've had a few drinks. And didn't text you all night."

He was making about 50 percent sense. "Where is he now?"

"Parker? Stumbled home. Has an early job."

"And yes, I've noticed you had a few drinks. Guess you're a happy drunk, huh?"

"Sure am."

"You said you didn't text me all night. What did you mean?"

"Mmm, that was a slip."

A slip? Mason didn't slip. That was the thing about him. Always under control. Maybe, until tonight?

"A slip, huh?"

"Yeah." He motioned his fingers like he was sealing his lips closed. "You're not getting anything more from me tonight."

"No?" I asked, suggestively.

He groaned. "Okay, maybe. But not about how hard it was not to text you or ask to see you."

I stifled a smile. "Another slip?"

"Maybe. Maybe not."

I kissed him on the nose. I liked this Mason.

"I don't want to abandon the girls," I said, disentangling myself from him but wishing I didn't have to.

He pushed me gently toward them, slapping me on the ass. "Go ahead. I'll just be over here eyeing you up while you do."

Laughing, I brought myself into the conversation with Delaney and Jules. Every once in a while, I turned back to see Mason talking to either the guy next to him or Beck, and mostly, doing exactly as he promised.

Watching me.

I liked this, being with him, and my own friends. I liked this a lot, actually.

Never fall in love.

Seemed like a pretty good rule if you wanted to guard your heart. Unfortunately, I was pretty sure it was too late for me to take that particular brand of advice.

31

MASON

"Morning, Captain," I said to my boss. "What can I do for you?"

I was on the back deck, feet up, cold beer open, marveling at how much we'd gotten done this week, when my phone rang. Aside from the weekend before, when Pia had gone out with her friends, I'd spent every waking moment either renovating or with her. It was a rare moment I was doing neither. She'd stayed over since last Friday night, and a few times I'd wanted to press her on it, to ask why she didn't want to stay this weekend, but I'd held back.

"You sound... chipper."

"It's the clean air. I can breathe up here."

"That makes one of us. How are you doing?"

A former Army guy himself, the captain had taken me under his wing almost from the start.

"I'm alright," I said, fully aware a certain blue-eyed vixen had at least partially soothed the grief that, in my moments alone, sat inside my chest. Lying in bed last night, I'd done something I hadn't, even at my father's funeral.

Crying for maybe the second, or third, time in my life, alone with thoughts of the man I was robbed of a chance to say goodbye to, the tears formed. And then fell. I hadn't known what to do with them except let them come, refusing to feel foolish. It was a natural consequence of being sad, even if foreign to me. Although when Pia asked if I was okay this morning, I hadn't told her.

"Glad to hear it. How's the innkeeping stint?"

How to answer that? *Better than expected. Going well. If we're talking about the inn's manager, fucking great.*

"Also alright," I said, knowing where we were headed. "Before you ask, I haven't made up my mind yet."

Silence.

Only my partner and the captain knew there was a possibility that my temporary leave might turn into a permanent one.

"Clock is ticking, Mace. You don't have much time until you're due back."

As if the fact wasn't seared onto my brain.

"I'm well aware."

"You have no idea what you're gonna do?" he asked in his thick Long Island accent.

"Honest answer?"

"The only kind."

"No."

More silence.

"Listen," he said finally. "I'm obviously biased. Clearly you've got to do what's best for you, but I do think you're more NYPD than innkeeper. You'd be bored out of your mind in weeks. I know you, kid. You were made for this job."

Was he right?

It had always seemed like the right path for me, and I did like helping people. I liked the job itself, if not all the bullshit that went along with it.

But bored?

I thought of Pia under me, hands gripping the pillow she lay on from both sides. Arching into me. Screaming my name.

Nah. I wouldn't be bored here.

Bring your stuff for the weekend.

As soon as the words left my mouth, I'd wanted

to take them back. Was I crazy? Here Pia was giving us space, and I was actively attempting to close it. I might as well ask her to permanently stay at the inn, like the guys. And then what? Tell her I loved her? Ask her to marry me?

Fuck.

"Maybe," I acknowledged. "My dad did hire a manager who is very capable." In more ways than one. "So either way, I don't have to sell."

"That's great news," he said.

I watched a rowboat make its way slowly past in front of me, down by the lake. Could this be more different than my apartment in the city?

Not a chance. The two places, lifestyles, were like night and day.

"You can have the best of both. Your dad's inn. And the job. What're ya waiting for?"

Good question.

"It's just a lot to consider," I hedged, not answering him directly. "I'll sort it out soon."

"If you need anything in the meantime, you know where to find me."

"At the deli?" I asked, referring to the deli just next to the station.

"Funny, Bennett."

I thought so.

"Thanks for calling, Cap."

"Just get your ass back here, will ya?"

"Yeah, yeah," I said, noncommittally. "Talk soon."

"Over," he said, hanging up.

I put down the phone. Stared out at the lake. The property. My home. Blinking, I saw my dad sitting on the edge of the dock, fishing. I couldn't tell if he looked peaceful, or sad. Maybe a little of both? He'd been sitting like that the day I realized he was never going to give up loving my mother, despite the fact that she'd been gone for more than ten years at that point. I'd asked him point-blank if he ever planned to date again, having heard from the grapevine a certain town widow had asked him out. A teacher with two grown children. A pretty woman who might have been perfect for him. I assured my father I was fine with him dating, but he'd said, "Thanks, son, but it's not for me."

Heartbreak. Cheating. Divorce. It was a stupid college pact, and yet...

"There you are."

I turned toward the sound of her voice. The combination of hearing her, seeing her and, as she walked toward me, smelling the scent that was uniquely Pia... my chest constricted in much the same way as it had the night before.

Heartbreak.

Love.

The two were, for all intents and purposes, one and the same.

"I brought clothes for the weekend," she said, almost shyly.

I could have kicked myself. Why had I blurted that? Was I a glutton for punishment, wanting what I could only have for a short time? Because there was no doubt in my mind, whether it was in a few weeks, or months, or even years, something would fuck this up. And it would shatter me.

"Good," I said, oddly meaning it even as these thoughts ran through my head. Because other ones replaced them as Pia leaned down to kiss me, like it was the most natural thing in the world. As our lips parted, our tongues tangled, I pulled her onto my lap.

I wanted to pull her so close to me that there was no beginning or end to either of us. That should be my answer to the captain's questions, and maybe it was. I just had to find the courage to do what was necessary, even if it wasn't what I wanted.

Unfortunately, the right thing wasn't always the easy thing.

A lesson too easily forgotten.

32

PIA

Something had been off with Mason all weekend. Though I couldn't put my finger on it, exactly, he was more like the Mason I'd first met than the one I'd fallen in love with.

Dammit.

I hadn't asked for it. Or gone looking for it. But there it was. When he'd asked me to stay the weekend, it took everything in me not to say "Yes!" Instead I played it cool, trying like hell to match his energy. Go with the flow. Be like water.

Inside, though?

"I didn't ask you here to work," Mason said, coming into the office. When I got up, he and Parker had already been installing windows. I'd gone over to the inn's kitchen to talk to Esther and caught up with the weekend guests, but apparently Mason had done that already when I was sleeping. For a guy who didn't think he'd be good at the innkeeping part of Heritage Hill, Mason was incredibly efficient and attentive.

Wandering back, instead of disturbing the guys, and not ready to go home, I'd wandered in here. Having chatted with Delaney earlier this week, I came up with a finalized plan for our initial phase of community partnership outreach and couldn't wait to get started. Although it was too late to plan something for the holidays, an idea of a New Year's Eve bash at Heritage Hill, catered by the Grapevine Bistro, was still doable.

"I know. But I had a dream last night that it was our first big event, and I forgot to order wine. One of the guests was a writer for *Wine Spectator* and left in a huff. It was a nightmare, actually, come to think about it."

Mason sat across from me. No kiss. No sex on the desk. In fact, we hadn't christened anything but his bed this weekend, and though it had been incredible...

"Your boss is an asshole," he said, paint splattered all over his white tee. He had no business looking so hot, mussed up as he was. But that was Mason for you. The man would look sexy in a potato sack.

"I don't think so. At least, not most of the time."

He smiled. "Meant to say, ex-boss."

"That I'll give you. But my wine nightmare has nothing to do with him."

"Sure it does."

I hated when he was so matter of fact. "No, it's about…" What was it about? Me not doing a good job? Something I never questioned until… "Fine, maybe a little."

"Pia," he said, sitting forward as I sank. "You are one of the most intelligent, capable, visionary people I know. It was his loss and our gain, so I'm glad he's an asshole. But I also hate that he's still making you question yourself, even for a second."

A warm, fuzzy feeling enveloped me at his words. I didn't want to need them.

"Thank you," I said simply.

"You're welcome." He grinned. "And I'm not saying that because we're sleeping together."

Sleeping together. That's all we were, I supposed. *Be like water.*

"You sure about that?"

"Positive."

No longer smiling, Mason cocked his head to the side, as if contemplating me.

"I have a question for you. Don't jump to conclusions, but... if I were to go back to the city, are you serious about managing the inn yourself? We could hire someone to help, of course, but it would still be a more intense job than you'd bargained for."

"You're going back," I said, aware my tone was flat. Aware I'd just jumped to a conclusion, as he'd asked me not to do.

"I'm considering it," he admitted. "But nothing's set in stone."

"Obviously you're considering it," I said, trying to keep the judgment out of my voice. "That's your career. It would be insane not to consider it."

But...

I left the rest unsaid.

But I thought you liked it here. Liked me. Just the other day when we sat on the back deck, you'd said the troubles of the city seemed so far away.

Maybe I'd read too much into that, but part of me thought it was an admission, of sorts. That you liked Cedar Falls more than Manhattan. That maybe, just maybe, you'd decided to stay.

"I talked to the chief on Friday."

It was odd he hadn't mentioned that earlier. "What did he say?"

"Just that he wants me to come back. Reminded me the clock is ticking, as if I wasn't fully aware of the fact."

"I see."

For a second I thought Mason would get up from his chair and come over to me. Lean in for a kiss, tell me not to worry, that we would be okay. I knew what we had talked about, but every day since then, we'd grown closer. Learned more about each other. This morning, waking up in his arms, I'd almost convinced myself all was well, and that we were a regular couple.

But we weren't. The ticking time bomb of Mason's two lives was about to explode.

He didn't move.

"I'm sure the guys are wondering where you went off to. Is Beck painting too?"

He nodded. "Yeah."

"I'll finish up here and head back soon to get ready for lunch with Delaney."

His brows drew together. "I didn't know you were meeting her for lunch today."

That was because I wasn't. But hanging around

here while Mason was working… while it had seemed earlier like a good idea, the picture of domesticity, now it didn't quite appeal. He was pulling back. So this was me just matching his energy.

"Last-minute thing," I said. So last minute, in fact, Delaney didn't even know about it yet.

"Hmm." Mason stood. "I'll let you get back to work."

I could have continued to look at him. Beckoned him with my eyes. Asked for him to come to me. I could have stood and gone to him. But I did none of those things. Instead I mumbled, "Sounds good," and turned to my laptop as if I were an air traffic controller about to prevent two planes from colliding.

Without another word, he left. Whether Mason was mad that I'd become closed off or was just distancing himself because he had already made a decision about heading back to work, I couldn't be sure.

One thing was for sure. Though no voices were raised or ill words spoken, Mason and I had just experienced our first fight. As a couple. Or not. Because we weren't a couple. We were just two people who wanted each other very badly, and one person who was dumb enough to catch feelings despite all of the warning signs that it was a bad idea.

I shut my laptop. There was no way in hell I could work today. With any luck, Delaney could actually go to lunch with me. I texted her, and it took all of two minutes for her to respond. She'd love to meet for lunch. Great.

Thank goodness for girlfriends.

33

MASON

The week went by in a blur.

After Sunday, nothing was the same between Pia and me. She came to work every day, leaving before I was finished painting. It was as if we'd come to a silent understanding, that if I were going back to the city, we were better off distancing ourselves now. More than once I'd wanted to march upstairs, head into her office and clear the desk again.

Or text her at night, asking what she was up to.

Or go to her apartment, as I had before.

The ache in my chest thinking of how good we were together was overshadowed only by the ache that developed when it hit me from time to time.

He was gone. Forever.

"You look like hell."

My hand froze in midair. It wasn't a voice I'd been expecting.

"Cole." I put the paint roller down, the guest room looking much brighter with the perfect shade of gray Pia had chosen. "What the hell are you doing here?"

"A guy can't come home for a weekend?"

"Sure," I said. "But no notice?"

He shrugged. "Maybe I like to be mysterious."

"You're as mysterious as a simple math problem, Cole. What gives?"

Judging by his bag, when Cole said he was coming home for a weekend, he meant here, at the inn. All four of us together, again, for the second time in just a few weeks? I wasn't complaining.

"I didn't have any classes," he said, tossing his duffle bag on the bed and sitting beside it. "I had plans to go out with a few colleagues. Just wasn't feeling it."

I picked the roller back up. "So you drove out of the city on a Friday? Bet that was fun."

"Quite." Cole adjusted his glasses. "So why do you look like you haven't shaved in days?"

"Because I haven't shaved in days," I said, glad to be almost finished for the day.

"That's not like you."

He was right. It wasn't.

"Guess I'll have to ask Parker and Beck what's up."

It would take Cole all of five minutes to find out that Pia and I were having trouble.

"Short version. I got involved with Pia. Hinted I might be heading back to the city. And now we're barely talking."

I didn't need to look at Cole to see his eyes rolling to the back of his head.

"Maybe a few more details?"

Sighing, I finished up a second coat in the corner of the room. "Fine. I got heavily involved with Pia. We agreed that if I went back to the city, we'd see other people. Since she agreed to take on a larger role if I didn't sell, I wanted to talk to her about that but lost heart after I saw her face. Pia has a terrible... no, nonexistent poker face."

With a few last rolls, this particular room was complete, and I surveyed the finished product. And finally looked at Cole, whose expression was a cross between confusion and disbelief.

"What?" I asked him.

"Heavily involved. Lost heart. Do you hear yourself?"

Clearly I was missing something. "Not copying you, Cole."

"You like her."

"Didn't I already say that?"

"I mean, *really* like her."

I couldn't argue that point.

"Mason," he started. And with that tone, I knew where this was headed. "You've got to be fucking kidding. What is the number one rule?"

Yep, exactly as suspected.

"Never say 'I do'?"

"Sure. Ultimately. But what comes before that?"

"I'm not in the mood for games."

"Love. That's what. No. Falling. In. Love. Easy enough."

"I'm not in love, asshole."

"No?"

"No."

"Sounds like it."

I started cleaning up. "First of all, if I was in love, I wouldn't give a shit about the pact and you know it. I don't deal with the worst of humanity on a daily basis—and that's NYPD and not even touching my military tour—to have my life be decided by anyone but myself. Second, I'm not in love."

What was the saying? He doth protest too much? Or something to that effect.

"Mace." Cole switched gears and now used his Mr. Professor lecture persona. "We made the pact for a reason. That's all I'm saying."

"I hear you loud and clear."

And I did. Even now I could see my dad sitting on that dock. Heartbroken after so many years had passed.

"Let's go get a drink," he said, the words we'd exchanged forgotten.

By the time I cleaned up and the four of us had all gathered in the kitchen, I'd hoped to have heard from Pia. When she left earlier, I had asked if she had plans tonight. She'd said it was another girls night, a new Friday tradition, but that she'd text me later.

So far, nothing.

"Are we heading to O'Malley's?" Cole asked, joining Parker and me.

"Sure," Parker said. "Or we can start somewhere else and head there. Up to you guys."

"You look like you're interviewing for head teacher at some fucking prep school," I added to Cole, for good measure.

"Or maybe some yuppie Ivy League college professor?" Parker asked.

"Shut the fuck up, both of you."

I was barely listening. No text. Should I get in touch with her? We hadn't been together all week, but giving her space to sort things out didn't seem to be helping. Instead Pia and I were growing farther apart.

Isn't that what you want?

"Earth to Mason," Parker said.

"He's in love." Cole just couldn't help poking the bear. I was about to lambaste him when Parker spoke up.

"Yeah, I know."

My head shot up. "What did you just say?"

"Yeah." He spoke slower and enunciated more clearly. "I know."

I glared at him.

"Come on, Mace. Tell me you aren't the only one who hasn't figured that out yet?"

Cole looked back and forth between us, a disgusted look on his face, as if falling in love were one of the worst crimes a person could commit.

"Is she coming to O'Malley's again?" Parker asked.

I put my phone away. "I don't know," I admitted.

The urge to text her was strong, but so was escaping to the city with Cole and resuming my career where I'd left off. I had a good life in Manhattan. Had never wanted to run the inn. Or live in Cedar Falls.

Or fall in love.

But I wasn't a complete idiot either. The guys were right, even if I'd chew off a finger before admitting it, especially to Cole.

I was in love with Pia Russo.

Fuck.

34

PIA

This was nuts.

Finally, after an agonizing night of staring at my phone, knowing Mason wasn't going to text since I said I'd reach out to him, I got out of bed. Took a shower. Ate a banana. Picked up my phone, looked at it, started to text Mason and put it down.

Delaney thought I should march right down to the inn and simply talk to him. We'd gone out last night with Jules, who I liked a lot, and both women agreed it was being in limbo about our relationship that was driving me bonkers. They also thought avoiding Mason was probably not going to solve the problem.

But they didn't know him like I did. If Mason had

answers, he'd have given them to me. He honestly had no idea if he wanted to be a cop or an innkeeper. If he wanted to live in the big city or small-town Cedar Falls. One thing he did know for certain? He wasn't ready for a serious relationship. So unless I was okay with status quo, or occasional hookups if he did go back, there was nothing much left to do except distance myself.

I'd been down heartbreak road already. It was a tangled, wild mess of a path that I was veering closer toward every day. Did we need to have a conversation? An official breakup? A "you were right, this was a bad idea from the start, let's go back to being boss/employee" talk? I supposed, yes, and that was what I was avoiding.

I did everything you're supposed to do when distracting yourself. Cleaned my apartment. Went for a long walk. Spent some time in nature, by the lake. But it all felt so hollow, visions of Mason and me together interfering every step of the way.

Still no text from Mason. As expected.

By the time I realized I'd skipped lunch, my stomach rumbled. I'd grab a hoagie at the deli, a bottle or two of wine from Emilio and go back to my apartment to watch movies about people falling in love. I might be a glutton for punishment, but romantic comedies always seemed to be the ultimate distractor for me.

Opening the door to the wine shop, I was immediately greeted with a smile. Usually Emilio's cheerful *"Buongiorno"* would be enough to make me smile back. Instead, I was just reminded of my family, the home I'd left, the failed promotion, Mason's rejection...

I tried to smile back, truly. But it must not have worked. Emilio came around from the counter and grabbed my shoulders as if he were my great-uncle, concern etched in every feature of his face.

"*Signora*, where is your smile?"

I tried again. "Here?"

"No, no. That is not a smile." He looked toward the door. "No boss today?"

That did it. Embarrassingly, tears formed in my eyes. I immediately wiped them away and then laughed, remembering the first time Delaney and I met. Emilio was not much more than a stranger to me, and here I was about to burst into tears because of a guy.

Shameful.

"*La mia povera ragazza*," he said.

I had no idea what that meant.

"Tell me." He guided me toward the register and

went back to his seat. Thankfully there were no other customers at the moment. "Go on."

"Mason is more than my boss. And may be going back to the city, back to his job and his real life. Even if he doesn't..." I shook my head. "I shouldn't be telling you this."

"Why not? If not an old man who's seen all of the good, and bad, life has to offer, who else?"

I laughed. "My mother. My sisters. My friends."

He waved that away. "They are too close to you. Even if he doesn't?" Emilio prompted.

"Even if he doesn't, I'm worried I may have caught feelings for him." Realizing at Emilio's confused expression he didn't understand, I added, "I may have fallen for him."

The words "fallen in love" refused to come from my lips.

"This is troublesome, no?"

"Very much so. Either way, he's still my boss. Which is exactly what Mason tried to warn me about. Turns out, he was right."

"And you are certain he does not feel as you do, *signorina*? I am an old man, and my eyes are not as sharp as they once were, but I've known Mason my whole life. And I would not presume to speak for him but..."

Emilio didn't speak for Mason, at least not with words, but his face said it all. Trouble was, it didn't matter. Even if there were feelings there—and I honestly believed there were, if just a little bit—he wouldn't allow himself to follow in his father's footsteps. Which I understood, or tried to. Mason made decisions based on calculation and risk, not emotion. It had kept him alive on probably more than one occasion. He'd opened up about at least one of those times—his Ranger life was something Mason was typically tight-lipped about.

"I am sorry to have burdened you," I said, meaning it. And then I remembered Mason's admonition about apologizing. That might work for him, but it didn't for me. I truly hadn't meant to make things awkward. Emilio knew Mason, as he'd said, his whole life. "I'm sure it will all be fine."

Emilio might not have the sharp eyesight he once did, but judging from the way he looked at me, there was nothing lacking in his ability to read a situation. He didn't believe me, rightly so. Nothing felt fine at the moment.

"The heart cannot be commanded, Pia. Do not judge yourself too harshly for attempting otherwise. My other advice, if you would have it?"

"Of course," I said, not foolish enough to look a

gift horse in the mouth. Emilio had much more life experience than me.

"Talk to him. And when you've finished the discussion, talk more. It is the only way, especially for two people still learning to love each other."

"He doesn't—"

"Talk to him," he interrupted. "*Capice?*"

I had a feeling Emilio wasn't going to take any other response than my own, "*Capice.*"

"You want wine to take to him?"

I hadn't planned on taking wine to him. Or even seeing him. But one thing Emilio said had penetrated. Avoiding the discussion wasn't going to solve anything. "Yes, please," I said, and he scurried away.

Heading to Heritage Hill with the guys there, or at least Parker, not to mention the distraction of an inn full of guests, wasn't going to cut it. Not for this talk. I pulled out my phone.

> Plans tonight?

I was surprised to see text bubbles form immediately.

> Nothing I can't change. What are you thinking?

That sounded so much like Mason that it made me smile, despite everything.

> My turn to cook.

He was avoiding me as much as I was avoiding him. Maybe he'd say no. Maybe this was the worst idea on the planet. It felt a little like I was laying the groundwork for my own heartbreak.

Talk to him.

Such simple, but wise, advice. And I hadn't come to Cedar Falls to hide in a corner, professionally or otherwise.

> What time?

Shit. He was coming. I fired off a quick text back just as Emilio reappeared.

"He's coming for dinner," I proclaimed proudly.

"*Molto bene.*" He handed me a bottle of wine. "On the house. Just be sure to come back and tell me about your dinner."

It was like having my own grandfather here in Cedar Falls. "*Grazie mille.* I will," I promised.

There was a lot to do between now and when

Mason came for dinner, starting with the grocery store and making my apartment presentable.

Talk to him.

Emilio had made it sound so easy, as if everything didn't ride on this discussion. My job. My heart. My peace of mind. No pressure at all.

With a deep belly breath, I put one foot in front of the other, heading toward the store. If nothing else, it was a start.

35

MASON

Opening Pia's door and calling "Hello" threw me back in time twenty years. I hadn't been this nervous to see a girl since I started dating.

"Oh, hey," she said, whipping around the corner from the kitchen. "Come on in."

My plan for tonight was to play it cool. To take Pia's lead, try not to think too hard and wait for the right moment to tell her that I finally, agonizingly, had made a decision. Was it the right one? Who the fuck knew? Only time would tell, I supposed.

So much for my plan.

When I reached for her, it was like someone had taken possession of my body. Being around her this week, not touching her, had been hell. The second Pia was in my arms, just the opposite.

Heaven.

Kissing her was even better. She fit so perfectly in my arms that my chest constricted with thoughts of the evening to come. One step at a time.

I released her.

"Wasn't expecting that," Pia said, looking thoroughly kissed.

I nearly said "Same."

"I've wanted to do that all week."

"Then why didn't you?" she asked. "Oh shit, dinner."

Taking off for the kitchen, Pia left me looking around the apartment. There was no good reason for her to have the extra expense. We'd have to talk about her moving to the inn, among other things.

Wandering into the kitchen, I asked if she needed any help. Pia assured me everything was under control, and by the time I poured myself a glass of wine from an open bottle, she was serving the meal.

"This is delicious," I said earnestly. "Risotto can be tricky."

"It's my parents' recipe. One of the things we're known for."

"Tell me more about the restaurant," I said. It wasn't something we talked about often.

Pia explained how her parents ended up in Oregon and the origins of their restaurant. As we talked, I remembered she'd told me once that she was an ocean girl. It was clear she missed it.

"You can paddleboard on the lake," I said. "I know it's not quite the same but—"

"At least it's water, and you're right, I do miss it. Thanks for giving me the office. Having that view makes me miss the ocean a little bit less."

Do it, Mason. This is the perfect opening to ask her to move into the inn and tell her.

"You're welcome. Pia, there's something—"

"Hold that thought. I am determined to make sure you try dessert," she said, clearing our plates. "This one," she called from the kitchen, "isn't a family recipe. One of the lodges I worked at was known for their tiramisu. I tried for months to wrestle the recipe from their pastry chef and finally managed it. I know you like coffee, so..."

She put the dessert in front of me.

"Even though you're not a big sweets guy, you've got to try it."

I did. It was delicious. So delicious I ate the whole thing in seconds, devouring every bite. "That was one of the best things I've ever tasted," I said. The second the words were out of my mouth, our eyes locked.

Pia swallowed.

"One of the best?"

Fuck. I'd had such good intentions until she looked at me like that. Coupled with the thought of tasting her, hearing Pia call my name... screw it.

I was out of my seat, pulling Pia up before I could even answer. A week's worth of need and longing had us tearing our clothes off like it was the first time. We didn't even make it to the bed. Naked, throbbing, I wanted nothing more than to be inside her. Instead, I led her to the couch, positioned myself between her legs, and held her knees open with my hands. I stopped only long enough to say, "This is the best."

With the first swipe of my tongue, Pia's hips buckled. With the second and third, her legs began to quiver. I pushed everything from my mind except her pleasure. Every moan, every call of my name, made me even more intent. It was only when she finally let loose, grabbing my head with an intensity that made me only want her more, that I relented.

Before Pia was fully finished climaxing, I was inside her. Pulling her onto the carpet beneath me, I buried myself so deep that for a second I thought I might have hurt her. One look at her face told me otherwise. She was still coming, so I didn't go gently.

"Yes, Mason. Don't stop."

I had no intention of stopping.

Kissing her, intent on making her come again, I used my thumb between our bodies. "Do that again," I whispered. Commanded. Just as she liked it. "Come for me again, sweet Pia."

"Oh God."

I snuck a peek at her face. So fucking beautiful.

"You are..." The words caught in my throat. I could have finished that sentence in so many ways, but instead, I drove into her as if it was our last time. "Come on, baby. Let it all out again for me. Come on."

"Mason." She grabbed me by the shoulders, circled her hips and cried out. I buried myself full hilt and stopped, wanting to feel every single throb. Every single sensation. Pulling her into my arms, we reached the summit together. And didn't come down for a long, long time.

Eventually, though, reality had to set in.

I rolled off her, completely spent and wanting only to head to Pia's bedroom, pull her into my side and take a nap. Then wake up and do it all over again and again.

That wasn't to be.

"We need to talk," she said.

I agreed.

"That's why I asked you to come over. Not for..."

Turning my head toward her, I couldn't help but laugh at her hesitation. "Pia. You can scream for me like that, and be more than fine with the dirtiest talk I can manage, but you can't say the word sex?"

"I absolutely can. Sex."

"There you go, you little vixen." Sighing, I rolled to my side, propped up on my elbow, and agreed. "We do need to talk. But we should probably get dressed first."

"Why?" she asked, properly suspicious.

"Guys can be very protective of their dicks," I said, only half-kidding.

"Why would you have to protect it unless...?" She sat up. Glared at me. "Mason?"

"I didn't expect this," I started. "Please don't get the wrong idea. I had no idea this was where things would go."

"Mason," she repeated in the same tone. "Why would you need to protect your precious..." She couldn't say the word.

"Dick," I provided.

"Dick," she said, as if she hadn't stumbled on the word a second ago. "Unless you were going to tell me something I don't want to hear."

There was no good way to answer her question. "I can't think of one."

Her eyes flashed. And this was why I wanted to get dressed first.

Fuck. This wasn't supposed to have happened. The talk should have come first. If my squad mates knew what a chicken shit I was tonight... but there was no other way to look at it. I'd been straight-up scared.

"I'm going back," I said finally.

She didn't need to ask what that meant. Instead, Pia calmly stood up, grabbed her clothes and walked away, into her bedroom.

I closed my eyes. Saw my dad on that dock.

But this time, the vision didn't make my decision any easier to swallow.

36

PIA

Dressed, I plopped on my bed, wondering how it was possible in just a few short weeks for me to have gone so far down this rabbit hole. Emilio was right about one thing. The heart could not be commanded, because if it could be I would make myself fall out of love with Mason this instant. He was probably also right about the whole talking thing, but I was too angry at the moment.

Mason knocked softly at the door. I did not tell him to come in.

The door opened anyway.

"Can we talk?"

Thankfully I was angrier than I was sad, at least

for the moment. That fact was the only reason I'd been able to hold back tears.

"Sure," I said as dispassionately as possible. While I wanted to throw my pillows at him, acting like a toddler wasn't going to get us anywhere. On the other hand, I simply couldn't let the obvious question go. "Why did you have sex with me knowing you were leaving?"

Mason sat on the opposite side of the bed from me. His jaw set, I could actually imagine him at that very moment in uniform, a military man who had been trained as a soldier. Who was more accustomed to giving orders than taking them.

I'd known he was a hard man from the day we met, and yet I fell for him anyway.

"I didn't have sex with you, Pia. We made love." He took a deep breath. "I've fallen in love with you."

Those were the very last words I ever expected to hear. As I stared at him in stunned silence, words escaped me.

"Even so," he continued, "I had no intentions of doing that when I came. I wanted you to be the first to know and was about to text you when you asked me to come over."

"You had all night to tell me," I managed, still in

shock over his words. It made no sense. He loved me. But was leaving?

"I know. And I should have done it sooner. But I don't want to hurt you, Pia. And I know full well that's what I'm doing by going back to the city."

"I don't get it. You just said you've fallen in love with me. But are you leaving?"

"Yes."

"Okay, I'm sorry. But that makes no sense."

"Can I come closer?"

It wasn't the words but the way he said them that dissipated any remaining anger. It was as if this was harder for him than me, which wasn't physically possible.

I nodded.

Mason scooted across the bed. Took one of my hands and clasped it between both of his. They engulfed mine completely. Protector's hands. But wasn't he the one I needed protection from?

"I've been scared before. Any Ranger who says otherwise is a liar. Or cop, for that matter. But I was trained for that. No amount of training has prepared me to deal with losing my father, being forced to make a major life decision so quickly or meeting you. I have no idea if this is the right choice, I just know that if I stay here, I will never be able to leave you."

"And that's what you want? To leave me?"

"Part of me doesn't want that at all. But there's another part of me that wonders if I'll miss the force if I quit now. I wonder, if I stay, will..."

He stopped. At the most important part of his speech, he stopped.

"Will what?"

If he wasn't clearly hurting so much, I'd pull my hand from his and punch him.

"Will I end up heartbroken."

Like his dad.

"Mason, you do understand that's a huge leap, to compare yourself and your father? I'm fine. Fit as a fiddle. Besides." I tried to add some brevity to an otherwise extremely heavy discussion. "We aren't even girlfriend and boyfriend. That's a long way away from something more serious."

"I know," he admitted. "But if I stay, it won't be."

Holy shit.

Was he saying that he was afraid if he stayed we would... get engaged? Married? How did a guy who couldn't even commit to a long-term relationship make such a leap?

Would I say yes?

Was that even a question? Telling him my own feelings, that I loved him too, seemed futile at this point. For all this talk, he was going back.

"I honestly don't know what to say. This is the most confusing breakup ever."

"Maybe it's not a breakup."

Had he truly lost his mind? "Meaning?"

"What if we take it one step at a time. Instead of defining anything, just take it as it comes."

"Practically speaking, that means what? Date other people? But when you come back for a visit"—I waved my free hand toward the bed—"end up here? Making love? Without the actual love part? I'm not sure it works like that."

"I wouldn't put it quite like that. I do love you, Pia. And maybe it can work like that, for now."

I wanted to tell Mason I loved him too. But if he truly loved me, he wouldn't want to see me with another person. But I held back. Was it possible for two opposite things to be true? Like when you loved someone but had to let them go, for your own well-being. But you were also sad even though you were the one to walk away.

Could I really love this man, watch him leave, and not fall apart every time we were together, but not *really* together?

"I honestly have no idea if that would work," I admitted. "I'm not a robot."

"Like me, you mean?"

I was going to tease, "If the shoe fits," but didn't think Mason would appreciate the humor right now. Plus, I wasn't really in the laughing mood.

"I don't have the answers, Pia. All I know is that quitting my job so unexpectedly doesn't feel right. Maybe with a bit of distance between us..."

This was ridiculous. "You'll find answers? Like me more?" I tried to pull my hand away. Mason held firm.

"It's not possible for me to like you more," he said. "If you think so, you haven't been listening. I get that this is unconventional. And selfish, on my part. I should let you go. I've never been this indecisive in my life and wouldn't blame you a bit if you told me to go screw myself. But this is also the most honest I've ever been, and the simple fact is... I don't know if I'm ready to retire as a cop. I don't know if I'd cut it as an innkeeper full-time. And I don't know if I can get past being scared as hell of enduring the kind of heartbreak my father did for most of his life. The only things I know for sure are that I'm confused as hell, and that I absolutely love everything about you, even though that scares me."

The pain in his eyes, the way his voice cracked as he spoke... This was an entirely different Mason. And also a truthful one. I never in a million years would have thought Mason would ever admit to being scared.

"My God, what a mess."

"I hate to say I told you so but..."

I swatted him with my free hand. "You're not helping."

He grabbed my wrist. Grabbed both of them actually. And in two seconds flat, he had me pinned to the bed. We stayed like that for what felt like hours, staring at each other. I told him, without words, that I'd fallen in love with him too. Mason told me, by the way he looked into my eyes, that he was as confused and sincere as he'd proclaimed.

It was messy.

Likely, would be disastrous.

Casually dating someone you loved, who was also your boss, might have been the worst idea in history. The only thing I could imagine even worse than that? Never making love to this man again.

So instead of giving him an answer with words, I lifted my head off the bed. Our lips met.

We were done talking, for now.

37

MASON

"How was your first week back?"

I still couldn't believe I let Cole talk me into coming to this yuppy bar. Positing myself with a view of at least most of the customers, I told him so. "Fine," I said. "But I really wish we could have met at Paddy's."

"Not enough shields here for you?"

"Too many uppity professor pricks, actually."

"Me being one of them," he said dryly.

"You're not a prick," I said, taking a swig of beer. "Most of the time anyway."

"Gee, thank you."

"No problem," I said, purposefully ignoring the obvious sarcasm. "It was fine," I added, answering his initial question. "Talked to a U.C. today with more time on the job than I'll ever see. Reminded me how little juice I have, despite my relationship with the captain."

I could see Cole's raised eyebrows even under his glasses.

"English, please?"

I thought back to what I'd said. "Undercover old-timer. Juice—"

"I know juice is unofficial power. U.C. was a new one. You people have more acronyms than actual words."

"My blue-collar people don't have your people's elevated vocabulary. We don't have time to be dicking around, looking things up in dictionaries."

"Good one."

"I thought so too."

We drank in silence, Cole raising his glass to the women at the other end of the bar who'd bought us drinks. I couldn't tell if the blonde and her friends were into him, me, or both. But it didn't matter, unless Cole was interested. Although Pia and I agreed we could see other people, I had no intention of doing that. Something the guys has teased me mercilessly about when I explained our "status" to them.

I took out my phone and looked at it. Nothing.

Pia and I texted every day, usually about the inn, sometimes about personal stuff. As she'd predicted, it was a weird balance to strike. I wasn't her boyfriend so couldn't ask if she was at O'Malley's with the guys without appearing too overeager. Asking Parker or Beck was out of the question.

"Let me guess who you're waiting on."

Cole hadn't held back sharing his opinion of Pia's and my arrangement. I think his exact words were, "That's the stupidest fucking thing I've ever heard," sounding more like me than his proper Cole self.

"I'm not waiting on anything," I lied.

"Whatever you say."

My phone buzzed. I cursed myself for not waiting longer before looking at it.

> Your girl's here.

It was from Parker.

> Tell her I said hello.

A few seconds later, he texted back.

> She says hello. And hopes you're having fun. I mentioned you were out with Cole.

> Tell her we're just hanging out at one of his college bars. No, wait. Don't tell her that. Sounds bad. Tell her I am and hope she's having fun too.

> JFC the two of you have your own phones.

Ignoring that, I said:

> Take care of her.

> Duh.

I put my phone down. Cole's expression had probably been honed to intimidate his wayward students, but it had little effect on me.

"What?"

"You know what."

Sighing, I tried to nip this in the bud. "Listen, I get it. You don't approve. I'll admit, it's not an ideal situation. But what do you want from me?"

"Cut the poor woman loose."

"I'm not cuffing her to me, Cole."

"No, but you're giving her false hope. We both know it's not going anywhere. You're back, she's upstate. How long are you planning to be long-distance dating? If that's what you're even calling it."

"We're not calling it anything. Why do we need a label? Pia's free to do whatever she wants and knows that."

"And if she does?"

The beer in my hand froze halfway to my lips. I'd forced myself not to think too hard on that since Pia didn't give any indication she wanted to date other people. On the other hand, she didn't say she *wouldn't* date other people. She hadn't said she loved me back.

A vision of her with some faceless man had me downing my drink and asking for another.

"Exactly," Cole said, ordering another Scotch.

Wanting to get the heat off my back, I asked Cole about his latest publication. Half listening, I watched the women peeking up at us. One of them was actually really pretty. The kind of pretty that probably never got turned down. How easy it would be to turn her down was the exact reason me being back was a good thing.

Pia had more than gotten under my skin. She

was in my blood. I woke up thinking of her. Went to sleep thinking of her. And every second in between that allowed for my mind to wander, I spent thinking of her. Wondering how she was doing. Wondering if I'd placed too big a burden on her even though she'd insisted.

Pia also agreed it made sense to stay at the inn and would be moving, with Parker and Beck's help, this weekend.

I should be there to help. Fuck that. I should be there to warm her bed the first night. And the second night.

But what bed? Mine? We'd be sharing a bed, a roof and a job. It'd be all but game over.

Was that so bad?

"Darts?" Cole asked, knowing he didn't stand a chance at beating me. He might be able to kick my ass at foosball, but darts? Nah.

"You sure?"

"Why not?"

It was only after darts, after turning away the very same woman I thought was pretty, and after I was lying in bed, thinking about the week, thinking about Pia, that I finally broke down and texted her.

She replied immediately.

38

PIA

I didn't have texting Mason for twenty minutes during my last night in this bed on the bingo card for tonight, but here we were.

> I think you're caught up, but I hardly know anything about your week.

Mason had first texted to remind me that, in addition to me moving into Heritage Hill tomorrow, we'd also be getting a shipment of carpet. Plus, the place was full, which would make for an interesting Saturday. Since Mason had left last weekend, it had been a whirlwind. But I'd vowed never to complain about a full inn, especially since the weekend before had been lighter than usual for this time of year. Not to mention, as fall turned into winter, we were headed into the leanest season yet.

But that would change.

I'd been hard at work on partnerships, and even conceived a reopening for early spring that would give us an opportunity to advertise something special for a typically down time until the weather turned.

The place looked great. New carpeting in all the bedrooms would make a world of difference too. The fact that I was excited about carpeting said all there was to know about this job. I loved it. Loved bringing Heritage Hill back to life. And would love to see it become a premier destination, the crowning jewel of Cedar Falls.

> Trust me, the less details I share about my day, the better you'll sleep at night.

> Speaking of sleep…

I sent a bed emoji. A cocktail or two, plus my big plush pillows, did that to me every time.

> Tired?

> Getting there.

Pause.

> Wish I was with you.

It was the first thing like that he'd texted. We were in work mode most of the time, and knowing we stood on extremely shaky ground, I personally hadn't been willing to fall through this particular crack.

> I wish you were too.

He sent a smiley face emoji, which, in turn, made me smile.

The first rule of a situationship? If you catch yourself smiling at your phone, block the other person immediately. Everyone knew that. But of course, instead of blocking him, or shutting down the conversation, I continued to smile at the fact that Mason was spending the end of his first night out in the city texting me.

Next thing I knew, a video call came through.

Answering immediately, and almost breaking down at the sight of him, I scooted up in bed.

"Hey there."

"Hey there yourself, cozy girl," he said.

"I am cozy. Last night in this bed."

"How do you feel about that?"

I pretended as Mason shifted the phone that I didn't notice his bare chest. Swallowing down a sigh, I concentrated on his face instead. "Good. It'll make things much easier. Thanks for leaving me with two roommates, by the way."

He laughed. It was one of my favorite sounds.

"It's good to see your face, Pia."

"Same."

"What is that on your shirt?" he asked.

If I'd known Mason was going to be seeing me, I'd have worn something a little sexier than a ten-year-old tank top. "Nothing." I yanked the blanket up. "Just a really, really old concert shirt."

"Damn. I wouldn't have said anything if I knew you were going to cover up."

The tone of his voice had taken a definite turn toward sexy town. Good idea or not, I was a willing passenger.

"That can be undone," I said, bringing the covers back to where they were before.

"Better. My God, Pia, you are so fucking hot. Have I mentioned that before?"

"Possibly. But you can never compliment a girl too much, you know?"

"Is that so? Can you get a girl off too much? Is that a thing?"

Telling Mason I liked when he talked dirty had been the best call I'd made since we met. Some of my other decisions might be questionable as hell, but this one wasn't.

"No. That's not a thing."

"Good. In that case, I want to see your hand slip underneath those covers immediately."

"That sounds like an order."

"It is." That tone, though. There was nothing to do but obey. At least, not in this case. "Very good. Now I want you to slip a finger inside, two fingers actually, and pretend they're mine. Can you do that for me?"

I nodded, watching as Mason's eyes hooded, and obeyed that too.

"Now I want you to move them, pretending those fingers are mine. Move them exactly as you like it. That's it. And don't you dare fucking hold back."

"From you? Never."

He smiled. "Good. Keep moving them, in and out."

"Mason," I panted, knowing what he'd say next.

"Louder."

Moving my fingers, pleasuring myself but pretending he was here with me, I did as he said. Called his name louder. And louder with each command.

"Come for me, Pia. I want to watch your face as you explode for me."

I was so close.

"I want to see your face so that I can hang up this phone and let you sleep while I go into my bathroom, take my dick into my hand—"

"Mason, please." He was giving me exactly what I wanted. But I begged anyway.

"And I'm going to picture this. You with your hand below the covers, inside that wet pussy of yours, thinking of me. I'm going to imagine your face, the way you call my name, as I pump myself, until I come as hard as I ever have in my life. All because of you."

That was it. The proverbial straw. I went right over the edge, my eyes squeezing shut as I throbbed around my own fingers. When I finally opened them, Mason was grinning from ear to ear.

"That feel good?"

"Mmmm. Very good."

"Maybe we should make this a regular thing," he suggested. "I like making you come just with my voice."

"I did use my fingers too," I reminded him, knowing that alone would not have done the job.

"True. And speaking of fingers and getting off, unless I want to clean a mess over here—"

"Go ahead." I almost asked him to take the phone too but was too embarrassed. Mason would laugh when I told him about this, me being embarrassed to ask. "I'm wiped. Even more so now," I added coyly.

"Good. Go to sleep and text me tomorrow anytime. I'm off."

I wanted to ask what he did on his days off, but I also didn't want to know. It made the fact that he wasn't away on a trip but had an actual full-time life away from Cedar Falls, away from me, too real.

Better to pretend he was just on vacation somewhere and would be coming back soon.

Might as well pretend the Easter bunny and Santa Claus were real too, while I was at it, I scolded myself as I drifted off to sleep.

You're getting deeper and deeper, Pia. Keep digging; it'll be one hell of a hole to get out of.

I'd worry about that tomorrow.

39

MASON

The first week, I'd been too busy reacclimating to do any deep thinking. The second, two of my colleagues had been shot during what should have been a standard domestic call. Coupled with a protest that forced me into mandatory overtime, I hadn't done much of anything but eat, sleep and work.

And get Pia off again during the wee hours of last Friday night. I hadn't gotten home until after midnight, but she'd told me to call no matter the time. So I did. And both of us were happy about the fact, me less so two days later when I'd spoken to Parker.

"You've got competition," he'd said when he called me about the hallway wainscoting project he insisted on doing, even without my help.

"Excuse me?"

"Competition. Pia and I went to O'Malley's last night. The oldest Baker boy split with his longtime girlfriend. I guess he's ready to start playing the field."

I'd just walked into my apartment after a long-ass shift and wasn't at all in the mood. But Parker had kept at it.

"He wasn't subtle either. Bought her a drink after asking me if we were a thing."

Fuck. He was a good-looking guy, a real-estate developer who'd been partially responsible for revitalizing Cedar Falls these past few years. The town considered him their golden boy because of it. Praise that was, I supposed, well-earned.

"What did you say?"

"What do you think I said? I'm pretty sure pretending she was my girlfriend so no one went near her would not have gone over well with Pia."

Obviously. But the thought of Pia with him, or any man, had jumbled my thoughts. Both then, and now. And every time in between when I thought of it. Despite the fact that Parker said Pia hadn't shown any more interest than just being friendly, could I expect her to never date anyone but me again? How long would she put up with that?

Not forever, that was for sure.

The third week, I actually asked for overtime to keep busy. To keep my mind off the woman who had hired an assistant and was now handling 90 percent of operations at Heritage Hill. Who was even more capable than I'd ever realized. As passionate as I expected, even after our first kiss.

What a fool I'd been, to think I'd ever loved a woman before Pia.

By the time I ate, showered and hit the sack, it was well after 1 a.m. Too late to text her. Since learning how to fall asleep anywhere, anytime... whether it was at the barracks or lying on the ground in the middle of a mission, a few hours of shut-eye necessary to function... I'd never had trouble falling asleep.

Until now.

One a.m. turned into 2 a.m.

Fuck it.

I turned on the lamp. My bedroom in this apartment was anything but homey, though I'd never minded before. I walked over to my dresser. Picking up a small shoebox, I started going through the few items of my father's I'd brought with me.

I picked up the ring. A modest diamond. Nothing to write home about, especially in this day and age.

Except... it was my mother's. So to me, it was the most valuable piece of jewelry in the world.

Turning it around and around in my hand, I remembered the day my father gave it to me.

"I know it's not much, but if you want it..."

We'd been sitting at the same kitchen island Dad and I had had many conversations around. I'd taken it from him, the pact firmly in place. One my dad knew about and thought had been ridiculous.

"It's everything," I'd said. Not wanting to hurt his feelings, I withheld my true thoughts at the time, which were along the lines of, "I won't be needing it."

Placing the ring back in the box, I pulled out an old polaroid. It was one of the only pictures I had of the three of us. Dad said he and my mother were too busy working to stop for pictures. I suspected it had more to do with how sick my mother was for so many years. Either way, I stared at the outdated picture for so long, my eyes began to blur.

They'd been so happy.

High school sweethearts with an inn, and a son, and a dream for the future that cancer stole. Instead, it had been Dad and me for all those years.

Putting the picture back into the box, I closed the lid.

And sat there for God knew how long. Sleep eluded me until it was absolutely necessary, unless I wanted to get myself killed by being anything less than 100 percent alert on the job tomorrow.

My last thought before dozing off was about that very job. The one I'd taken to help people. But in reality, if I were honest, being a cop was as much about helping myself as others. I had no control over my mother's illness. No control over the course of my life.

But if I could control the outcome for others... do some good...

My father's job, being the innkeeper of Heritage Hill, might not be the same as saving people's lives. But wasn't making people happy a worthy occupation too?

The only answer that came to me was the silent darkness of sleep.

40

PIA

Walking into the Big Easy, I didn't see Maggie anywhere. Since we'd decided not to include a kitchen upgrade in phase one of the renovations, now that we were over budget, getting local restaurants to partner with for events into the following year had become a priority. I could work with caterers easily enough, but I wanted partners. If we were going to put Cedar Falls on the map in a big way, make it stand out among the many cute towns dotting each of the Finger Lakes, doing it as a community just made sense.

"Hi, can I help you?" a woman from behind the hostess stand asked.

"Yes, I have a dinner reservation. But I also wondered if Maggie was around?"

"Sorry, she's off tonight."

"I didn't realize she took days off," I said just as Delaney joined me.

"She doesn't usually but her son and his wife are in town for the weekend."

"Oh, nice." I'd seen the pretty, long-blonde-haired waitress before but didn't know her name. For all intents and purposes, even though Heritage Hill wasn't technically mine, I was a business owner. Getting to know everyone and anyone in this town was high on my priority list. I stuck out my hand. "Pia Russo. I manage Heritage Hill."

"Gaia Love," she said, pushing up the dark-framed glasses that made her look like a sexy librarian.

"That's a cool necklace," I said, gesturing to the multi-colored beaded one around her neck.

"Thanks. A local woman made it. She has her stuff in a few shops around town."

I was about to ask which shops when a large group came in behind us. Not wanting to hold them up, I let Gaia show us to our table instead.

"I always wonder how Maggie manages to pack

this place every weekend outside of tourist season," Delaney said as we sat.

"Technically, it's still in-season until the leaves completely drop," I said, thanking the waiter for the menus.

"Right, but still. There are probably as many people here as the population of Cedar Falls."

Though it was a serious exaggeration, I got what she was saying. "Well," I said, not sure if Delaney really wanted the answer or not, but I'd give my best guess, "she's established a strong local word of mouth. She's got too much overhead to rely on tourists alone."

"Hmm." Delaney looked over the menu she likely knew by heart. "Still. I mean, the food is amazing..."

"Good food. Live music. A warm, inviting atmosphere. And unique enough to stand out. Plus being here. I have a feeling tonight is rare, that Maggie lives and breathes this place. That's one thing my parents always told me about the restaurant business, or any hospitality business really. It's either all in or don't bother. No one will take care of your place like you."

"Luckily for Mason, he found an exception to that rule."

Mason.

I hadn't heard from him in three days. It was a longer stretch than most, but I supposed his job kept him pretty busy. If I needed to, I could reach out. Which was something I wanted to talk to Delaney about.

Waiting until after we'd ordered, I dove in.

"I don't think I can do this," I said, blurting out what had been on my mind for days. Weeks, actually, if I were being honest.

"I'm not catching what you're throwing."

"Mason."

"Oh."

All of my piled-up thoughts came tumbling out. "I came here to put Heritage Hill on the map, in no small part thanks to my dickhead ex-boss who made me question myself, something I swore never to do again. It's great things are coming together, better than I could have hoped for, on that front. But it's like one step forward and two steps back. I wanted so hard to be like water. To go with the flow. But those are just words that I can't make real, in my actual life. You know?"

Delaney looked thankful when our drinks came. She shook her head, taking a sip. "I'm not 100 percent sure I do."

"I can't do it. Be casual like that with someone I care about so deeply. It's driving me nuts, replaying every one of our conversations over and over. Making me question myself, again. How do you let someone go that you love, even if you know it's the best thing for your own well-being?"

"I'm actually not sure," she said. "If I knew the answer to that, I'd probably be single."

I sat up straight, realizing she was right. "Damn, that's pretty self-aware."

"I never said I wasn't self-aware, just a bad decision maker. So yeah, I do get it. And I agree it would be a brave thing to do for yourself. Provided you can actually pull the trigger."

Could I do it? Could I tell Mason that this wasn't working for me? Have nothing more than a professional relationship with him? What was the alternative? Wondering every day why he didn't choose to stay? Why I wasn't enough to make him change his mind about love?

"Love isn't always enough," I said.

"Sad, but true," Delaney agreed.

I thought about what Emilio had said. "I guess I could try to talk to him. Tell him how I feel and see if there's a way to work it out. I hate the idea of giving up on him so easily. But on the other hand..." I sighed. What else needed to be said? On the other hand, he left. And wasn't coming back anytime soon.

"It just won't work," I said. "I've got to choose me."

Delaney looked at me as if I were a superwoman. "I admire you," she said.

"Don't admire me yet. Deciding to do it is one thing. Actually saying the words is another."

"What are you gonna tell him?" she asked as the sax player began his song. Fittingly, it was a slow, sad song that perfectly fit my mood.

"That I love him," I said, having given it a lot of thought. "Which is why I've got to let him go."

"Wowza. Are you sure about this?"

"Not at all. It's not like I can cut him off completely or go full-on no contact. He's still my boss. I should have listened to him in the first place when he said we weren't a good idea."

"Don't do that," Delaney said as our food came. She waited until our plates were placed and the waiter left before finishing. "Don't go backwards. What's done is done. No sense worrying about something you can't change."

"True. Forward, not backward."

"To moving forward," she said, holding her glass in the air. "And you are braver than me."

"I'll toast to the first, but not the second. You are plenty brave."

We toasted, but I could see Delaney didn't believe me. I got it, though. A few weeks ago, I wasn't brave enough either to tell Mason how I really felt, and because of it, we were in this limbo, which just wasn't working for me.

"So what's the plan?" she asked as we ate.

It was a perfect night. New friends, good food, great music. A job I loved. While I missed my family, Cedar Falls felt more and more like home every day. But the heaviness in my chest at her question underscored all of it.

"I don't want to do it over text. We video call every Friday night—"

Her head snapped up. "Oh really?"

I tried not to smile thinking about the nature of those calls. We'd had our last one, Mason just didn't know it yet.

"Really. So I'm thinking of telling him then. We don't talk as much during the week anyway, so it shouldn't be difficult to manage the status quo until then. It's afterward I'm worried about."

Delaney finished chewing her red beans and rice. "It'll be okay. There's bound to be tough times ahead, but like you told me the first time we met, 'I eventually got over it. And you will too. I promise.'"

"Way to use my own words against me."

She laughed. "Just imparting your own wisdom."

"Thanks," I said wryly. "Your turn. Catch me up."

Delaney talked about the job she mostly hated and the boyfriend she suspected of cheating. I wanted to tell her to dump his ass, but who was I to give relationship advice? Instead I just tried to be a good friend by listening.

But as the night went on, all I could think was that we were one day closer to Friday. One day closer to me choosing myself. So why did it feel so damn crappy?

41

MASON

"She said no."

I'd spent over two hours in traffic and was finally free of it only to have Beck call to tell me there was a problem.

"What do you mean, she said no?" I said, my phone on speaker as I drove.

"I mean, she said no. She doesn't want to go out tonight. I think her exact words were, 'Thanks for the invite, but I'm going to stay in and get some work done.'"

"On a Friday night?"

"I guess. Honestly, she doesn't seem like herself at all. This morning when I brought in a plate of breakfast from Esther—"

"Wait a minute," I cut him off. "You did what?"

"She doesn't like to eat a big breakfast every day but makes an exception for Fridays. Says it's her favorite day of the week, or something about kicking off the weekend. I dunno. But I usually bring her breakfast from Esther. Granted, it's a late breakfast. I'm back to closing up on Thursdays."

Beck. Delivering Pia breakfast. I shook my head. The relationship between the two of them was... interesting. Usually Beck had only one use for women. I'd never actually seen him be friends with one before.

"So what did she do this morning?"

"Nothing. That's my point. Usually when she's finished she comes down with her empty plate, asks me if I need anything, and then goes over to the rooms to check on guests. But she never came down. I went up to check on her, and she hadn't eaten. Seems odd to me."

"You guys have a regular routine over there, it seems."

"That's what you're worried about?"

He was right.

"We've got to get her out. Maybe Parker can ask."

"First of all, she's not going to say yes to him after she said no to me." Beck seemed to take it as a personal affront that Pia would even consider such a thing. Despite myself, despite the stakes, I smiled at the effect she had on my friend. It was a shame Cole hadn't gotten to know her as well as Parker and Beck. But I supposed that was the least of my concerns at the moment.

I looked at my clock, as if it mattered. I had no idea what time Delaney worked, or if she'd be there today at all.

"Listen, I need another favor."

"Shoot."

That he hadn't even asked what it was made me thankful for having him in my life. I might not have parents, or siblings, but I had three best friends.

Shaking off the rare moment of sentimentality, something that had become more common as of late, I asked Beck to find Delaney.

"I have no idea if she'll be there, but it's worth a shot. Tell her everything."

"Let me see who's on day shift. If I can sneak over there now, I will. If not, I'll send Parker. He mentioned finishing up a job and getting back early today."

"Either way, talk to her. See if she can convince Pia to go out."

"Dumb question, but why can't you call the pharmacy?"

Shit. Confession time. "I actually did, just before I left. There was a busy signal for more than an hour. I think something's up with their phones."

Silence.

"You called her first?"

"This isn't a popularity contest, Beck. And to be fair, I texted both of you assholes and no one got back to me."

"Maybe if you waited more than a half hour..."

"Can we debate that later? I still have a few calls to make."

"Fine. We'll keep you posted."

"Thanks," I said, cursing at the dipshit who slammed on his breaks. "Fucking New Jersey drivers are the worst."

"Not gonna argue with you there. Talk to you later."

"Later," I said, my heart pounding. Last time I'd been this keyed up was day one of Ranger training. At least then I knew what to expect even if I hadn't known if I could hack it. This was an entirely different matter. I had zero clue what was going to happen tonight, what Pia would say or if I'd be coming down this highway in the opposite direction tomorrow...

Or never again.

42

PIA

"Sorry to bail on you guys, but I think I'm tapped."

Delaney, Jules and I had just finished dinner at Bella Luna. At first when Delaney had asked, I'd told her the same as Parker and Beck... that I was planning to stay back and catch up on some work. Truth was, tonight was the night I'd planned to tell Mason that I couldn't do this anymore. That I was getting way too attached, which sounded better than "I love you too much to be casual." Because of it, I just wasn't in the mood to be social.

But Delaney wouldn't take no for an answer. Told me she knew why I was moping (okay, maybe I was moping a little) and that I should at least come to dinner.

"One more drink," Jules prodded.

Was it my imagination, or did she and Delaney just exchange a look?

"I'll grab the waitress and tell her one more round of wine," Delaney said before I could stop her. If I'd known Jules better, I'd ask about that look. Something was off, but I couldn't put my finger on it.

Also, my nerves were absolutely shot, so more likely, it was all in my head.

"Couldn't wait," Delaney said, sitting back down. "You were 100 percent going to bail."

"True. But I also hadn't wanted to come in the first place."

Jules was caught up on the Mason drama so knew the real reason I'd planned to stay home.

"Are you glad you did?" Delaney asked.

"I am. That manicotti rivaled my mother's. Please don't ever tell her, though."

"I would never," Delaney said.

We finished our wines, talking about our jobs, Jules's writing, and finally, when the thought of breaking up completely with Mason popped into my head for the millionth time, I pulled out my wallet.

Again, the two women seemed... off. Delaney got on her phone, presumably to text her boyfriend. When she finished, she finally agreed to let me go, and the three of us paid and left. Although it was only a few blocks off the main square in town, the two insisted on walking me back to the inn.

As expected, the house was quiet. Beck was working, and Parker had headed to O'Malley's. There hadn't been any messages, but I still headed over to the guest section of the inn. All was quiet there too.

I'd taken a shower before heading out, but since I was too keyed up to head to bed, and my brain would definitely not function to do any work, I took another. Made a coffee—probably a terrible idea. Paced the kitchen for a while. And then finally, knowing Mason was home by now, and with no other choice, I headed to my bedroom and called him.

He answered on the first ring.

"Hey there," he said, sounding more cheery than usual.

"Hey," I said, aware my voice sounded as opposite as possible from his. "Why is it so dark over there?" I could barely see him.

"Too exhausted to turn on the lamp," he said. "How's it going?"

I sat up. Pooled the words together in my head. "It's going," I said, trying to figure out how to start.

"You look like you could use a little pick-me-up."

I shook my head. "I'm not feeling it, to be honest," I started, figuring he'd given me a good opening. I took a deep breath.

"How about you let me give you one anyway," he said, cutting me off. "Come on into my bedroom."

What did he just say?

"Excuse me?"

"I said, you look like you could use a little pick-me-up. Come into my bedroom, and I'll give you one."

He was making absolutely no sense.

"Mason. That's not possible."

"Sure it is. Get out of bed. Walk down the hall. And come into my bedroom."

My heart thudded inside my chest. He couldn't possibly be serious? If Mason was here, he'd have told me he was coming. Wouldn't he?

"Come on, sweet Pia. I'm waiting for you."

With that, he was gone. Mason had literally hung up on me.

I'm waiting for you.

It wasn't possible.

Even so, I swung my legs out of bed, stopped at the mirror briefly, looking at my reflection, and then numbly made my way down the hall. Feeling foolish, I stood in front of his door, looking around.

Nothing.

And then I pulled it open. Gasped. And nearly fainted.

There were white flower petals and candles everywhere. But the reason all breath was sucked from me was Mason himself.

Down on one knee, waiting for me.

Before I could register that fact fully, he began talking.

"I was scared, Pia. And still am. But I realized that being afraid of losing you was a ridiculous fear since I was already doing just that."

If he only knew how true his words really were, what I'd almost done tonight.

Mason was here. On one knee. It was taking some time for it to all sink in.

His hand rose up between us.

"It was my mother's. Nothing grand, by any means. Will you marry me, Pia? I love you and want to run Heritage Hill with you. Make the heritage our own."

His mother's ring.

Will you marry me?

"Your job?" was all I managed.

"Retired cop doesn't have as ominous a ring to it as I expected."

He was retiring from law enforcement. Staying here.

Asking me to marry him!

"Mason," I said, as if he were sitting across from me at the kitchen island and not kneeling below me, hand raised with his mother's ring, asking me to marry him. "I never told you I loved you."

"Do you?"

"Of course I do."

He knew it all along. As if I'd hidden it well.

"I do," I said, still in shock. "I do love you, Mason. So much that I was going to tell you tonight, I couldn't do it. There's no way I could be in a casual relationship with you."

"Can you be in a long-term committed one? As in, the rest of our lives?"

To get engaged after so short a time? On the same night I thought we were breaking up? It was madness. But life was short, and nothing felt more right than being with Mason.

"Yes," I said, the tears flowing before he could get the ring on my finger. It didn't fit, so he put it on my pinkie.

"We'll have to fix that."

It was so imperfect. Our relationship. Our engagement. Not at all like the movies or the way things were supposed to go. But none of that mattered. Only he mattered.

Mason stood up, reaching for me. I was in his arms, our mouths melding, before either of us could say another word.

A bang at the door, followed by a loud curse and exclamation of "Beck, seriously?" had Mason pulling away. With a look of *sorry* he stalked to the door.

Parker and Beck all but tumbled inside.

Mason folded his arms but neither of his friends seemed at all contrite.

"Well?" Beck asked. "We couldn't hear a thing. Guess these old doors are made pretty well."

I stifled a laugh and held out my hand. "Didn't quite fit," I said. "Was his mother's."

The brevity of that statement wasn't lost on them, even Beck. He whistled and came into the bedroom. There were hugs and congratulations all around, and it wasn't until Parker looked at the room that he said, "Guess we're interrupting here."

I changed my mind. It wasn't imperfect, just unconventional. These guys were his family, and I knew Beck usually closed on Friday which meant he had left early to be here.

"Not at all."

Mason cleared his throat, glaring at me.

I smiled. "I know you have at least one bottle of champagne downstairs. Let's go celebrate. After I get some clothes on," I said, the oversized tee with my legs sticking out not exactly a party outfit.

"You sure?" Mason asked.

"Absolutely. We'll meet you downstairs," I said to the guys. When we were alone once more, I confessed what I'd been about to do. "I thought we were going to break up tonight," I admitted.

As expected, Mason didn't seem very pleased. "Is that why you didn't want to go out?"

Suddenly, the look that passed between Delaney and Jules flashed back through my mind. "You got Delaney to ask me out to dinner." I waved my arms around the room. "To do this?"

"Guilty as charged. You said no to the boys so..." He shrugged.

"She knew? Jules too?"

"I assume so, but can't say for sure. But I will tell you, Delaney gave me an earful first about treating you right. And something about you being so brave, and she hoped I appreciated that. She was talking so fast I couldn't really catch it all."

I'd have to thank Delaney for that one. "I'll explain later."

"Why don't you change, and I'll blow out these candles."

Though I said, "Good idea," I didn't move.

He seemed to understand. Mason scooped me up in his arms, kissed me again, and we stayed that way with the scent of vanilla and roses around us.

No, not imperfect at all. Just the opposite.

43

MASON

It was done.

I was now retired from the military. Retired from the NYPD. A fiancé. An innkeeper.

I made my way down to the dock, but I didn't sit, like the memory of my father, on its edge. I wasn't fishing. Or mourning. But instead, celebrating.

A new life. One I never could have seen coming.

Pia and I had only been engaged a few days, but those days had been as perfect as possible. I took the ring to get resized. Filled out a mound of paperwork for my early retirement. Made love to my fiancée, a lot.

It had been a good week, but there was one thing missing.

I love you, Dad. Wish you could have met her. I should have talked to you sooner, but I didn't know what to say. Or how to do it. I've thought so often over the past few weeks of you sitting here, on this dock, looking sad. But I wonder if I had it wrong all along, remembering the way I wanted to remember, to protect myself. Maybe you weren't sad, but content. Every time I asked if you would ever remarry, you insisted you were happy. With me. With the inn. That it was enough. I never believed you, but maybe I should have.

I love you. And miss you. But I know you'd be proud of what we're doing with the place. It's looking better than ever, and next spring we're giving Heritage a fresh coat of paint and a new roof to cap the renovations off. Pia has so many good ideas, ways to put us on the map. She doesn't just want to turn a profit but wants to make this the crowning jewel of Keuka Lake. Knowing her, of all the Finger Lakes. And she'll do it, too. We'll do it together.

I'm glad to have you along for the ride.

"Trying to prove former Rangers don't get cold like mere mortals?"

Beck joined me on the deck.

"I didn't expect to find myself down here," I admitted, realizing the T-shirt and cold weather really didn't go hand in hand. "Just kind of wandered down."

"I'm headed into town. Need anything?"

"Nah." I shook my head. Then, remembering I'd grabbed the money yesterday, I pulled out my wallet and handed Beck a wad of cash. "For the pot."

"Didn't think it would be you to go first."

"First? You say that as if I won't be the last."

"You won't. Parker will be next."

"He doesn't even have a girlfriend."

"And you did?"

"Fair point. What about you?" I asked, already knowing his answer.

"No fucking way. One woman? For the rest of my life? Nope."

"I might have agreed with you at one point."

"But then... Pia."

"But then Pia," I agreed. "She really is incredible."

"Look at you." Beck was about to burst out laughing. "Where's the straight-faced Mason I know and love?"

"You don't love that Mason. How many times have you said I was grumpy as hell?"

"Ahh, there he is. I was beginning to worry."

"You're fucking insane."

The lake was quiet today. So peaceful. I hoped my dad was at peace too. "What do you think he'd say about all this?"

Beck sighed. "He'd say, 'It's about time.'"

My head whipped around to Beck. "You think so?"

"I know so. Papa Bennett told me."

My eyes narrowed. "What d'ya mean?"

"One of the nights he was in the bar. Asked if you were dating anyone. I said not really. He said he hoped you found someone to marry someday. Despite the fact." Beck chuckled on that last bit.

"He said that?"

"Yeah."

"Why didn't you tell me?" I asked, incredulous. "We talked about this."

"Yeah," he said again in typical Beck fashion. "I know."

I crossed my arms. Ones that were getting colder by the minute, but ignoring that, I put all of my energy into staring down Beck. "I know? That's it?"

He shrugged. "Didn't want to let that influence your decision. You needed to decide on your own."

"Are you serious right now? I specifically asked what you thought he'd say."

"And I gave you a straight answer. He wouldn't have been like, 'You know, Mason. I've always wanted you to get married. So you should leave the police force, move back, and marry Pia.' Who wasn't even your girlfriend at the time."

"He'd have me marry, despite what happened to Mom."

Beck frowned. "Of course. You think he'd rather you shack up with your bachelor friends like it was college all over again for the rest of your life? Speaking of—"

"You guys can stay," I said, cutting him off.

"Because we're still renovating."

"No. Because I want you to. And so does Pia. For some reason, she's fond of both of you."

"Smart girl." Beck clasped me on the shoulder. "Then again, she has agreed to marry *you*."

"Funny."

"Speak of the devil."

As if we'd summoned her, Pia appeared on the wraparound deck, coffee in hand. She wore a thick cream sweater, her hair piled on top of her head in a messy bun.

In short, she was perfect.

"Come on," I said, beginning to walk.

"You go ahead."

I couldn't help holding back. Beck's voice was unusually quiet, almost somber.

"I'm fine. Just gonna hang here for a few minutes."

To say Beck and quiet contemplation weren't a *thing* would be an understatement.

"You sure?"

"Yeah."

Beck's favorite word. I waited a second or two, giving him a chance to elaborate. But he didn't. So I left that dock, left behind the vision of my father mourning his beloved, replacing it with a man content, still believing in love.

As I approached, Pia peered at me from above the mug. In a few days, we'd be flying to the west coast, leaving Heritage Hill in the maybe-capable hands of my two friends to celebrate our engagement with Pia's family for a few days.

With every step, I replayed our time together, one thing left I'd been wanting to say to her.

"I'm sorry," I called up, when I was close enough that I knew she could hear me. "For kicking you out that first day."

"I thought you didn't apologize," she called back.

"I don't."

Pia opened her mouth, likely to explain how I'd

done that very thing just now. I beat her to the punch.

"There are rules. And exceptions. You, my sweet Pia, are an exception."

"Exception? Or exceptional?"

Finally, I reached her. "Both."

EPILOGUE
PIA

"Happy New Year," everyone cheered around us. I kissed Mason and surveyed the room. Our first major gathering in the newly renovated meeting space was, for all intents and purposes, a success. The fact that we were sold out on a weekend that was typically only half-filled, and that we'd made so much progress in just a few months, was almost as fulfilling as kissing the man who would be my husband.

"Look at this," he said with a sweep of his hand. "This is all you."

"Not all me," I argued. "I'd say it was both of us."

"Fine. Mostly you."

"I'm just sorry Beck couldn't make it with work."

"You're not sick of him?" Mason asked as the revelry continued around us. The sax player whose name we got from Maggie began to play once again—the New Orleans-themed party was a perfect opportunity for our first Heritage Hill and the Big Easy partnership.

"Not yet. At least Parker's here," I said as Mason's friend joined us.

"Nice job, you two."

"Thanks to you," I said, snatching a glass of champagne from the caterer's tray, "we have a space to do this. I still can't believe how different it looks without the wall."

"And with some paint, a new floor and windows, among other things," Parker said, looking around.

"Speaking of paint and a new floor," Mason said. "How's the new job coming?"

Parker's face said it all.

"Guess we don't want to know?" I asked.

"No. You don't."

"Jack?" Mason frowned.

"Always."

"They say people don't quit their job, they quit their bosses." I smiled knowingly at Mason.

"Thankfully we're partners. Or will be soon," he

said. "Don't want to worry about you quitting on me."

"No chance of that," I said.

"While the two of you continue to fawn all over each other, I'm going to hit the chocolate fountain," Parker said.

"You don't even like chocolate," Mason said.

"Exactly." Parker walked away, leaving Mason and me laughing. Until he got that look in his eye.

"Oh no. I know that look."

"Speaking of fawning all over one another," he said, confirming my suspicions. Mason grabbed my hand and tugged it. "I need to ask you a private question."

Although I let him guide me upstairs, I had to remind him we were the hosts.

"Mason," I said, the second he closed our bedroom door behind me. "We—"

His mouth covered mine while he lifted up my short dress. Apparently he understood without me having to remind him that we needed to be down there since it was our party. When he stopped long enough to strip me of my thong and feel that I was, indeed, more than ready for him, Mason undid his pants. With my help.

Without even moving to the bed, he hiked me

up, my legs straddling him. And just like that, we went from mingling to making love. I wanted him with the same intensity as that first time, and Mason knew exactly how to please me.

When we finished, he helped my panties back up, but stayed kneeling before me.

"Don't even think about it," I said, pushing his shoulders back.

"Too late." Mason's hand ran up both of my bare legs. The thought of him down there, between my legs, almost had me changing my mind, despite the fact that someone might need us.

"Oh man," I murmured, about to give in to the delicious sensations, and sight, of Mason in that position. Until I remembered the sax player finished at twelve thirty. It had to be close to that, and he needed to be tipped.

"We can't," I said. "I need to tip the saxophone player. It's got to be close to twelve thirty by now."

With a sound that was suspiciously close to a growl, Mason stood up, hauled me against him and kissed me. Hard. "Fine," he said, clearly displeased.

Join the club.

"Raincheck?"

"It depends. When?"

"When the party's over?"

With a kiss on the neck, Mason murmured against me, "I don't think the party will ever be over with us, sweet Pia. I am so fucking in love with you."

"So sweet," I teased. "With that mouth of yours."

"I happen to know you like my mouth."

Couldn't argue with that.

"New rule," I said. "Quickies can only involve one orgasm. Otherwise, they aren't quickies."

Mason groaned. "You know how good I am at following rules."

I tossed my arms around his neck. "Never fall in love. It's a dumb rule to begin with. Who can actually prevent themselves from falling in love?"

"Apparently, not me."

Mason kissed me, a kiss full of that very love he wasn't supposed to have felt. A kiss full of the warmth I hadn't realized he was capable of when we'd first met.

A kiss full of promise for a partnership, in work and play, that was just beginning.

BONUS SCENE
PARKER

"I still can't believe, after all these months, you never met Delaney," Pia said, tidying up the kitchen.

"I can get those," I told her as Pia tossed empty beer bottles into the recycling bin. We'd been pre-gaming a night out. Nothing special—just a short walk to O'Malley's so Beck didn't pout that we were leaving him out.

"I got 'em."

Sitting back on the kitchen stool, I responded to Pia's observation. "She's out of town a lot, visiting her boyfriend."

"True, but still. She wasn't at the New Year's party either, was she?"

"Nope."

"Wait a minute. Didn't you guys meet once at the Big Easy? I remember you being there together."

I thought back, but honestly couldn't remember. "I'm not sure. Hey, speaking of friends, did Mason tell you Cole's coming in next weekend?"

"I did," Mason said, walking into the kitchen. "Told him he's nuts, that there's nothing up here this time of year but piles of snow and an Irish pub we've been to a million times."

"Hey," Pia said as Mason kissed the top of her head and looked around for his beer. I motioned with my hand that Pia had dumped and tossed it. She had a thing for tidiness. Leave something lying around, and it was getting tossed.

"No disrespect," he said. "I wouldn't be anywhere else in the world, obviously. But Cole loves hobnobbing and drinking good Scotch—"

"And using big words that people actually understand," I added.

"Exactly." Mason stood behind Pia, wrapping his arms around her.

Engaged. I was happy for them. Surprised Mason was the first of us to go down. Glad he seemed at peace with his decision to go from big bad Ranger and NYPD cop to small-town innkeeper—something else I had never expected to happen. And that probably never would have if not for Pia.

"I think you guys will get along great," Pia said in a way that gave me pause. She was looking at me way too expectantly.

"I don't like that look."

Mason craned his neck around to see Pia's face. "Oh no," he said, confirming my suspicions. "I don't either. Pia, she has a boyfriend."

"A really shitty one who makes her anxious and doubts herself and all kinds of bad things that have no business being a part of a loving relationship. But I can't tell her that."

"Why not?" I asked.

"For obvious reasons."

This was why I found dating women almost impossible. We really did live on two different planets. "If it were obvious, I wouldn't have asked."

Mason chuckled.

"It's not like Mason and I were any paradigm of a perfect relationship. Who am I to judge?"

"But we are now," he argued, almost wounded.

Another reason not to have a long-term girlfriend. I almost missed the surly guy with a chip, or ten, on his shoulder.

"Pia." I hopped up from the stool. "I won't argue

with you on whether or not you can, or should, give relationship advice to your friend. But I will say, matchmaking is never a good idea."

"Never?"

"Very rarely," I amended. "Especially when one of the two parties is attached."

"But if she found someone better? A handsome someone with arms of steel and abs to match who is a great friend, nice to everyone, charming, adventurous—"

"Okay, that's enough," Mason cut in.

"Do go on," I told her. "I'm enjoying this."

"I'm sure you are." Mason unwrapped his arms and tugged Pia off her stool.

"All I'm saying," Pia finished, "is that you are both awesome. And extroverted. And fun. And Delaney is really, really pretty."

"She's also in a relationship. Something I have no interest in."

"Mason didn't either."

Pia seemed so excited by the prospect of her friend and me that I didn't want to crush her, but I also wanted to set realistic expectations. So I said, in as firm a voice as I could with someone as sweet as Pia, "I am happy to meet your friend. But I have no interest in anything more than friendship, boyfriend or no boyfriend. The last thing we need are more complications in this house. Because," I added as Mason shot me a "you can stop talking now" look, "it worked out with the two of you, but it won't with your friend and me, even if she were single. So let's not complicate things."

Pia pouted.

Mason laughed.

I almost walked myself back, not wanting to hurt Pia's feelings, but instead left things as they were so expectations for tonight were crystal clear.

"Besides," I added for brevity, "I don't plan on losing our bet. Mason might be okay with coughing up his hard-earned cash to give to the rest of us, but I don't plan on doing any such thing."

Case closed.

ACKNOWLEDGEMENTS

A heartfelt thank you to my family and friends for your unwavering support and encouragement. To my editor, Megan Haslam, my agents, Andrea Hurst and Katie Reed, and the entire team at Boldwood—thank you for helping bring this book to life.

ABOUT THE AUTHOR

Cissy Mecca is the author of the American small-town romance series such as 'The Bachelor Pact' and 'The Boys of Bridgewater'. She also writes spicy romantasy under the pen name C. L. Mecca. She lives in Northeast Pennsylvania with her family.

Sign up to Cissy Mecca's mailing list for news, competitions and updates on future books.

Follow Cissy on social media here:

facebook.com/MeccaRomance

instagram.com/meccaromance

tiktok.com/@clmeccaauthor

ALSO BY CISSY MECCA

Fallen Hearts

Cissy Mecca writing as C. L. Mecca

Whisper of War and Storms

LOVE NOTES
LOVE IN EVERY CHAPTER

WHERE ALL YOUR ROMANCE DREAMS COME TRUE!

THE HOME OF BESTSELLING ROMANCE AND WOMEN'S FICTION

WARNING:
MAY CONTAIN SPICE

SIGN UP TO OUR NEWSLETTER

https://bit.ly/Lovenotesnews

Boldwood

Boldwood Books is an award-winning fiction publishing company seeking out the best stories from around the world.

Find out more at www.boldwoodbooks.com

Join our reader community for brilliant books, competitions and offers!

Follow us
@BoldwoodBooks
@TheBoldBookClub

Sign up to our weekly deals newsletter

https://bit.ly/BoldwoodBNewsletter